AND THE TRUTH IS...

JAMEY MOODY

As an independent author, reviews are greatly appreciated

And The Truth Is...

©2021 by Jamey Moody. All rights reserved

Edited: Kat Jackson

This is a work of fiction. Names, characters, places, and incidents are the product of the author's imagination or are used fictitiously. Any resemblance to an actual person, living or dead, business establishments, events, or locales is entirely coincidental.

This book, or part thereof, may not be reproduced in any form without permission.

Thank you for purchasing my book. I hope you enjoy the story.

If you'd like to stay updated on future releases, you can visit my website or sign up for my mailing list here: www.jameymoodyauthor.com.

I'd love to hear from you! Email me at jameymoodyauthor@gmail.com.

❦ Created with Vellum

CONTENTS

Also by Jamey Moody   v

Chapter 1	1
Chapter 2	7
Chapter 3	13
Chapter 4	21
Chapter 5	27
Chapter 6	35
Chapter 7	43
Chapter 8	50
Chapter 9	59
Chapter 10	67
Chapter 11	75
Chapter 12	84
Chapter 13	93
Chapter 14	102
Chapter 15	110
Chapter 16	118
Chapter 17	128
Chapter 18	138
Chapter 19	145
Chapter 20	155
Chapter 21	164
Chapter 22	171
Chapter 23	178
Chapter 24	185
Chapter 25	193
Chapter 26	200
Chapter 27	208
Chapter 28	215
Chapter 29	223
Chapter 30	231
Chapter 31	240

Five Years Later	249
About the Author	259
Also by Jamey Moody	261
No More Secrets	262

ALSO BY JAMEY MOODY

Live This Love

The Your Way Series:
Finding Home
Finding Family
Finding Forever

It Takes A Miracle

One Little Yes

The Lovers Landing Series
Where Secrets Are Safe
No More Secrets
And The Truth Is...

1

"Tara is here," Krista said, sounding surprised. She looked down at her phone then over at Melanie.

"Are you going to let her in?" Melanie asked, raising her eyebrows.

Krista went to the back door and opened it. "Come on in. Why didn't you just knock?"

"I didn't want to interrupt anything. You *are* kind of like newlyweds," Tara said, walking into the room.

Krista and Melanie both smiled at her. They'd fallen in love thirty-two years ago, but couldn't get past the obstacles to actually be together. Three months ago Melanie had turned her business over to her daughters, sold her house and announced to Krista that she was never leaving her again.

"If this is our honeymoon then it's been great, but why haven't we seen you? I thought you'd be back after the Ten Queens meeting," said Krista.

Ten Queens was the production company they had formed with eight other actresses, directors, and producers to make quality movies with an LGBTQ+ storyline. They'd met the first week of June to discuss future projects.

"I had things to take care of in LA," Tara answered.

"Take care of? Like what? Or should I say who?" Krista teased.

Tara smirked at her. "Believe it or not, there was no one."

"I was just teasing, Tara. What's going on with you?"

"How long have you had Lovers Landing now? Three years?" she asked.

"We just finished our fourth summer," said Krista.

Lovers Landing was a lake resort she and her best friend Julia had bought three and a half years ago. They'd worked there as kids when it was a vacation spot on the lake. As adults, she and Julia had made it into a hideaway for closeted Hollywood lesbians. Krista had been a beloved actress in Hollywood for decades and one of the obstacles she and Melanie had faced was coming out. Krista had waited for years in fear that coming out would negatively affect her career. When she and Julia had the chance to buy this place, they made it into Lovers Landing in hopes of helping queer women that were afraid to come out, just like Krista had been for so long.

"I was serious about looking at property around here," said Tara.

"What about all your friends in LA?"

Tara laughed sarcastically. "What friends? You know as well as I do that we don't have any real friends in Hollywood."

"Are you ready to retire then?" Krista asked.

"I'm fifty-seven years old. What kind of roles do I have to look forward to?"

"Are you kidding me?" Krista said, bewildered. "You won an Academy award last year!"

"I know and I'm grateful, but come on, Krista. Look at all we gave up for fame and fortune. We knew then the consequences that would come along with it. Sitting here looking at the two of you, though, makes me happy," said Tara.

"If I could do it all over again," began Krista.

"Stop," Tara said, interrupting her. "None of that matters. You're finally together, so don't waste a minute."

"Oh we haven't," said Melanie, smiling at Krista with love in her eyes.

"Good," Tara said firmly. Then she chuckled. "You know, I never told you this, but I knew how jealous you were when Krista and I were together."

Melanie narrowed her eyes at Tara, but didn't say anything.

"I laughed to myself because I knew you two would end up together," Tara said.

"You did?" said Krista.

When Krista was twenty-two she begrudgingly went to Hollywood, Melanie couldn't come with her because her daughters were so young and she was starting her own business. Times were different back in the early nineties when they were trying to navigate being in a gay relationship with kids while starting a business and Krista beginning her acting career. They'd broken up and Tara was there to comfort Krista in her loss and they had been together for several years. Tara was ready to come out at that time, but Krista wasn't, thus their relationship had ended.

"Kris, I know you loved me, but Melanie has always been the only one for you. And thank goodness you found your way back to one another. There's no one like that for me, but the real friends I have are here. That's why I want to have a house nearby. Could you stand me as your neighbor?"

"Is that the reason you want a place here or is it your real estate agent?" Krista asked with an accusatory tone.

"Lauren is my friend. I've heard you every time you've told me she's not the one for me," said Tara, obviously frustrated.

"I didn't say that!" Krista said, sighing. "I know she means something to you, Tara. Julia and I have known Lauren since we were in grade school. She married her high school sweetheart and had two amazing kids. Then they raised those kids and grew apart. It was hard for them to end their marriage."

"But you think she's curious about women, right Kris?" asked Melanie.

"When Julia found out this place was for sale she had me come home. Lauren was the agent and asked us questions about how we knew we were gay and so forth. Then later when it was just her and I, she had more questions. I think she is open at this point because she was unhappy in her marriage and wants more out of life. She wants the passion that you and I have that you read about in romance novels." Krista looked at Melanie and reached for her hand.

"Who wouldn't want what you have!" Tara exclaimed.

"She and Marcus didn't have anything but the kids in common and she asked me if there was more to life than that. For me there was, but getting it sure was challenging," she said, glancing at Melanie. "I'm glad I didn't give up, though, because look what I have now."

"Look what *we* have," added Melanie, squeezing her hand.

"That's why I still have hope. I may have been a player since you and I split, but not anymore." Tara shrugged.

"Since we split? That was over twenty years ago!"

"I've had a couple of relationships that were serious, but

neither lasted more than three years. It's hard to have anything lasting in Hollywood," said Tara. "You know that relationships like Allison and Libby have are rare."

Allison Jennings and Libby Scott were both very successful actresses that had starred in several blockbuster movies, and were both members of Ten Queens. They had hid their twenty-year relationship and only came out three years ago.

"I think Lauren was looking for that passion too and had to decide if ending her marriage was worth taking that chance. It took her three years, but right now I think she's finding out who she is without Marcus. She knows she may never find what she's looking for, but she's open to all possibilities. That is courage, that's being brave," said Krista.

"You'd know," said Tara.

"I'm not the brave one, Tara, or Mel and I would've been together thirty years ago. Melanie is the brave one in our relationship."

"You've had your moments, babe. You're not acting anymore or even doing much with Ten Queens. You're only entertaining couples at Lovers Landing because you knew I wanted to do this with you," said Melanie.

"I like having these couples here. They get to spend a week with no worries of being outed or pictures showing up on social media. All I do is give them the experience you and I had that summer we fell in love here all those years ago. Who doesn't love the lake, the beach, dancing, karaoke, and your own private luxurious cabin?"

Tara chuckled. "You can tell you love your work."

"I do! And now I have this hot partner that helps out," she said, wiggling her eyebrows at Melanie.

Melanie rolled her eyes. "You still haven't told us why you're here, Tara."

"Lauren called and said there is a property she thinks I'll like that hasn't come up for sale yet. They're putting it on the market next week and if I like it I can have first dibs."

"Oh wow! You really meant it when you said you were looking at property. Did she say where it is?"

"No, but that's one reason I'm here. Would you both like to come along when we look at it?"

Krista and Melanie looked at one another.

"Fuck yeah, unless... Do you want your real estate agent to yourself?" teased Krista.

Tara looked up and sighed. "I'm telling you, we're friends. Did you ever think that while Lauren is finding out who she is as a single woman that I may be doing the same?"

"What!" Krista exclaimed. "You've made your reputation as a single woman!"

"What I mean is that maybe I'm finding out who I am without someone on my arm," explained Tara.

"Oh," Krista said, eyeing her friend. "I guess that's true. You do always have someone you're dating, even if it's brief."

Tara nodded.

"Tara, we'd love to come along and you're more than welcome to be our neighbor," said Melanie kindly.

2

Lauren Nichols smiled as she recognized the car coming up the road toward her. She was meeting Tara to show her a property that Lauren thought was perfect for her. The smile grew and she waved as the SUV came closer. Krista got out of the driver's seat and came around the front of the car while Melanie got out of the passenger's side along with Tara.

"I see you've brought your most trusted advisors with you," Lauren joked, hugging Krista and Melanie.

"I thought I might need them. My real estate agent can be very persuasive." Tara grinned, raising her eyebrows. She held out her arms for a hug.

Lauren's heart fluttered for a moment. She knew Tara Holloway had a different woman on her arm most nights in Hollywood, but she was so charming. Her shoulder-length raven hair shone in the sunlight and those bright blue eyes looked at Lauren and sparkled.

They had been friends for a little over three years now. Since selling Krista and Julia Lovers Landing, Lauren had been a regular singer at karaoke night and met Tara one week when she was here. Their friendship was steadfast and it surprised Lauren that Tara had never tried anything with her. Surprised may not be the right word; there was a bit of disappointment mixed in. But Tara knew Lauren's marriage was on the rocks and when she needed a friend that didn't know her husband, Marcus, like Krista and Julia did, Tara was there. She listened and let her rant or held her when she cried. It was much better this way, Lauren told herself. She needed Tara's friendship more than she realized.

The joy she felt when Tara had asked her to look for property in the area was obvious on her face. She remembered Tara asking if she was excited to make a sale or excited she would be here more often. Lauren answered quickly by hugging Tara tightly and telling her she'd love for her friend to live here. Tara had wavered and told her it wouldn't be a full time move. Lauren just nodded, knowing that once Tara experienced the slow, enchanting magic of the lake she wouldn't want to go back to Hollywood.

She had just the place picked out for her and couldn't wait to show it. With her best smile Lauren said, "This house is going to do all the persuading, I'm just along for the ride." Then she winked. "Right this way."

They walked over the neatly trimmed grass to the front porch. There were two rocking chairs facing the private road that led to the main highway. This place was secluded and offered killer views of the lake.

Tara looked at the rocking chairs and then at Lauren skeptically. "Can you see me rocking in these?"

"Don't knock it until you've tried it," Krista said, sitting in one of the chairs and leaning back.

Melanie joined her. "Look through there." She pointed just across the clearing and said, "I'm sure deer would come up here every morning to have coffee with you."

Tara followed Melanie's eyes, but didn't say anything.

"I can see that smile at the corners of your mouth," Lauren said softly.

Tara looked at her and let the smile light her face. "I can't imagine the quiet— deer too?"

"You know how quiet it is around here," Krista said, astonished. "You've had your own cabin at Lovers Landing."

"I know, but that's not my own place. It's your little resort." She looked at each one of them and said rather shyly, "I've never been one for quiet places. There's always something going on, you know." She quickly looked away and stepped toward the front door.

Lauren made a mental note to find out a little more about what Tara wasn't saying. She walked to the front door and unlocked it. Before she let Tara in she waited until Tara looked at her. "I thought of you when I walked in here," she said with an affectionate smile.

"You did?"

"You'll see," Lauren said, her face delighted.

Tara walked into the great room and stood still, clearly awed. The room had high ceilings with exposed beams. The back wall was solid windows with a breathtaking view of the lake. It was bright and inviting at this time of day, but at night the lights on the lake would give the room a mysteriously warm aura. Off to one side was an open, state of the art kitchen with a dining area that also looked out over the lake.

Lauren gestured for Tara to walk further into the room so she could see a hallway that led to the bedrooms. Behind them was a stairway that led to the master suite which took up the entire upper floor. There was a loft that looked down on the great room, as well as out to the lake.

"Why did this make you think of me?" Tara asked, turning towards Lauren.

"Because it's big, bold and beautiful, just like you," Lauren said with another high wattage smile.

"Big?"

Lauren chuckled. "You are a five foot ten inch goddess that is bigger than life."

Tara pointed and wiggled her finger at Lauren. "Careful, Lauren, I'll think you're flirting with me." She paused then said, "Oh wait, now you're giving me the sales pitch aren't you?"

"Not at all. This place will sell itself. I'm being honest with you. Don't you believe me?" Lauren thought that maybe she was flirting with Tara just a little, not that it would matter. There were times over the years when she'd danced with Tara at karaoke and liked the way she held her so close. But again, nothing had come of it because they were friends and Lauren was married. *I'm not married anymore.* The thought popped into her brain without warning.

Before Tara could answer, Krista and Melanie walked in and whistled. Lauren didn't notice how Tara tilted her head and stared for a moment.

"Wow, Lauren!" Melanie exclaimed.

"I know! Isn't it gorgeous," she replied.

"It is!"

"Are you rethinking our decision to stay in the cabin?" asked Krista, equally amazed as she looked around the room.

Melanie chuckled, putting her arm around Krista's shoulders. "Not at all. We'll come visit Tara all the time after she buys this place." She grinned at Tara.

"Oh, you want to use my money," Tara said, laughing

with her and turning to Krista and Melanie. "I do seem to keep accumulating it. Did I tell you I have a new financial wizard?"

"You have not shared that with us," said Krista, feigning seriousness.

"Your daughters really impressed me when I met them back in May. I decided to give them a little money and see what happened."

Melanie had opened an investing firm when she and Krista were falling in love years ago. Krista was one of her first clients and she'd made them wealthy. Melanie had built it into a multinational company and her daughters joined her in the business after college. They were now running the company and Krista was the only client Melanie had kept.

The girls were just as talented as their mother in making money. Afterall, they'd learned from the best.

"And now instead of just being filthy, you're filthy rich," Krista said. "Oh wait, that didn't come out right, did it?"

"Ha ha, very funny," Tara deadpanned.

"I hope they've done a good job for you," Melanie said.

"Of course they have; you wouldn't accept anything less, would you?" Tara said to Melanie.

Melanie smiled at Tara's knowing stare. "I wouldn't. Investing other people's money is a great responsibility."

"I'm very pleased and in the process of moving my business to them. I should've done that a long time ago, but I guess I couldn't give you my money when I knew you were going to get Krista too. I don't mean that as possessive as it sounds. You were going to end up together and I knew that. I may not have liked it, but I knew it." Tara shook her head. "I still don't know why it took you so long."

"As a good friend told me," Melanie said. "It doesn't matter now."

Tara smiled. "A good friend? I *am* your friend, Melanie, and have been for a long time."

"I just didn't know it," Melanie said, shrugging.

Tara laughed. "Anyway! I have money, I want to move here part-time and we're standing in the middle of a gorgeous great room. Tell me more, beautiful real estate broker?"

3

Lauren was momentarily thrown off balance by Tara's compliment. What was wrong with her today? This was Tara, her friend. It had been a long time since someone told her she was beautiful, but come to think of it, Tara had said so several times when they were dancing. She shook those thoughts out of her head and got back to business.

"Let's walk out on the patio before we go through the rest of the house," she said, walking to an end table and reaching in the drawer. She pulled out a remote control and pushed a button.

Before their eyes the back windows began to slide into one another, opening the room to the outside.

"I was not expecting that," said Tara.

"I think Allison and Libby have a sliding wall like that at their place in the canyon," said Krista. "Libby was saying how much she enjoyed it. Maybe we should hold our next meeting there."

"I'm sure they'd love that," Tara said, gazing out where there were once windows.

"Are you kidding me? You know how Allison loves to show off," Krista said, walking up beside Tara.

"Maybe we'll have the next meeting here." Tara nudged her with her shoulder. "What Hollywood actress in our group doesn't like to show off?"

Krista chuckled. "How true."

"Okay my unpretentious, humble friends, right this way," said Lauren.

"You know we're kidding, right?" said Tara, suddenly serious.

"Of course I do." Lauren tilted her head as she met her eyes. "Come on," she said, taking Tara's hand and leading her out to the patio.

The patio was made of natural stone and had several levels that flowed down toward the water. To one side was a covered outdoor kitchen and there was a table with chairs for outdoor dining. On the next level was a smaller table with chairs for enjoying the view, working, relaxing, or whatever. And finally there was one more level that had two adirondack chairs facing out over the water, waiting to be enjoyed.

"Wow," Tara said, again sounding awed. "I'd be out here all the time."

"It is beautiful, but I have one other spot you might like as well or maybe even more," Lauren said, standing next to her as they looked out over the water.

"This is something," Krista said. "I had no idea this was here. You have to be coming to this area on the lake to know about it. It's very private, Tara. Just like you like it."

"The dock is brand new and the boat comes with it if you want it. We can walk down there after I show you the rest of the house," said Lauren.

"You are really good at this," Tara commented as they turned around and walked back toward the house.

"What did you expect? Of course I'm good at this. I sold an old run-down family lake camp to two good friends and they're still my friends," she said with a laugh.

Tara laughed. "Of course you did! And I didn't mean any disrespect; I meant it as a compliment."

Lauren smiled and nodded slightly. "Then thank you."

She showed them the downstairs bedrooms and bathrooms and an office or TV room. Then she led them up the stairs to the loft that overlooked the great room and had views of the lake through the expansive upper windows. The high ceiling coupled with the A frame roof made the room and lake even more dynamic from this upper perch.

"Is this the spot you think I might like better than the patio?" asked Tara as she took in the panoramic view.

"Nope. Take a minute and then I'll show you," Lauren said, building Tara's anticipation.

"This just keeps getting better," said Krista.

"Yeah it does. If you don't buy it, we will," said Melanie.

"Back off bitches," Tara said playfully.

They all laughed and then Tara turned to Lauren. "I can't imagine what this master suite is going to look like after the rest of this place."

"Well, let me show you," Lauren said, deepening her voice. She led Tara to her left first, into the bedroom.

Tara looked around the room and Lauren watched as she took it all in. The bed was against the outside wall. To the right was a sitting area that looked out over the backyard. The wall was covered in large floor to ceiling windows. When they walked closer they could see down to the patio and out over the entire cove.

She turned from the window and looked at Lauren with a broad smile. "This is it," she said softly.

Lauren nodded. "This is it. Can you imagine waking up to this?"

Krista and Melanie had joined them in the sitting area and gazed out at the lake.

"Look, babe," Melanie said, pointing out the window to the right. "You can just see our mountain on the other side of the cliffs."

"Hey, you can! We'll have to look the next time we go over and see if we can see Tara's place from there," said Krista.

"Hold up. Your mountain? My place?"

Krista chuckled. "Melanie took me to a lovely little spot on that mountain right over there for our anniversary," she said, showing Tara. "It's become our favorite place on the lake."

"I think I know where you mean. Is it just past the swim area behind the cliffs?" asked Lauren.

"Yes, there's a hint of a trail up to the top."

"I'm sure it's beautiful up there," said Lauren. "I don't think I've ever been there."

"We'll take you sometime," said Melanie, smiling.

"You don't have to do that if it's your place," said Lauren.

"Anyone on the lake can get there. Of course you're welcome," said Krista. "Now, you are going to buy this place. Right, Tara?"

Before Tara could answer Lauren jumped in. "Wait now, she hasn't seen everything. There's still the master closet and bathroom. This way."

They walked to the back of the room where a door opened into the master bath. It wrapped around the loft and included a huge custom closet. The bedroom, bathroom, and closet took up the entire top floor along with the loft.

All the fixtures in the bathroom were high end, including a beautiful soaking tub and shower with multiple shower heads. The closet had custom shelving and cabinets complete with mirrors and an upholstered bench.

"This is it!" said Krista, walking into the closet. "Tara is a sucker for a closet like this. Let's see, what did you used to tell me?" Krista closed her eyes then she said, "If you're going to stay in the closet then it may as well be a luxurious one."

Tara laughed. "I did say something like that."

"Let's make our way back downstairs and go out to the dock. We can talk more there and I can answer any of your questions. We can also look through it again," Lauren said pleasantly.

There was an exit from the closet to the loft or they could go back through the bathroom to the bedroom. Krista and Melanie stepped into the loft and made their way back downstairs while Tara and Lauren went back through the bathroom.

Tara paused in the bedroom and asked Lauren, "How would you arrange this room?"

Lauren waited a few moments and looked around the room. When she'd first viewed the property she'd had the same question. She would rearrange this bedroom to take full advantage of the lake view.

"Well, I'd take the bed off that wall and put it in the middle of the room. Just imagine, you could lie back on pillows at night or in the morning and see directly out to the lake. I'm not sure, but I think you'd get the sunset right over your cove."

"You've thought about this," Tara said, looking into her eyes. "You'd make the bed the center of attention."

Lauren looked away shyly. "The windows and the view are obviously the main attraction, but I'd put the bed where they could be enjoyed the most."

"I totally agree. You know, if I bought this place, I'd have to redecorate. The way it is now is not my style."

"I know that, but it is a beautiful place and I can see you here."

Tara smiled. "You know me pretty well, Lauren."

Lauren returned her smile. "I think so. I could see you happy here."

"Would you help me redecorate?"

"Oh, I'd love to," she said excitedly.

Tara nodded, the smile still on her face. "Let's go see this dock."

They walked down to the dock to meet Krista and Melanie and looked over the boat carefully. There was a nice area for swimming. The double decker dock provided shade on the lower level and tanning or jumping off the upper level. There was a platform that lowered into the water to dock jet skis and there was plenty of storage that could house paddle boards, canoes, life jackets, and other floatics.

"It has everything," said Krista. "You don't have a beach, but you don't need one here. The water is deeper and perfect for swimming."

"Lauren, you're right. This really does fit Tara. Nice job," said Melanie.

Tara narrowed her eyes at Melanie. "You almost sound like you want me to move here."

Melanie threw her head back and laughed. "I do! I no

longer have to be afraid you're going to take Krista away from me again."

"What?" Krista and Lauren said at the same time.

"Look, Tara and I have a different dynamic. We both love Krista, but I'm in love with her and have her heart for all time," Melanie said, gaining speed as the words flowed out. "And there was a time when insecurity set in and I was afraid."

"Then your very smart brain kicked in and you realized you were the only one Krista ever wanted to be with and I was simply holding space until you both could get your shit together," said Tara.

"Did you know this?" Lauren asked Krista.

"Not exactly. I know they are both protective of me and Mel was jealous of Tara back in the day."

"But we are friends now and someday I'll be with my true love. I know it," said Tara confidently.

"Wow! That's uncharacteristically romantic for you," said Krista.

Lauren couldn't help but share her optimism, yet she wondered if Marcus was that for her. There had to be more, she just knew it. She met Tara's eyes and said, "Me too."

"How about we all go out to dinner and talk about your new home," said Krista enthusiastically.

"Like a double date?"

"Well, we double date with Julia and Heidi unless there's something y'all aren't telling us," Melanie said with raised eyebrows.

"Not you too," said Tara, frustrated. "I told you. I know Lauren is off limits."

"What's that?" Lauren said, confused.

"Don't you remember when we met, Krista told me to leave you alone?"

"No, I didn't." Krista sighed. "I told her you were going through a rough time," she explained, looking at Lauren sympathetically.

"Yeah, but that was a long time ago," said Lauren, annoyed.

"I told them you could take care of yourself," said Melanie.

"Can we drop this? We were having such a good time," Lauren said.

"I'm so sorry," Krista said to Lauren. "I should've kept my mouth shut. Please don't be angry."

"I'm not angry at you. It's okay; I know you were looking out for me, but I can handle Tara," she said confidently.

Tara's face lit up with delight. "Oh you can?"

"I can," she said. "Come on, let's go."

"I'll ride with you," Tara said, hurrying to Lauren's car with a delighted grin.

4

On the fifteen minute drive into town and to the restaurant Lauren asked, "Are you going to tell me what you think?"

"We can talk about the house at the restaurant. I've barely seen you since I got to town. How are you?" Tara said, glancing at Lauren with genuine concern in her voice. "I know it's been a few months since the divorce was finalized."

"I should've done it years ago, but I had to be sure. Thirty-five years is a long time, you know," Lauren replied.

"You were married thirty-five years! You never told me that!"

Lauren looked over at Tara and chuckled. "We may as well have been. We started dating our last year of high school and all through college. We got married as soon as we graduated and then I had Justin a couple of years later."

Tara patiently waited for Lauren to continue.

"I feel like I'm starting a new life," she said eventually.

"You are!"

Lauren smiled. "Marcus is a simple man. He likes to

hunt, fish, and loves the Dallas Cowboys. I know there has to be more to life."

"I get that."

"Really, I'm a simple woman."

"Oh, I don't think so at all," said Tara, shaking her head.

"I am. I love my job. When I first walked through that house all I could think of was you. And if you don't love it then I'll find one you do love. I love helping people find their dream homes, or the home they want or need at the time. I love helping older people get the best price for their homes when they want to move nearer to their grandchildren. It brings me joy. And when I come home at the end of the day, I want someone there that's happy to see me. Don't get me wrong, my dog was happy when I got home," Lauren said, grinning at Tara.

"I can't imagine someone not being happy to see you," Tara said in disbelief.

"Aw, you're just being sweet. You said you're looking for your true love; I suppose I am too. I had to divorce Marcus so I could be open to possibilities."

"I'm open, but I know it will have to be a woman," Tara stated plainly. "What about you?"

Lauren looked over at Tara with a soft smile. "I don't know. I'm open."

Tara smiled back at her. "Krista told me that you've asked her questions about women and being gay. You know, you can ask me."

Lauren scoffed. "No I can't."

"Why?" Tara asked, pulling her brows together.

"I might want to try what Krista tells me on you," Lauren said, grinning.

Tara's mouth fell open and then she gave her a sly grin. "Are you flirting with me, Lauren Nichols?"

"I might be practicing; it's been a long time."

"So which is it?"

Before Lauren could answer, her ringtone filled the car. She pushed a button on her steering wheel and said, "Hi Krista."

"Hey," Krista's voice came through the speakers. "I saw Matt's car in the parking lot. We can go somewhere else."

"It's no problem. Let's eat here. I want Tara to have some real Texas Barbeque."

"Okay, let's park."

Lauren ended the call and Tara said, "Who's Matt?"

"He's my ex brother-in-law."

"Do you not get along?"

"He was vocal about the divorce, but it's fine now. He won't bother us."

"Are you sure? I can have barbeque another time."

"I'm positive," she said, parking next to Krista. "Let's go." She gave Tara a dazzling smile and got out of the car.

They went inside and were seated at a booth and given menus. Their waitress came up to take their drink order.

"Hi Tammy," Lauren said. "How are you today?"

"Hi Lauren. Hi Krista. I'm well, how are things at the lake?"

"Wet," Krista said, chuckling.

"Ha ha, good thing you can act and sing," Tammy said, winking at her.

Krista laughed. "Ain't that the truth. Tammy, this is my wife Melanie," she said, gazing at her with a smile. "And this is our friend Tara," she said, nodding toward her.

"I'm so glad to meet you," she said, smiling at Melanie. "I wondered if she was ever going to bring you in here."

"It's nice to meet you," Melanie said with a big smile.

"Welcome to our little town," Tammy said to Tara. She

leaned in and said, "I know you hear this all the time, but I love your movies, especially the last one."

"Thank you, Tammy. I'm so glad you liked it," Tara said with a friendly smile.

"What can I get y'all to drink? The brisket is excellent tonight," she added.

They gave Tammy their orders and handed her the menus.

"You liked introducing Melanie as your wife," Tara said to Krista, grinning.

Krista grinned back. "I did. I haven't gotten to do that yet."

"Yes you have. You introduce me as your wife to every group that comes to Lovers Landing," Melanie said.

"I know, but this is different. It's the town," Krista said.

"I've come to town without you and everyone is very friendly," Melanie said.

"They love Krista, so they love you too," Lauren said. "Small town life," she added.

"So when do you move in?" asked Krista.

Tara laughed. "Damn Krista!"

"She's right. What are you waiting on? You won't find a better house that fits you more perfectly," said Melanie.

"Wow, I didn't realize you knew me so well," Tara teased.

Melanie simply smiled and stared at Tara.

"Do you have any questions? Seriously, y'all stop the hard sell," said Lauren.

Tara looked over at Lauren and bumped her with her shoulder. "Is the price accurate? I'm not going to quibble because I have money, but I also don't want to overpay for something either."

"Do you want it? If you do, I'll work up an offer that's

fair. No one is going to take advantage of you because of who you are. I won't let that happen," stated Lauren.

Tara tilted her head and looked into Lauren's eyes. "Thank you. You have no idea how many people try to do just that."

Lauren smiled at her. "I'll work it up in the morning."

"We're getting a new neighbor, babe," Krista said.

"Welcome to the lake," Melanie said.

"Well, well, look who we have here," a man said, walking up to the table. "So you're hanging out with the queers at the lake, huh Lauren."

Tara looked up at the man and then stood, reaching her full height, bringing her nose to nose with him. Before she said anything, Lauren grabbed her wrist and said, "Hello Matt."

"What's the matter, Matt? You don't like our money?" said Krista, her tone friendly.

"Oh hey, Krista," Matt said, his voice losing its edge. "I didn't see you. No offense."

"Who were you trying to offend then?" said Tara, narrowing her eyes.

Matt looked her in the eye and then looked down at Lauren.

"It's okay, Tara. Matt doesn't realize he has the opportunity to make a lot of money on your renovation if he doesn't fuck it up," Lauren said nonchalantly.

Matt stood a little straighter, looked down at Lauren and then back at Tara.

"You didn't mind taking money from Julia and me when we bought our place," said Krista.

"We may be queers, but we're rich queers," Tara said with a snide smile.

Melanie stood up and held out her hand. "We haven't met. I'm Melanie, Krista's wife."

Matt looked confused and then shook her hand. "It's nice to meet you."

"This is my friend Tara Holloway. She might look familiar; she's a movie star," Melanie said, introducing Tara.

Matt nodded and said curtly, "It's nice to meet you."

"Matt owns the hardware store in town and is a contractor. Tara's looking at the Hogans' place and wants to make some changes."

"I see. I'd be happy to take a look. Lauren has my contact info."

"Thanks," Tara said.

"You'd better get going, Matt. I'm sure April is waiting on you," Lauren said.

"Nice to meet y'all," he said, walking away.

"What a dick," mumbled Tara.

"You don't have to do business with him," Krista said. "My cousin Brian is a contractor and did the renovations at Lovers Landing."

"He's really not a bad guy. He's always looked up to Marcus and doesn't understand why we divorced."

"Then I feel bad for his wife," said Melanie.

Lauren chuckled. "April is nice enough. She goes her way and he goes his. But enough about my ex and his family. Here comes Tammy with our barbeque," she said cheerily.

5

Tara's phone pinged and her watch vibrated with a text message as she got back in the boat.

"I heard a ping, is that you?" said Melanie from the water. "I'm waiting on a text from Jennifer."

"Yep, it was me," Tara called to her.

When Tara didn't say anything Krista said, "Is everything all right?"

"I don't know, it's Lauren. She wants to know what I'm doing," Tara said as she held her phone to her ear. When the call connected she said, "Hi! I'm on the boat with Krista and Melanie."

"What a life," Lauren said teasingly. "Can you meet me at the lake house? We may have an issue. Krista can get you here on the boat."

"Okay, hold on," Tara said. She looked down at Krista in the water. "Lauren said there's a problem with the house. Can you take me over there in the boat?"

"Sure," Krista said, swimming towards the boat. "Tell her it'll take us about ten minutes."

"We'll be there in ten," Tara said into the phone.

"Okay. I'll wait for you on the dock," Lauren said, ending the call.

Tara shrugged as Krista and Melanie got into the boat.

"Don't worry. Lauren is the best at her job. Everything will be fine," Krista said as she climbed into the driver's seat.

"I'm sure it is. I trust her completely." Tara smiled tightly.

Krista started the boat and soon they were flying across the lake. Tara sat in the back looking at the sparkling water and the cliffs on her left. She would never tire of this vista.

She recognized the lake house as it came into view and stood between Krista and Melanie where they sat in the seats. Krista pulled the throttle back, slowing the boat.

Lauren stood on the dock and waved to them.

"Look at her," Tara said fondly. "Marcus is an idiot."

"Yeah he is," agreed Melanie, leaning back with a knowing glance toward Krista.

Krista guided the boat to the empty stall at the dock.

"I've got you on this side," Lauren said. "Give me your hand, Tara."

Tara walked behind Melanie's seat and took Lauren's hand. Her heart skipped a beat, but it always did when she touched Lauren. She'd danced with her many times and it always made her heart thud in her chest. She figured it was her body's way of fucking with her since Lauren was off limits.

Krista caught the boat on the other side and jumped out with a rope to tie them off.

"Watch your step," Lauren said to Tara as she guided her to the back of the boat where it was easier to get out.

"Thanks," Tara said, looking into Lauren's eyes, searching for a clue.

"Where were y'all swimming?" Lauren asked as Melanie and Krista came around the dock to stand next to them.

"Over by the cliffs," said Krista.

"Oh, did you jump?" she asked.

Tara shuffled from one foot to the other, her anxiety beginning to show.

Melanie answered, "No jumping today."

Lauren nodded then looked at Tara. "You're awfully antsy there, Tara. Do you meditate?"

"What? No, I don't meditate!" Tara exclaimed. "What's the problem with the lake house?" she asked, angst wracking her voice and posture.

"Well..." Lauren hesitated. "Here's the thing. I hope Krista and Melanie won't have an issue with their new neighbor." A smile couldn't be contained on her face. "Because this is *your* lake house!" Lauren raised her arms out wide.

"Really?" Tara said skeptically.

"Really," Lauren said with a wide grin.

"Hallelujah!" Tara said, grabbing Lauren around her middle and swinging her around.

"All right!" Krista and Melanie exclaimed.

Lauren wrapped her arms around the taller woman's neck and held on, laughing.

"Oh, sorry," Tara said, putting her down.

"I'm so happy for you," Lauren said, hugging her close again.

Tara pulled her arms tighter and her heart nearly beat out of her chest. She'd held Lauren many times, but this felt different. Maybe Lauren wasn't off limits any longer.

"We need to celebrate," Tara said.

"Honey, I've got you," Lauren said, stepping out of Tara's arms. "Follow me."

They walked up to the patio where Lauren had champagne chilled and glasses waiting.

"Here you go," she said, handing Tara the bottle.

"You're not going to shake it up and spray it everywhere?" Lauren asked as Tara opened it and poured everyone a glass.

"No way Tara's going to waste good champagne." Krista chuckled.

"That's right. We're drinking it." Tara grinned. "To my new home and the best realtor ever." Tara clinked her glass with Lauren's.

"Aww, thanks. I told you I loved my job and this is why!" she exclaimed, taking a drink of the bubbly.

"You're right, Tara," Krista added. "She's the best."

"To Lauren," Melanie said as they clinked glasses again and drank.

"Oh wow, I can't believe it," said Tara.

"I think you were more excited about this than we knew," said Melanie.

"I am. Since the very first time I came running down here to save Krista from Brooke, I've loved it here."

"Yeah, you did a good job on that one," Krista drawled.

Tara shrugged. "I've loved coming to Ten Queen meetings here and the best part is karaoke and dancing with you," she said, clinking her glass with Lauren's again.

"Those are fun nights." Lauren smiled and her cheeks turned pink.

"I loved having my own cabin and then it hit me that if I love it here so much why not move here," Tara said. "That's when I called Lauren."

"Move here?" said Krista. "I thought this was a vacation home."

Tara shrugged. "You never know. What do we have to do next?" she asked Lauren.

"I set up a meeting here for you tomorrow with Brian. We have a few documents to sign, but there shouldn't be any problem completing the sale. I thought you may as well get started."

"You'll be here tomorrow too, won't you?" Tara asked, suddenly nervous.

"If you want me to, I will," Lauren said.

"I need you," Tara said. "I know my home is beautiful and I always look good, but I don't do it on my own."

Lauren chuckled. "What makes you think I know anything about decorating?"

Tara scoffed. "You couldn't look more stunning at this moment. I know you know your shit."

Lauren's cheeks pinkened. "Thank you. Okay, I'll be here tomorrow, too."

Tara let out a relieved breath. "Good."

Lauren brought out a little snack tray and they celebrated.

Later Krista said, "We'd better get going before it gets too dark."

Tara turned to Lauren. "Would you mind giving me a ride back to my cabin? I'd like to go inside and look around again and make a few notes."

"I'd be happy to. You need to sign a few documents anyway," Lauren said, smiling.

"Okay then, we'll see you tomorrow," Krista said, giving Tara a hug. "You know, everything's better when you're nearby."

"I know," Tara said, hugging her back. She caught Melanie's eye and said, "In a completely friendly way."

Melanie chuckled and hugged Tara. "It's okay, I know who she's sleeping with tonight."

Tara laughed. "I'm looking forward to hanging out more with you."

"Oh no!" Krista said. "That won't be good."

"It may not be good for you, but it'll be entertaining for me." Lauren laughed.

* * *

They walked inside and Tara roamed around the main floor. Lauren had a folder with a few forms for her to sign on the coffee table. She waited and watched as Tara explored this time as the owner. When Tara walked back into the great room she looked at Lauren. "What?"

"You look happy," Lauren said, sitting in the chair opposite the couch.

Tara sat down on the couch and spread her arms on the back and took in the room and then directly at Lauren. "Thank you so much for finding this place for me."

"You're very welcome. It gives me joy to see you happy like this. However... "

Tara looked at her expectantly. "However?"

"You may not find very many women around here, but I'm sure you don't have problems with that." She smiled at Tara. "Oh wait, there's always Lovers Landing."

Tara shook her head. "Those are couples. I'm not like that."

"Is that why you never hit on me?" Lauren asked. Tara definitely made her heart beat fast and had made her lose her breath more than once over the years, but Tara never did anything inappropriate. But then again, why would Tara want someone like her? She was a now divorced woman trying to find herself. What could be more unappealing?

"I've never hit on you because you were married. Don't think I didn't want to, Lauren. But I know you needed a friend more than a fling with a lesbian. And despite what Krista says, I'm not like that anymore. I'll admit I have dated a lot of women, but that doesn't mean I had sex with all of them. The tabloids can paint a picture that isn't necessarily true."

Lauren smiled and her heart was stuck in her throat knowing Tara wanted her at one time. She swallowed and said, "I know who you are. And I'm no longer married."

They stared at one another for several moments and Lauren could hear and feel her heart pounding. She was quite sure her cheeks were flaming and she could see how dark Tara's blue eyes were now.

"We'd better get these papers signed," Lauren said, leaning forward and taking the documents out of the folder. "Let's go in here." She got up and led Tara to the large island in the kitchen.

Tara signed where Lauren indicated and when she was finished she put the papers away and turned to Tara with a huge smile.

"Hold out your hand," Lauren said. Tara did as requested. "It is with great pleasure that I give you these." Lauren dropped the keys into her hand.

Tara chuckled and closed her fist around the keys.

Lauren leaned in and said softly, "I'm not really supposed to give you those yet, but I think I can trust you." She winked.

"I won't do anything without checking with you first," Tara assured her.

They locked up the house and Lauren drove her over to her cabin at Lovers Landing.

Before Tara got out she leaned over and kissed Lauren on the cheek. "Thank you, Lauren. You've made me very happy."

"I'm glad," Lauren said softly as her mouth went dry.

Tara got out of the car and waved as she walked to the door. Lauren backed out and in her rear view mirror she could see Tara wave one more time then go inside. She reached up and touched her cheek where Tara's lips had just been and wondered what it would be like to kiss Tara Holloway.

6

Tara drove up to the lake house and smiled. *This is my lake house now!* She grabbed her keys and got out of the car just as Lauren drove up.

"I can't imagine what you're smiling at," Lauren said, getting out of her car.

"I really love this place," Tara said shyly. "It surprises me how much."

"Aww, I think this home is going to bring out parts of you that you haven't seen in a while," Lauren said thoughtfully.

Tara quirked an eyebrow. "Let's hope it's the good parts because believe me there have been some bad."

"I don't believe it!" Lauren teased.

Tara chuckled as a pickup pulled up. "Hey Brian," she said.

"Tara! It's been too long!" he said, pulling her into a hug.

"Yeah it has."

"Welcome! We need a badass like you around here," he said with a smile.

"I don't know about that," Tara said.

"Hi Lauren," Brian said, giving her a quick hug.

"Good to see you, Brian."

He looked up at the lake house and whistled. "What a nice place, Tara. Show me around."

They went inside and Tara pointed out the changes she wanted to make in each room. When they got back to the kitchen Brian looked over his notes.

"You've mainly given me paint color changes and the floor in the master bedroom," he said. He looked around the kitchen. "I suggest that if there's anything else you want to change, do it now before you move in. Do you like these cabinets? How about the appliances? Do you like the vanities in the bathrooms? What about the light fixtures?" He held up a hand and smiled. "I realize that sometimes you have to live in a place for a while to find out the things you'd like to change. Why don't you and Lauren walk through one more time and look a little closer. I'll make a few calls down here to give you an idea of when we can start."

"That's excellent advice," Lauren said. "Let's go upstairs first, okay?"

"Okay," Tara said, following her to the stairs.

Once they were in the master bedroom Lauren said, "How long do you plan to stay?"

"I don't really know. All I have going is a movie premiere at the end of the month."

"Were you going to stay during the renovations?"

"I have no plans to go back to LA until I have to."

Lauren smiled and nodded.

"I see that smile," Tara said. "Are you happy I'm staying?"

"I am," she said as the smile grew on her face.

Tara smiled back at her. "What would you think if I lived here full time?"

"I think it would be wonderful."

Tara walked to the window and looked down on her patio.

"I've actually got a paint idea for this room if you want to see," Lauren said hesitantly.

Tara whirled around. "Of course I do."

Lauren opened her iPad and showed her the colors. "I'll get paint samples for you tomorrow, but I hope you can get the idea from this."

Tara looked at the device and then looked around her room. "I love it. I wouldn't have considered that color." Tara sighed.

"What's wrong?" Lauren asked.

"This is a bit overwhelming. I have so much trouble choosing paint colors."

Lauren tilted her head and smiled kindly. "It's okay. I'll help you," she said, rubbing Tara's arm.

"Will you help me with something else?"

"Name it," Lauren said.

"Will you teach me how to drive my boat? I've driven a few times with Krista, but I could really use a few lessons." She shook her head, exasperated. "I'm sorry, Lauren. I keep asking you for help. You're going to be sorry I'm moving here."

"No I'm not. I'm happy to help. I promise you, Tara. I love doing this and especially for my friend."

Tara exhaled in relief. "Thank you," she said, pulling Lauren into a hug. "I couldn't do this without you and I really want to be here."

"I've got you, Tara."

"Thank goodness," Tara said. She didn't normally let anyone see when she felt vulnerable like this, but she trusted Lauren.

They walked into the bathroom and through the closet. Then they went downstairs and did the same.

Brian looked up when they came back into the kitchen. "Well?"

"I didn't see anything else that we haven't already talked about."

"Okay then. We'll get started on the floor. You choose paint colors and we'll get this ready for you," he said.

Tara looked over at Lauren. "Lauren has the color for the master."

Lauren pulled it up on her iPad and showed Brian.

"Oh, very nice," he said, nodding. "You know your stuff, Lauren."

"Thanks, but I want to get a sample and paint a little on the wall first. Okay, Tara?"

"If you say so."

"Give me a couple of days to get the materials and we'll get started. I'll give you a call."

"Thanks Brian," Tara said.

"Welcome home," he said, grinning.

After he left, Lauren looked at Tara. "I guess we'd better get to the hardware store and find your colors."

Tara exhaled. "Lead the way."

* * *

A few days later Lauren drove up Tara's driveway and saw her rental car and also a pickup. The door was open so she went inside. She could hear voices and then Tara's rich laughter echoed through the room. A woman's voice she didn't immediately recognize said something and Tara laughed again. A pang of jealousy shot through Lauren. She stopped and took a deep breath, composing herself before walking into the room. *Where did that come from*, she thought.

She recognized the other woman as Alexandria 'Lexie' Masingh. She was the painter that worked with Brian. Lexie wasn't as tall as Tara. She had black hair with light brown eyes and a great smile. Lauren knew she'd spent years in martial arts, giving her an athletic body. Even in work clothes with paint all over her, Lexie still turned heads. She was known to date women and be exceptionally charming.

Tara was listening intently to some story Lexie was telling and Lauren's stomach burned with jealousy once again. Something must have caught Tara's eye because she suddenly looked her way.

"Hey," Tara said, beaming a smile her way. She walked toward Lauren. "Look." She pointed to the wall in the kitchen that was halfway painted.

"Hi. That looks great," Lauren said. "Hi Lexie," she added with a forced smile.

"Hey Lauren. How's it going?" Lexie said, turning back to her work.

"I'm glad you're here," Tara said.

"I wanted to show you an idea I had for this room," Lauren said, her stomach unclenching with Tara's attention.

"Show me."

Lauren took out her iPad once again and showed Tara the colors.

"Oh Lauren, how do you do that? I wouldn't think to put those colors together, but it would look great in here," Tara said, looking from the tablet to the walls.

"I brought samples if you want to try them on the walls," she said shyly.

"You know I do."

They walked out to her car to get the paint. "What were you and Lexie laughing about?" she asked nonchalantly.

"She was telling me about some guy at the hardware store."

"Oh," Lauren said, her voice clipped.

"You okay?"

"Sure, I'm fine."

"Did I do something?" Tara asked, taking the paint from Lauren.

"No. I don't want to interrupt you and Lexie," she said, closing the car door a little harder than she intended.

"Interrupt us?" Tara said, her brow furrowed. Then recognition hit her. "Lauren, you sound kind of jealous."

"Jealous?" Lauren said, walking off.

Tara caught up to her and grabbed her arm. "What's wrong?"

Lauren let out an exasperated breath. "Nothing's wrong. I'm sorry." She smiled at Tara. "Lexie is a beautiful woman and I guess I've gotten used to having your attention," she said honestly.

Tara tilted her head with her hand still on Lauren's arm. "*You* are a beautiful woman and I'd give you more attention, but you have a job and can't be here with me all day," she said, widening her eyes.

"I wasn't fishing for a compliment."

"I know you weren't. I'd tell you that every day, but you wouldn't believe me."

Lauren began to feel more like herself and said playfully, "Try me."

Tara laughed. "I will."

"Let's see how this paint looks on your walls and then I thought I'd give you a boat lesson."

Tara's brows flew up her forehead. "Oh good!"

They went back inside and showed Lexie the paint.

"We'd like to paint a little on both walls so I can show Tara the effect," Lauren said.

"No problem," Lexie said, grabbing a couple of brushes and a tool to open the paint cans. Lexie took a can and went to one wall while Lauren and Tara went to the other.

Lauren opened the can and handed Tara the brush. "Here. You'll be giving love to your new home."

Tara looked at her skeptically and slowly took the brush from her. She dipped it into the can and ran the brush over the lip to leave the excess. She swept the brush over the wall and spread the paint.

Lauren looked on and smiled as she watched Tara's face begin to brighten.

"Hey Lauren, I saw you out with Jeff a couple of weeks ago. Is that the first time you've been out? I know it's hard to date again after so long."

Lauren saw Tara stop painting and look over at her. She didn't meet Tara's eyes, but turned to Lexie.

"It wasn't any big deal," she said.

"Wow," Lexie said. "Y'all, step back and look." She waited for them to do so and added, "It's like you brought the lake inside the room. I love the deeper blue of this wall and the lighter of yours. As much as I like the brighter blues, our lake is not that. I'll remember this, Lauren. You've always had such a good eye."

"Thanks," Lauren said, smiling at Lexie. "But what's important is you, Tara. What do you think? This is your home."

"I love it," Tara said without emotion.

"Okay," Lexie said, not noticing the change in Tara. "I'll get it ordered."

"Are you okay?" Lauren asked Tara quietly.

"Yep," she said, laying the paint brush down and putting the lid back on the paint.

"Are you ready to go in the boat?" Lauren asked, unsure of what just happened.

"Sure," Tara said, not meeting Lauren's eyes. "See you later Lexie," she said, walking toward the back door.

7

They walked down to the dock and Lauren could still see the tension in Tara's demeanor. She gave her a few instructions as they got in the boat.

"I always like to start it before leaving the dock to make sure there's nothing wrong with the engine."

"That makes sense," Tara said curtly.

"If you keep your hand out and gently keep the boat off your side of the dock you won't have to worry about the other side," Lauren said.

Tara listened and watched as she backed the boat out of the stall. Once clear of the dock Lauren got up and said, "Your turn."

Tara got in the driver's seat and waited for Lauren to sit down. She eased the throttle forward and looked to see if there were any boats nearby. With the coast clear, she jammed the throttle forward as far as it would go. The boat's nose shot in the air and Lauren fell back into her seat. As the boat picked up speed the nose trimmed down and they flew over the water.

Lauren studied Tara's profile and could see her

clenching and unclenching her jaw. Her brows were scrunched together and her cheeks were red. She got up and put her hand on Tara's shoulder and reached across her to pull the throttle back and slow the boat. Tara's muscles were tense under her hand and Lauren felt a throb of heat pass through her. This woman was alluring even when she was angry and Lauren was pretty sure Tara was mad about something. She turned the key to shut off the engine as the boat slowed.

"What is going on with you?" she asked, sitting back down in her seat.

Tara took a deep breath and turned toward Lauren. "Who's Jeff?"

Lauren could see the jealousy shooting out of Tara's eyes. She started to tease her, but thought better of it. "Jeff is a realtor," she began slowly, looking into Tara's eyes. "I heard that the Hogans were talking to him about putting their place on the market. He's asked me out at least a hundred times, so I agreed to go out to dinner with him in hopes I could get you a look at the place before it went on the market."

Tara's eyes softened, but then they narrowed. "What did you have to do?"

Lauren's eyebrows shot up her forehead and then she laughed. "Dinner, that was all."

Tara leaned back and laughed with her. She ran her hands over her face. "I'm so confused." Her eyes met Lauren's then she leaned over and grabbed her hands.

"I'm sorry I teased you about being jealous of Lexie earlier. Here I am so jealous of some realtor that I almost got us killed in a boat that I have no business driving."

"No you didn't," Lauren said, squeezing Tara's hands and

smiling. "I was jealous of Lexie and I keep giving you paint ideas like I'm going to live there too. I'm sorry."

Tara stared at her and kept rubbing her thumbs over Lauren's knuckles. Suddenly Lauren could feel her pulse pounding in her ears and she wasn't sure she was breathing.

"I know you're divorced now and open to all possibilities. I want you to know that the first time I met you my heart stopped and then fluttered in my chest, but something told me that you weren't just any woman. So we danced," she said, smiling. "And we sang and had fun and became friends."

"We did." Lauren nodded.

"It was later that Krista told me what was going on with you and honestly Lauren, I wanted to whip Marcus' ass. I could not understand what was wrong with that man, but what I did know was that I wanted to be in your life. And I told myself that if I ever got the chance I was going to treat you like you should be treated."

"Tara..." Lauren said breathlessly.

"Wait. You still make my heart hammer in my chest and I'd like you to go to my movie premiere with me as my date. We'll get all glammed up and go to the movie and the after party."

Lauren's hands covered her mouth in surprise. Tara sat there with a hopeful look on her face.

When she didn't say anything, Tara said, "Or we can go out somewhere here if you don't want to go to Hollywood."

"I'd love to go with you," Lauren said, finally gathering herself.

Tara tilted her head. "To Hollywood or here?"

Lauren laughed and grabbed her hands. "Both!"

Tara blew out a relieved breath.

"I'm flattered you asked me because the enchanting Tara

Holloway could have any woman she desires on her arm," Lauren teased.

"I've told you the tabloids and magazines like to make it look like I date a lot of women, but it's not true. I'm not like that."

"And I told you, I know who you are," Lauren said, cupping the side of Tara's face.

Tara kneeled in front of Lauren and she could see yearning in her eyes.

They both leaned forward and Lauren closed the distance between their lips. It seemed like the most natural thing in the world to kiss Tara Holloway. But what she didn't expect was how soft Tara's lips were on hers or how their touch sent an electric charge zapping through her body. She didn't expect the moan to escape her throat when she felt Tara's hand on her neck and her fingers entwine in her hair. She wondered why they hadn't done this before. She wondered why she'd ever want to stop doing this, but then Tara pulled away slightly.

"I hope I didn't just ruin our friendship," she said hoarsely.

"You didn't," Lauren said quickly, crashing her lips to Tara's. She wrapped her arms around Tara's neck and pulled her closer. She could feel Tara's hands on her thighs where she sat in the passenger seat of the boat. In perfect sync, their lips parted slightly and when their tongues touched Lauren heard Tara moan. This brought a new rush of heat flying through her and she thought her heart might pound out of her chest. The kiss had to be one of the best Lauren had ever experienced and she didn't want it to end, but when they parted all she could do was smile.

Tara smiled back at her, but didn't move. "Have you ever kissed a woman?"

Lauren grinned. "I have now. And you know what?"

"What?"

"I want to do it again," she said. And then she added, "With you."

Tara chuckled. "It'd better be with me!"

"Oh yeah?" Lauren teased, liking the way her arms felt around Tara. "I do seem to remember you have a jealous streak."

Tara wrapped her arms around Lauren's middle and pulled her close. "Kiss my worries away," she dared her.

Lauren's teasing smile turned softer and she gently placed her lips on Tara's and licked across her bottom lip. Tara parted her lips, inviting Lauren inside. She entered and explored with abandon. Tara moaned and pulled her closer as Lauren kissed her with all the passion she'd been searching for and had now found. As Lauren had her way with Tara she suddenly realized where they were and what she was doing.

She eased away and groaned. She put her forehead against Tara's. "As much as I'd like to keep doing this, I do have a client to meet in a little while."

"One more thing," Tara said, leaning back. "When I told you to ask me your questions instead of Krista, it's because I want to show you. I want to show you what it means to be loved by a woman, by someone that cares for you, by someone that puts your pleasure and your feelings first."

"Good God, Tara," Lauren said breathlessly. "How am I supposed to go to work now?"

Tara smiled. "I want to give you something to look forward to."

Lauren dropped her head and Tara got back into her seat and started the boat.

Lauren leaned back in her seat and looked over at Tara.

"Now I know why all those women in the photos are looking at you that way."

Tara killed the engine and turned back to Lauren. "I didn't want any of them the way I do you. I'm not playing around, Lauren."

Lauren smiled at her, got up and put her hands on Tara's shoulders. "I know you aren't. And I want you more than all of those other women, Tara. It surprises me, it scares me, but mostly it excites me. I don't know that I've ever felt quite like this and I want all of it with you." She leaned down and kissed Tara tenderly. "But you've got to take me back to the dock," she added sadly.

Tara grinned and once again started the boat. Before she sped up she said, "Who knew jealousy could kick your ass in gear!" Then she hit the throttle and they sped back to her house.

When they got back to the dock Tara glided the boat expertly into the stall with Lauren's help.

"Such a quick learner. You've got this," Lauren said, her voice full of pride.

Tara had already hopped out of the boat and tied it to the pole in front. She went to the back and offered Lauren her hand. When she stepped out of the boat she stumbled into Tara's arms.

"I've got you," Tara said.

Lauren looked into the most beautiful blue eyes she'd ever seen. She'd marveled at Tara's eyes from time to time because they changed colors with her mood. And right now they were a deep cobalt blue with a sparkle that Lauren knew was just for her.

She couldn't have stopped their lips coming together again if she tried. Her lips were made for Tara's and she'd just found her favorite new thing to do. All she wanted was to keep kissing Tara Holloway.

"We've got to stop," Lauren said, breathless, as she pulled away. "I promise I'm not like this."

"Like what?" Tara asked.

"Out of control," Lauren said with her arms still wrapped around Tara's neck.

"You are in perfect control, Lauren, and I hope you stay that way."

Lauren smiled and kissed Tara chastely then let her go. She reached out her hand and said, "Come on."

They walked back up to the house. Lexie waved as they continued out to Lauren's car.

"Are you going to be busy all night?" Tara asked.

"I shouldn't be."

"Let's meet at my cabin for dinner. I hear the moon over the lake is very romantic."

"Oh you have?" Lauren said, opening her car door. She got in and rolled the window down.

Tara leaned down and kissed her through the open window.

"Will there be kissing?" Lauren asked, stroking the side of Tara's face.

"I hope so," Tara said.

"Count me in. I'll see you around 6:30." Lauren started her car, grabbed Tara by the shirt and kissed her one more time before pushing her away. She winked and then backed out.

Tara stood there grinning like a kid at Christmas as she drove away. "Holy shit! She is *so* in control," she said out loud and laughing.

8

Tara had a few hours before her dinner with Lauren and rushed to Krista's house. She couldn't believe what happened and needed to talk to someone. When she walked around the back of the cabin she found Melanie reading on the patio.

"Hi Melanie," she said, looking around.

"Well hey there, Tara. How's it going?"

She grinned. "I invited Lauren to go to my movie premiere with me at the end of the month," she blurted out.

Melanie put down her book and sat up. "Sit." She patted the chair next to her. "Tell me all about it," she said excitedly.

Tara exhaled and sat down. "I've had a thing for Lauren since I first met her, but I knew she needed a friend more than a lesbian lover," Tara said, exaggerating the last few words. "And I didn't need Krista to tell me that. Sometimes she gives me no credit for being sensitive to others."

Melanie smiled. "I think she is very protective of Lauren because Julia and Heidi have teased her about Lauren's crush for years."

"Well, she didn't need to protect her from me. If anything, I'd protect Lauren."

"I know you would. So tell me what happened."

"She brought some paint samples by the house and asked me how long I was staying. I have a movie premiere at the end of the month and I really want her to go with me. Since I've been back this time, things are different between us. I mean, it feels different. I don't know if it's because the divorce is final or me moving here or what."

"What do you mean by different?" Melanie asked, quirking an eyebrow.

"There's been flirting and we've been spending a lot of time together and there's been jealousy," Tara explained.

"Jealousy?" Melanie said, her eyebrows raised.

Tara chuckled. "Yeah, jealousy. Do you know Lexie Masingh?"

"That works with Brian? Yeah, I've met her a couple of times. Very fit, flirty, and gay."

"That's the one. She's painting at my house. Lauren walked in and heard us laughing and got a little jealous. I teased her about it and learned quickly that it's not funny."

"Why? What did she do?"

"Lauren didn't do anything. She actually apologized, but later I got a taste for myself." Tara hesitated. "Lexie mentioned seeing Lauren out with a guy named Jeff."

"Oh," Melanie said, surprised.

"Yeah, needless to say I got jealous, but did not handle it as well as Lauren did," Tara said.

"What did you do?"

"Oh, I just drove us across the lake as fast as my boat would go because I was so, so..."

"Jealous?" Melanie chuckled.

"Exactly."

"How did you end up in the boat?"

Tara grinned. "It all started because Lauren came over to give me lessons driving the boat. I don't feel very confident and she was helping me out. When Lexie asked her about Jeff, my stomach dropped and I could barely speak."

"Go on," Melanie encouraged her.

"We got in the boat and Lauren backed us out and we switched seats. When I knew she was sitting, I jammed that throttle down as far as it could go. I was confused. I didn't know what to do, so I drove."

"Oh my God," Melanie said, trying not to laugh. "I know it wasn't funny."

"It is a little, now." Tara chuckled.

"What happened next?"

"Lauren got up and calmly slowed us down and asked me what was wrong. I asked her who Jeff was and she sweetly explained that he was the realtor the Hogans were talking to and had asked her out many times. She agreed to go out with him so I could see the property before it went on the market."

"Oh my God!" exclaimed Melanie, putting her hand over her mouth.

"I know! Am I an idiot or what?"

"Well," Melanie said, not finishing her sentence. "What did you do then?"

"I was honest with her. I told her how she makes me feel and that I wanted her to go to the premiere with me."

"She said yes?"

"Yeah she did," Tara said, remembering the feel of Lauren's lips on hers. That was the best first kiss she'd ever had and now all she wanted to do was keep kissing her.

"Tara? Hey, where'd you go?" Melanie said, trying to get Tara's attention.

Tara shook her head bringing her back to the present. "She said yes and then we kissed," she said, smiling at Melanie.

"Uh oh," Melanie said, her eyes getting big. "That must have been some kiss."

"Do you remember how it felt to kiss Krista for the first time?"

"Oh yeah. I didn't want to stop."

"That was this kiss. So we didn't stop, but then she had to go show a house. I don't know what to do, Melanie," Tara said, sighing.

"What do you mean?"

"I don't want to overwhelm her. She's never been with a woman, but at the same time I also want to show her what it's like. I want to love her like she should be loved. I want to devour her!"

Melanie smirked and nodded.

"It's not funny!"

"I'm not laughing! I know exactly what you mean because that's how I feel about Krista. One look and I have to have her."

"I'm so confused and happy and scared all at the same time. We're supposed to meet at my place for dinner tonight."

"You're in love with her, aren't you?" Melanie asked softly.

Tara smiled. "I have been for a long time."

"I thought so. I've mentioned it to Krista, but she didn't believe me."

"I've got to figure something out for dinner."

"I've got just the thing."

"You do?"

"Yep, come with me," Melanie said, getting up and going

into the house. Tara followed her. She reached in the refrigerator and took out a couple of containers. "I'm going to make you a sweet picnic supper that y'all can have by the water. She won't expect something like this from you. Do you have wine?"

"Yes."

"Perfect."

"What is all this?"

"Fruit, crackers, nuts, crusty bread, and my special pimento cheese," Melanie said as she packaged the food.

"Pimento cheese?"

"I'm telling you, it's magic with Krista. I have a feeling it will be with Lauren too."

"Thanks Melanie. I really appreciate this."

Melanie stopped and looked at Tara. "I want you and Lauren to have the love Krista and I have. You both deserve it."

"I want that, but I don't know about Lauren just yet. I've got to romance her, show her how special she is," replied Tara.

Melanie smiled at her. "Lauren loves you too. I've seen it when you're together or when you talk about one another. This," Melanie indicated the food, "can be your first little romantic dinner. I even have a picnic basket."

Melanie walked to a closet at the other end of the room and pulled out a picnic basket and set it on the table. She pulled out plaid napkins and a small plaid blanket that matched.

"Oh Melanie, Lauren will love this. I love this!"

Melanie laughed. "This is fun," she said, packing the food in the hamper and putting the blanket on top. "You're on your own for dessert," she said, winking.

"I told her we'd sit by the water and watch the sun set,

but I think I'll take her over to the new house. The view of the water and the sunset is perfect from that place on my patio where the two chairs are," Tara explained.

"Owww, that would be perfect, Tara," Melanie said. "Go romance your girl." She grinned.

"Thanks for helping me with all this." She remembered she'd come over to talk to Krista and asked, "Where's Krista?"

"She's at the office with Julia. Can I tell her what's going on?"

"Only if you can keep her from coming after me. I wanted to tell her that Lauren was going with me to the premiere."

"I'll make her understand. Besides, she'll be happy for you. Like I said, she's protective," Melanie said. Then she put her hand on Tara's shoulder and added, "Of both of you."

* * *

Lauren finished with her client and decided to go by Lovers Landing to see Krista. She needed to talk to someone because she couldn't get Tara and those kisses out of her mind. If she closed her eyes she could feel Tara's lips on hers and her strong arms holding her close.

She pulled up to the restaurant and went inside. Voices coming from the back reached her ears, so she walked through the bar and into their office.

"Hey! If it isn't my favorite real estate agent," said Julia cheerfully.

"How did we get so lucky?" asked Krista.

"Well," Lauren said, drawing the word out and sitting down across from them.

Krista and Julia both studied her and Julia smiled. "What have you done, Lauren Nichols?"

Lauren smiled back at her, obviously pleased with herself. "I've got a date. Well, actually two dates," she said, tilting her head.

Krista and Julia looked at one another and then at Lauren. "Well?" they said in unison excitedly.

Lauren was still smiling and said, pointing, "Julia, you're going to like it and I'm not sure about you, Krista."

"Let's hear it!" said Julia.

"Tara asked me to go to her movie premiere at the end of the month. We're going to get glamorous," she said, pretending to hold a mirror in front of her. "And then go to the after party."

"That's wonderful," said Julia. "You're going to have the time of your life. I don't know anyone that deserves it more."

"Thanks Julia," Lauren said. "What about you?" she asked, eyeing Krista.

"I think it's wonderful, too!" Krista answered.

"You do? Then why are you always trying to keep Tara away from me?" Lauren said, suddenly upset.

"I wasn't trying to keep her away," Krista said, sitting up.

"You're always telling her I'm off limits, Krista! It's not funny. I'm a grown woman and can handle Tara Holloway. For your information I'm going out with her tonight. I've kissed her and I'm planning to do it again." Once Lauren started speaking she couldn't stop and all the words tumbled out.

"Fuck yeah!" Julia yelled.

Krista's eyes were wide and she stared at Lauren. She finally said, "That's awesome! What happened?"

"You think it's awesome?" asked Lauren, narrowing her eyes.

"Yes I do. I'm sorry, Lauren. I wasn't trying to keep Tara from you. I just wanted her to know that you had a lot going on in your life."

"Tara has been the friend I needed over these last three years. Y'all have known Marcus as long as I have. I needed someone who didn't know him, who could be objective and listen. She's been that and more. Nothing happened between us until today and it has me asking myself why I waited so long," Lauren explained with a smile growing on her face. "I feel strong and emboldened when I'm with her. I know when you think of the two of us you'd think that of her, but it's me." She leaned forward in her chair. "I didn't know kissing could be that much fun."

Julia grinned and nodded. "There's other things that are even more fun."

"Oh no!" Lauren said, panicked. "I won't know what to do."

"Yes you will," said Krista, reassuring her. "Tara will show you, if that's what you want to do. I mean, you can take your time," she stammered.

"Are you kidding? After that kiss, I want it all! I've got to know!" Lauren exclaimed.

"I'm so proud of you, Lauren," Julia said. "You will be fine. We all had a first time. Remember that. I am proud that you've opened yourself to whatever is next. You're not only giving yourself a chance, you're going out and taking what you want."

"Thanks Julia. That doesn't mean I'm not afraid. I love Tara. We have a friendship like I've never had before and I don't want to mess that up," Lauren said. Then she laughed.

"What's so funny?" asked Krista.

"After we kissed for the first time, Tara said she hoped she didn't mess up our friendship. I quickly told her she didn't and ravaged her mouth." She giggled. "All I can think about is kissing her. What am I? Sixteen?"

Julia and Krista both chuckled. "You're in love with her?" asked Krista.

Lauren nodded. "I have been for a while now. Good Lord! What do I have to offer *the* Tara Holloway?" she said, panicked again.

Krista smiled. "Everything. You are exactly who Tara has always wanted and needed. You, Lauren Nichols, just as you are."

"Ditto," said Julia.

"I hope you're right. We're having dinner tonight. What do I bring?"

"Yourself. That's all she wants. It's not going to matter what you eat or drink or even what you do. As long as you're together, that's all that matters."

Lauren stood up and smiled. "I've got to go get ready."

9

When Lauren pulled up, she saw Tara sitting on her back patio with the picnic basket. She looked up when Lauren's car approached, then she grabbed the basket and walked to the car before she got out.

"Let's go over to the new house and eat on the patio. I think there's a perfect spot to watch the sunset and have a picnic," Tara said, her eyes sparkling.

"That's a great idea. Hop in," Lauren said. She watched Tara walk in front of the car. The sleeveless top she was wearing showed off her toned, tanned arms. Those were the arms that were wrapped around her earlier, holding her tight. She had paired that top with loose fitting linen shorts that made Tara's legs look even longer. Lauren wondered what it would be like to slide those shorts down those long beautiful legs and slide her hands back up them. She'd fantasized about Tara from time to time, but tonight it could happen and the thought made her mouth go dry.

After putting the picnic basket in the backseat, Tara got in the car and Lauren smiled at her. They looked at one another for a moment and then as if they were both magnets they leaned in and shared a sweet soft kiss. "Hi," Lauren said dreamily.

"Hi." Tara grinned.

Lauren blew out a breath and chuckled. She backed up and drove to Tara's new house. Lexie was gone for the day and they went through the house to the back porch. Tara led them down a couple of steps to the private little area off to the side. It had a small table and two chairs and was separated from the main part of the porch and patio with a few strategically placed potted plants.

"I wondered how you might use this little area," Lauren said.

"I thought it would be a perfect place to enjoy the view with a friend or lover," Tara said seductively.

Lauren curled an eyebrow, "Which am I?"

"I hope both," Tara said, setting the picnic basket on the table. "You look absolutely gorgeous in that dress," she added.

"This old thing?" Lauren teased, turning from side to side.

Tara laughed. "I wonder how many movies that line has been in."

"You're the movie star. You tell me," Lauren said.

Tara stopped what she was doing and gave Lauren her full attention. "You look beautiful and I know you went home to change."

"Thank you." Lauren inclined her head slightly. "You look awfully scrumptious yourself, showing off those beautiful arms and long legs."

Tara smiled. "Thank you." She went back to setting the food on the table and opening the wine. "How was your client meeting?"

"It was good. I had a few problems focusing, but other than that, it was fine," Lauren said, accepting the glass of wine Tara handed her.

"Problems focusing?" Tara asked.

"Yeah, I couldn't stop thinking about your lips on mine," she said, looking over the top of her glass.

"I may have replayed those kisses a few times since I've seen you too," Tara said shyly.

Lauren smiled. She loved this vulnerable side of Tara that she knew other people rarely saw. "This is quite a picnic you've prepared for us," Lauren said, taking a berry from the bowl.

"Melanie did most of it," Tara said, opening containers. "I went by to see Krista but she wasn't there. Melanie and I got to talking and she knew I wanted to do something special for you."

"Why would she know that?"

"Because I was glowing and she could tell something had happened," Tara said, taking the lid off the pimento cheese.

"Pimento cheese!" Lauren exclaimed. "It's one of my favorites."

"Oh good," Tara said, with a relieved sigh, passing Lauren the bread.

"You know, anything we had tonight would be special because I'm having it with you," Lauren said, smoothing the spread on a piece of bread and handing it to Tara.

"You're the one that is special and I'm going to show you every day from now on," Tara said, taking a bite.

Lauren stopped and stared at Tara for a moment. *I don't know how I've made this woman interested in me, but I hope I can keep her.*

"Why are you staring at me?" Tara asked, taking a napkin and wiping her mouth self-consciously.

"Because you're beautiful and I can't believe I'm the one you choose to be kissing." Lauren smiled softly.

"Am I not the lucky one since you're kissing me? Because that's how I feel. You could have anyone you want, Lauren, but here you are having a picnic with me. By the way," Tara said, excitedly. "They are supposed to be finished upstairs tomorrow and the furniture will be here the day after that."

"Oh, that's great. I can't wait to see your bedroom. It's going to be a sanctuary."

Tara looked at Lauren while she served herself fruit. "I know what I want to worship there," she said softly.

Lauren smiled and looked up from her plate. Then her face turned serious. "I'm scared I won't know what I'm doing. What if..."

Before she could finish Tara said, "You will know. Do you trust me?"

"Of course I do," said Lauren.

"Please don't be afraid and if you are, you have to tell me. Okay? I don't care what it is, please know you can tell me anything. I don't want you to be scared," Tara pleaded.

Lauren got up and stood in front of Tara. She took her face in her hands and gazed into the most beautiful blue eyes she'd ever seen. She saw love and knew Tara should be able to see it in her eyes as well. They may not have said it out loud to one another yet, but Tara had shown her love in so many ways. She lowered herself into Tara's lap and said, "I trust that you will tell me what you want and help me give you that if I need it."

"I will," Tara whispered.

Lauren slowly closed her eyes and touched her lips to Tara's. She felt like she could breathe again and at the same time she lost her breath. It was such a collision of emotions and sensations, but she welcomed it. She'd wanted to kiss Tara again as soon as she saw her and now that her lips were where they wanted to be she couldn't get enough. Their tongues danced to the music of their moans. Lauren could feel Tara's fingers weaving through her hair. Her other hand rested on Lauren's hip and slid down the outside of her thigh. Oh how she wanted that hand to slide under the skirt of her dress.

Tara pulled back slightly, her eyes boring into Lauren's. "The first time we make love is not going to be in a chair," she said softly. Then she began to kiss Lauren's neck.

Lauren leaned her head back and wrapped one arm around Tara's shoulders to give her better access. A sexy chuckle deep in her throat rumbled out. "I hope that doesn't mean we'll never make love out here."

Tara looked up and chuckled. "It doesn't. I want to make love to you all over this place." She took her finger and stroked it down Lauren's cheek to the middle of her chest. "I'm going to kiss every inch of your beautiful body, too," she said as her eyes followed her finger. It rested in the vee of Lauren's cleavage and then trailed down to her thigh. Tara looked back up into Lauren's eyes. She splayed her hand over Lauren's thigh and then slid it under her skirt, resting it on the outside of her leg.

Lauren could see Tara's chest heaving and saw the want in her eyes. She felt powerful knowing Tara wanted her this much. "You make me feel mighty and strong," she said, taking Tara's chin in her hand. Then she kissed her passionately and felt Tara's arms tighten around her. This was what she dreamed of, to be wanted as desperately as she wanted. It wasn't just about desire; she and Tara had built this relationship on friendship and wanting to be there for one another. Their passion was more than sex; it was love, devotion, respect, and trust.

They finally pulled away to catch their breath. "You!" Tara said, panting.

Lauren laughed, panting right along with her. "Us!"

Tara joined her laughter and slapped the side of her ass. "Why did we wait so long to do this?"

"Because I had to find out who I was and you patiently waited like the friend you are," Lauren said affectionately.

"I want to be more than your friend," Tara said.

"You are more than my friend and I'd better be more to you," Lauren said, pinning Tara with her eyes.

"You know you are. Why do I keep coming here to visit? It's not to see Krista. Why did I drop everything and come here when you called? Why do I talk to you and text you everyday? Why are you the only one I dance with?" Tara narrowed her eyes at the end of her statement.

Lauren playfully put her finger to her mouth and looked up. "Hmm, I wonder."

Tara laughed and tickled Lauren. She squirmed and then jumped up, laughing.

"Come on," Tara said, standing and holding out her hand. "Let's go down to the dock before we miss the sunset."

Lauren grabbed her hand and they walked down the steps, knocking shoulders together.

"So Melanie could tell you'd been up to something? Meaning me," Lauren asked.

"She could tell. I went by there because I wanted Krista to know I was serious about you."

"How funny. I went by her office and found her and Julia."

Tara bumped her shoulder again and said, "And?"

"I told Krista I didn't need protecting, that I could

handle you," she said with a smirk. When Tara didn't say anything Lauren said, "Well?"

"Well what? You're right. Do you remember when you said this afternoon that you are not normally out of control?"

"Yes."

"Honey, you've been in control the entire time. I can admit it and I don't care what anyone thinks."

Lauren smiled and squeezed Tara's hand. "I don't know about that."

"You just said you feel strong and mighty," Tara said, dropping her hand and raising both arms, flexing.

Lauren's eyes widened. "Damn, do that again."

Tara chuckled. "Look Lauren, we're in this together. We have been for a while now. It takes both of us—sometimes you lead, sometimes I do—but ultimately it's we, not you or me."

"I knew there was a reason I loved you. It's because you're smart and you have a way with words," Lauren said, sitting on the dock and gazing at the sun as it began to fall from the sky. When Tara didn't sit next to her she looked up and saw that Tara was smiling down at her with a look of wonder on her face.

Lauren looked up at her confused and then her eyes began to widen and she put her hands over her mouth. "I said that out loud, didn't I!" she exclaimed.

"You love me," Tara said softly, awe in her voice.

"Sit down, baby," Lauren said, patting the dock next to her. "I didn't expect to say it quite like that, but you know I do."

"How exactly did you expect to say it?" Tara chuckled, regaining her composure.

"Well," Lauren said, grabbing Tara's hand and kissing

the back of it. "I thought it would be in the heat of passion and breathlessly," she said, feigning being out of breath.

"I don't care how or when you say it because it will always sound like music to my ears, make my heart skip a beat and make my knees weak. Come to think of it, that happens anytime I see you or think of you."

"It does?" Lauren said happily. "Because that's how I feel."

Tara caressed the side of Lauren's face and looked into her eyes. "I love you too, Lauren." Then she brought their lips together in a sweet kiss that quickly heated to blazing. This kiss sealed their love and promises to come and was full of possibility.

Lauren looked into Tara's eyes and said, "This is the best date ever."

Tara chuckled. "This is better than any sunset," she said, once again caressing Lauren's face.

10

"I'll be down at the dock, Lexie," Tara said as she walked out the back door.

"Wait," Lexie said, looking up from painting around the fireplace. "Everything is finished upstairs if you want to take a look."

"Okay. I'll go up when Lauren gets here."

"You and Lauren, huh?" Lexie said.

Tara stopped and turned around. She couldn't hide the smile that appeared on her face whenever she heard Lauren's name. "What?"

Lexie smiled casually. "I think it's cool. Lauren is one of the best people I know and I haven't seen her this happy." She shrugged then added, "Ever."

"I plan to keep it that way," Tara said, raising her eyebrows.

"You're a lucky woman, Tara."

"Believe me I know it," Tara assured her.

Lexie cocked her head. "I think Lauren is lucky too. I don't know you that well, but I can tell you love her and y'all make a good team."

"Thanks Lexie," Tara said, considering her words. "A good team. I like that."

Lexie went back to painting and Tara walked out to the patio and bounded down the steps to the dock. Lauren was supposed to stop by between appointments today and she couldn't wait. Tara was trying to keep busy, but her thoughts kept going back to the previous night. Lauren had let it slip that she was in love with her, but Tara was glad. She didn't have to worry about holding in the truth. *And the truth is that I am passionately and completely in love with Lauren Nichols!*

When Lauren took her back to the cabin last night Tara thought she'd stay the night. But Lauren was afraid that she wouldn't make her meetings this morning because she said she knew what would happen if she stayed. Tara smiled to herself knowing Lauren was right.

She busied herself cleaning out the boat and tidying up the dock area. At one point she stopped and relived yesterday's kiss in the middle of the lake. That kiss had released so many emotions. It brought her joy and made her happy and it gave her a taste of what was to come. She couldn't wait and she knew Lauren was ready too. That was one thing she appreciated about Lauren; she knew what she wanted and although this was new to her, she didn't let Tara take the lead. Lauren was bold and vocal.

Tara was brought out of her thoughts and chores by a shout, but it was the sweetest shout she'd ever heard.

"Hey gorgeous!" Lauren yelled from the patio.

Tara came out from under the covered dock and looked up toward the house. Lauren was standing on the patio in a tight straight skirt and a sleeveless top waving at her. "Do you want to fool around?" she yelled at Tara, grinning.

Tara shook her head and hurried up the steps. She took Lauren in her arms and spun them around.

Lauren shrieked with laughter, wrapping her arms around Tara's shoulders. "I thought that would get your attention." When they stopped, Lauren's eyes widened and she crushed her lips to Tara's. She bit down gently on Tara's lip and tugged. "God, what are you doing to me?" she murmured as she softened and deepened the kiss.

When they pulled back to get a breath Tara was panting. "Wow," she whispered.

Lauren grabbed Tara's face with her hands and then chuckled. "Damn!" They both laughed.

"You look good enough to undress," Tara said.

Lauren giggled. "If you'd ever get that bed maybe I'd let you."

Tara grinned then pouted "I can't believe you didn't stay last night."

"You know why I didn't," Lauren said. "We'd still be there."

"Probably," Tara said, giving her a quick kiss. "Do you want to see upstairs with me? It's finished."

"Owww," Lauren said. "How does it look?"

"I don't know. I was waiting on you so we could see it together."

Lauren looked at her affectionately. "You did?"

Tara shrugged and grabbed her hand, leading them both into the house. They walked up the stairs and into the loft.

"This looks nice," Lauren said, spinning around the space with her arms out.

"Let's look in here," Tara said, holding her hand out to Lauren and nodding toward the bedroom door. Tara felt like that was something they should do together. After all, Lauren had helped her with paint colors, furniture, and even how to set up the room. It had begun to feel like their home to Tara, not just hers.

They walked through the door and Tara immediately smiled. "Oh, yes," she said, squeezing Lauren's hand.

Lauren looked around, nodding. "It's beautiful." She pulled them over to where she'd told Tara the bed should be placed. "This is the spot," she said, looking out toward the windows and then at Tara.

Tara nodded, then slouched, dropping her shoulders and head. "Why can't the bed come today!"

Lauren chuckled. "It's okay, darlin'. Only one more day, right?"

"Yes. I called them this morning hoping it would be today."

Lauren turned toward Tara and put her arms around her neck. "This will be a beautiful room."

"You can be here tomorrow when they set everything up, right?" Tara said, resting her hands on Lauren's hips.

"Yes. You already asked me. Gosh, I feel like this is my place too," Lauren said teasingly.

"It could be," Tara said, her tone serious. "You've heard the stereotypes. We lesbians move fast," she said more playfully.

"I'll stay with you tomorrow night," Lauren offered.

"You have to!" Tara exclaimed, grinning. "But what about tonight? You could stay at the cabin with me."

"Did you forget we're having dinner with Krista and Melanie tonight?"

Tara's shoulders dropped. "I did."

"We'll figure it out," she said, staring into Tara's eyes. "I know you want our first time to be special, but I'm pretty sure that every time is going to be special with you."

Tara smiled at her and then kissed her softly. Lauren

pulled her closer and deepened the kiss. *Lexie was right*, Tara thought, *I am a lucky woman*.

"Mmm," Lauren murmured as she kissed Tara's neck. "Maybe we should go back to my place."

"Don't tease me like that. I know you have showings this afternoon," Tara replied, running her hands down Lauren's back and cupping her butt.

"God, I love you. Whew," Lauren said, pulling away and swatting Tara's ass. "I'll pick you up at 6:30 tonight," she said, swinging her hips as she walked towards the door. She stopped and turned around. "What are you doing?"

"Just watching, babe."

Lauren gave her an innocent look.

"Don't even pretend you don't know what you're doing," Tara said, joining her. "And I love it," she added, putting her arm around her as they walked into the loft. "That skirt looks lovely on you and will look even lovelier as I take it off."

Lauren giggled. "I'll remember to wear it again soon."

"You do that." Tara winked.

"I heard a lot of happy laughter coming from upstairs," said Lexie once they'd gotten back into the living room.

"The bedroom looks great, Lexie," said Lauren.

"Thanks. I think the color is perfect. That's all you, Lauren."

"I'll walk you out," said Tara.

Once Lauren was in the car Tara leaned in and kissed her. "See you later."

"You will."

* * *

"Come in, come in," Krista said warmly.

Lauren and Tara walked in the back door. "I love the familiarity here at the lake," Tara said. "Do you ever use the front door?"

Krista and Lauren looked at one another and chuckled. "Not for family," Krista said. "And you two are definitely family." She smiled.

"Hey you two. I'm so glad to see you," Melanie said, coming in from the bedroom.

"Hi Melanie," Lauren said. "Thanks for having us. And thank you for the picnic last night. Pimento cheese is always a winner."

Melanie looked at Tara quickly and smiled. "I kind of thought you'd like that."

"Listen, I wanted to apologize to you both," Krista said, sounding anxious. "I'm sorry if anything I said kept you apart. I can see how happy Lauren is and if I in any way–" she stammered.

"What are you talking about?" Tara said.

"I know I said things to make you back off from Lauren and I'm sorry."

Tara laughed. "You didn't make me back away."

"Lauren made it very clear yesterday that she could take care of herself and I didn't give her the respect I should have."

"I should tell you this without an audience, but since we are family," Tara said, looking from Lauren to Krista and Melanie, "I knew the minute I met you, Lauren, that I wanted more than a night or two when I came to visit. You danced right into my heart that first night."

"And you were patient and gave me time to find out who I was," Lauren said to Tara. "I'm not sure Krista thought that a small town real estate agent could handle the big Hollywood movie star." Lauren grinned.

"Was *she* wrong?" Tara laughed and put her arm around Lauren.

"Why do you think I kept asking you questions about being with women?" Lauren asked Krista.

"I thought you were exploring the possibilities. You said that you knew there had to be more than what you had in your marriage."

"I knew my marriage was over long ago. I asked you because I was falling in love with Tara. I didn't think there was any way she could look at me like she did those other women, but was I ever wrong," she said, smiling lovingly at Tara.

Krista laughed. "And you were falling in love right under our noses."

"I tried to tell you," Melanie said, putting her arm around Krista's waist.

"Yeah you did. So, we're okay? Y'all aren't mad at me?" Krista asked.

"No. We knew what we were doing," said Lauren. "Sort of." She laughed.

"Tell us about the new house," said Melanie. "How's it coming?"

"Good. Brian has Lexie painting and she finished the upstairs. The furniture is supposed to be delivered tomorrow and I can't wait," said Tara. "The downstairs won't quite be ready so we'll keep the furniture in the office or spare bedrooms, but the master should be set up by tomorrow evening."

"Oh and I can imagine what will be going on in there," Krista teased.

"Let me ask y'all." Lauren gave Tara a teasing look. "I had Tara in a rather compromising position yesterday," she explained. "And she told me that our first time was *not* going to be on the patio."

Melanie laughed. "I understand that. The same thing happened with us."

"What? Tell me," said Lauren.

"Well, we were skinny dipping," Melanie said, then paused.

Lauren and Tara's faces lit up.

"Yep and I told her we were not making love for the first time in the lake."

Tara chuckled. "I did, however, say that it didn't mean it wouldn't happen on the patio sometime. But come on, as much as I wanted to..."

"*You* wanted to!" Lauren exclaimed. "So did I!"

Krista and Melanie laughed.

"I'm so happy for y'all!" Krista said, putting an arm around each of them.

"Let's eat and tell more embarrassing stories," said Melanie, laughing.

11

After clearing the table and putting the leftovers away Krista turned and said, "Let's go out and sit by the water. It's beginning to cool off at night."

"Are you sure we can't help with the dishes?" asked Tara.

"It won't take any time. Krista and I will do it later," said Melanie.

"One thing I'm looking forward to is cooking in my new kitchen. Did you see those appliances and how it's set up? As much as I used to love cooking years ago I have about as much business in that kitchen as I did driving my boat." Tara chuckled.

"You know how to drive that boat just fine," Lauren said with a wink.

"I see a story in that wink." Krista chuckled as they grabbed their glasses and went outside. "I know who can help you in the kitchen."

"Who?" asked Tara.

"Emily, Lauren's daughter. She's helped us out at the restaurant and she is amazing," said Krista.

Tara looked at Lauren. "What do you think?"

"I think she'd love to come cook in that kitchen. I thought of her when I first saw it."

"Do you think she's going to have a problem with this?" Melanie asked, pointing between Lauren and Tara.

"I don't think so. She has gay friends," said Lauren.

"But will she have a problem with you being with someone new?" continued Melanie.

"No. When we decided to divorce I talked to her and explained what happened and how I felt. She knows I love her dad, but I'm not in love with him."

"What about Justin?" asked Krista. "He was pretty upset about the divorce, wasn't he?"

"Oh, Justin. Who knows with that kid. He didn't understand at first why we couldn't still be married and just be friends. I think he's been so focused on his job and making money that his heart is a little closed off."

Tara looked at Lauren with concern.

"Isn't he close with his Uncle Matt?" Krista asked.

"Yes, but Matt isn't so bad. He sees it like he's taking up for his brother when he's being an ass to me. He won't always be like that," Lauren said, taking Tara's hand in hers. "Besides, Justin will probably think it's cool because he loves your movies."

"Would it upset you if Marcus was dating someone else?" Melanie asked.

"Not at all. We've even talked about it. I know he's been out on a few dates."

"Your town doesn't have a problem with Lovers Landing, so they shouldn't have a problem with us, right?" Tara asked.

"Why would they? It doesn't matter who I love," Lauren said.

Tara exhaled and smiled. She'd never get tired of hearing Lauren say that.

"We need to have a house-warming party for you," said Krista.

"We do!" Melanie exclaimed.

"I don't know anyone around here but you and Julia and Heidi."

"Lauren knows everyone. That would be a good way to introduce you to our friends," said Krista.

"I don't know," Tara said hesitantly.

"It's okay, Tara. I was a little nervous meeting all their friends too," said Melanie.

"It's not that I'm nervous. I just don't want anyone to give you a hard time and I'm afraid someone will," Tara said to Lauren.

Lauren squeezed her hand. "Honey, I know that's going to happen. There's always going to be someone that has something to say, but I have you and that's all that matters to me."

Tara smiled. "You do have me, but Lauren, people can be cruel."

"She's right. There are hateful, spiteful people, even in our little town," said Krista.

"It's okay, y'all. I'm in love with you, Tara. When did you let what someone said stop you?"

Tara scoffed then a big smile lit her face. "I love you too, and I am one lucky woman."

"We can all agree on that," Lauren said, leaning over and kissing her on the cheek while Krista and Melanie laughed.

* * *

The delivery people had finished unloading the furniture and were upstairs putting the bed together. When they had finished with the others, Tara had shown them where to place each piece. All that was left was the bed.

She was in the living room pacing from the front window to the back door when Lexie said, "You're going to have to replace that floor if you keep that up."

"Lauren was supposed to be here," Tara began.

"And here she is," Lauren said, walking into the room and seeing how anxious Tara was. "Hey baby," she said to Tara, grabbing her hand. "Lexie, if you'll excuse us," she said, dragging Tara into the office.

She pushed the door closed and grabbed Tara's face. "This is so exciting!"

"I know!" Tara rested her hands on Lauren's hips.

"I want you to breathe with me," she said, inhaling deeply. "Come on." Tara did as Lauren instructed. "And let it out slowly." Lauren exhaled. "Let's do that again."

They repeated the deep breaths in and out a couple more times.

"Isn't that better?" Lauren said, her eyes sparkling.

"I'm better because you're here. I've never been this excited to move into a new

house. This feels like home and I haven't had that in a long time. You make it feel like home."

Lauren smiled at Tara and kissed her softly. "I'm excited too. Let's go upstairs and see how it looks."

They walked up the stairs and when Lauren stepped into the bedroom she gasped. "This is so beautiful."

"It will look even better when we get something on the walls."

"Is this where you wanted it, Ms. Holloway?" asked the delivery man.

Tara glanced over at Lauren and she nodded.

"That's the spot." She grinned. "Thanks guys."

"I think that's the last of it. I'm going to go down and check the truck," he said.

"Thanks again for the autographs."

"No problem. Thank you for all of this," Tara said, spreading her arms wide. She reached in her pocket and pulled out cash to tip each of them.

When they left the room Lauren turned to Tara and said, "This looks awesome.

Stay there, I'll be right back."

"Wait, what?" Tara turned around and she was gone.

Lauren came back into the room a few minutes later and found Tara gazing out the window. "What a nice view," she said.

Tara turned around and saw her holding a bottle of champagne and two glasses.

Lauren handed her the glasses as she opened the bottle. She poured them both a glass and held hers up. "Welcome home," she said, clinking her glass to Tara's.

They both took a sip and then Lauren took their glasses and set them on the table by the windows. "The thing that I like about this bed is that you didn't get a footboard," she said, backing Tara to the end of it. "So I can do this," she added, placing her hands on Tara's chest and pushing her back on the bed. Tara grinned up at her.

Lauren crawled on top of Tara. "I sent Lexie home for the day and locked the door. This may not be the way you thought our first time would go, but Tara, I can't wait any longer." She sat up and pulled her shirt over her head. When she reached behind her back to unfasten her bra Tara stopped her.

"Let me," she said, her voice husky. She reached behind

Lauren, unhooking her bra and slowly pulling the straps down. "You are so beautiful," she whispered.

Lauren smiled at her and pulled Tara's shirt over her head and quickly unhooked her bra. Then she pushed Tara back down on the bed and took a deep breath. She hooked her fingers into Tara's shorts and pulled them and her panties off at the same time. Then she did the same to her own as Tara inched up the bed. Lauren couldn't take her eyes off this stunning woman. She may have never made love to a woman before, but Tara made her feel confident and in control. Her eyes shone with love, but they were blue-black with desire.

Lauren smiled. "We'll do it your way next." She leaned down and pressed her lips to Tara's and kissed her slowly and seductively. Then she began kissing a path from her neck up to her ear. "I love your soft skin," she murmured. "But I'm not sure what I'm doing. I want to show you the love that's grown in my heart for three years now," she whispered.

"Touch me and watch what your love does to my body," Tara said softly.

"You're so beautiful," she said breathlessly. "I know I keep saying that, but you are." Lauren took her fingers and gently trailed them where she'd kissed Tara's neck and then down the middle of her chest. She took one finger and circled Tara's nipple and watched it harden as goose bumps appeared in the wake of her touch.

"See? My body feels your love," Tara said, her chest rising and falling quickly.

Lauren met her eyes and smiled. She cupped Tara's breast and then rolled her nipple between her finger and thumb. Tara's eyes closed briefly and she moaned.

"That feels so good," she said, opening her eyes.

Lauren kissed her again harder as she continued to squeeze her breast. They were both breathing hard now. Lauren pulled away and kissed down Tara's chest to her other breast. This time she used her tongue to circle Tara's nipple and then sucked it into her mouth.

"Oh God, Lauren," Tara groaned as her fingers ran through Lauren's hair.

"Mmm," Lauren moaned. "I like this."

Tara giggled. "So do I!"

Lauren smiled against Tara's breast and then her hand began to roam across Tara's stomach and down her outer thigh. Her kisses were on Tara's neck again as her fingers found her short hairs. Tara gasped and moaned deep in her throat.

"Thank you for giving me your body in this moment. I want to make you feel the love mine feels from you."

"I do, Lauren. Touch me, feel me, do what you feel comfortable with."

Lauren ran one finger into Tara's wetness and she groaned louder. "You're so wet," she said softly.

"You do that to me."

Lauren began to explore, running her finger between Tara's folds and around her throbbing clit. "You are hot and I don't mean to look at. God, Tara, I love touching you."

Tara blew out a breath. "I'm loving it too."

"You are so patient with me and make me feel emboldened," Lauren murmured as she found Tara's opening and circled it. Then she slowly pushed her finger inside and Tara moaned Lauren's name.

"Oh baby," Lauren said. "I've never felt anything so soft and warm and perfect."

"That is so good," Tara groaned.

"Like this?" Lauren said as she began to slowly move her finger in and out.

"Oh yes," Tara breathed. "Add another finger." Lauren did and Tara moaned again. "Oh baby, that feels so good."

"Mmm, you feel good," Lauren murmured as she kissed Tara. Her tongue was inside Tara's mouth just as her fingers were inside her and Lauren thought she might come right then. This woman she loved trusted her and let her seek and search for her most sensitive spots and that filled Lauren's heart to overflowing.

"A little faster, babe," Tara said, her hips matching Lauren's rhythm. "Oh yeah."

Lauren could feel Tara's hands on her back and her hips began to slow down. She pushed a little deeper and felt Tara's arms tighten around her.

"Oh God, I'm close, Lauren. Kiss me, baby," Tara said between breaths.

Lauren kissed Tara hard, getting caught up in the moment with the movement, the sounds, and the scent.

Tara pulled her lips away and said breathlessly, "I've got to hold you close."

Lauren pushed in deeper as Tara's arms tightened around her even more. "I love you, Tara," she exclaimed.

Lauren felt Tara's body stiffen as she held on tight. She could feel the orgasm roll through Tara and didn't dare move her fingers as she was clamped down on them. It was the most exquisite feeling and when Tara fell back on the bed she said, "Oh Lauren, I love you, too."

Lauren smoothed the hair off Tara's damp forehead and kissed it and then kissed her cheek. "That was amazing," she whispered.

"My God, Lauren," Tara finally said, rubbing up and down Lauren's back.

Lauren pulled back and looked in her eyes, unsure if it had been as wonderful for Tara as it had been for her.

Tara smiled and curled a lock of Lauren's hair behind her ear. "You are incredible."

"It was all right?"

"It was more than all right. It was perfect. Do you understand what I mean about what you do to my body now? You just filled my heart with love and made my insides sing."

"I love you so much, Tara. I do."

"I know. Let me show you how much I love you."

12

Tara gently pushed Lauren onto her back. "My way included sheets, but I'm glad you couldn't wait. That let me know how much you wanted me."

"You couldn't tell from all the kisses and longing looks and frustrated sighs I've given you over the last two days?" Lauren chuckled.

"I know you want me, but I like how you take charge," Tara admitted.

"Really? You let me do that. I don't know what it is, but I feel confident as well as curious and I know I'm safe to ask questions and be unsure, knowing you won't judge me."

"I want all of you and I want you to be whoever you want to be," Tara said, smiling down at her.

"Right now I want to be your lover," Lauren replied. Tara gave her a sexy smile that made Lauren wet all over again. "My God, Tara," Lauren swooned. "And you're all mine." She pulled her down for a scorching kiss.

"I love you," Tara whispered in her ear and kissed the pulse point in her neck. She nipped and licked and Lauren moaned.

"Mmm," she panted.

Tara kissed down her chest and over to one of her ample breasts. "So beautiful," she murmured as she circled her nipple. Then she took it in her mouth and gently bit down.

"Oh shit, Tara," Lauren said as her hands cradled Tara's head.

Tara continued to lick, suck and nibble as Lauren pulled her hair, combing her fingers through it.

She replaced her mouth with her hands and began kissing Lauren's stomach. She kissed the faint scar from a C section and ran her tongue along the puckered skin. Her right hand stroked down Lauren's leg. She bent it and opened her legs wide.

Lauren's chest was heaving up and down. She didn't think she'd ever wanted to be touched as much as she did at this moment. And she only wanted Tara. When she felt Tara's breath on her sex she gasped. "Oh Tara." The anticipation was maddening and glorious all at the same time.

But Tara didn't tease her, seeming to be just as turned on as Lauren was when she said, "My love." Then her tongue found Lauren's opening and she licked up from there and Lauren almost came undone. Her hands slammed down on the bed as her hips bucked, trying to get closer to Tara's glorious mouth.

She swirled her tongue around Lauren's engorged clit and when she sucked it into her mouth Lauren rose up and her hands grabbed Tara's head. "Dear God, Tara, yes!"

Tara went to work worshipping this most sensitive part of Lauren and her moans only encouraged her. Lauren felt how much Tara loved her. When she gently circled her finger around Lauren's opening and pushed inside, Lauren felt her love even more.

Lauren's hands tried to fist the mattress cover and when

there was nothing to hold she flattened them against the bed and pushed her hips up. She wanted all of Tara: she wanted her love, she wanted a life together, she wanted forever.

"Kiss me, Tara," she groaned, grabbing for her head.

Tara hovered over her as her fingers moved in and out. "I love you, Lauren," she said fiercely then crashed their lips together. Lauren threw her arms around Tara and held on. She loved this feeling of Tara everywhere. She never wanted it to end.

The orgasm ripped through her with such intensity she'd thought she'd explode into thousands of pieces if Tara wasn't holding on to her.

"I've got you," Tara whispered.

Lauren held on and let the waves roll through her again and again. *So this is what it feels like*, she thought, *to be loved and love your person, your soulmate*. She and Marcus had had good sex and they'd loved each other, but it never felt like this. This felt like every part of her was loved by every part of Tara. She touched and loved every part of her being; in her soul and in her heart. She hoped, no, she *knew* that Tara felt it too. There was no way she could be apart from her ever again.

"Are you okay?" Tara asked softly.

Lauren hugged Tara close. "I'm loved," she responded.

Tara pulled back so she could see into Lauren's eyes. "You are loved, by me." She grinned.

Lauren grabbed her face and kissed her tenderly.

"You're not saying anything," Tara said nervously.

"That doesn't happen to me very often." Lauren chuckled. "You know I'm honest and say what I think with you," she said tentatively.

"That's something I love and you'd better be honest now," Tara said.

Lauren saw her swallow and lick her lips. There was apprehension in her eyes and Lauren wanted to ease that. "I felt you everywhere," she said, smiling. "And I never wanted it to end. I don't want us to ever end. This part may be new for us, but loving you and wanting a life with you isn't. I've wanted that for a long time, but didn't exactly know how to tell you."

Tara looked at her, seeming relieved. "I cannot tell you how happy I am to hear that. Lauren, I feel like I touched your soul just now. I gave you my heart—or you took it," she said, smiling. "You take what you want, but please know, I don't ever want to be without you either."

"You didn't just touch my soul; you took my heart," Lauren said, smiling lovingly. "Now you are stuck with me."

Tara rolled over on the bed next to Lauren and let out a big breath. "I've never been happier."

Lauren laughed and rolled over on her side, gazing at Tara's profile. "Do you realize this could be a lot of fun for you because I'm new to this?" she asked, running her hand down the middle of Tara's chest.

"This is a lot of fun for me, but what do you mean?"

"There's all kinds of things you can show me that I've never done before."

Tara chuckled. "Like what?"

"I don't know," Lauren said, rubbing her hand over Tara's stomach. "I've heard about toys."

"Oh you have." Tara smiled. "It may surprise you to know that I've never used any toys before."

Lauren cut her eyes from watching her hand to look at Tara. "Really?"

"That's right. So, if you want to experiment then it will be new to both of us," Tara said.

"You'd do that for me?"

Tara rolled over to face Lauren and cupped her face. "I'd do anything for you." She leaned in and kissed her. "One thing I don't like about living here is that you can't order take-out and have it delivered when you've worked up such a hunger."

"That's when you have to think ahead, and lucky for you..." Lauren said.

"Lucky for me I have you," said Tara.

"That's right, and I brought a few things by this morning while you were out riding bikes with Krista."

"You did? Lexie didn't say you'd been by."

"I told her not to, that it was a surprise."

"She said we were a good team and she's right."

"We are a good team, but there's something else I want to do first," Lauren said, crawling on top of Tara. She kissed her lips and then began to kiss lower and lower until she licked around her belly button. "This looks like a lot of fun. I know how good it feels and I have a feeling you taste divine," she said with a wicked grin.

"Lauren," Tara said. "You don't have to do that."

"I know that, babe. I want to. Do you have any idea how incredible you just made me feel?" she exclaimed.

"Yes I do because you told me."

"I want to do this. I've wanted to for a long, long time," said Lauren.

Tara stared into her eyes. "A long time?"

"Yeah, I had to find my courage and confidence that you loved me more than a friend and would give me a chance. But that didn't stop a girl from dreaming."

"Just when I think I know you, you surprise me like this."

"You know me. You're the one that gave me the time, remember?" Lauren raised up and kissed Tara sweetly. She deepened the kiss and could feel her heart speed up again. "I want all of you, Tara. I want all of your body," she said softly.

"I'm yours," Tara said breathlessly.

Lauren kissed her way back down the body she loved.

* * *

"Is this what lesbians do? Eat in bed after having lots of sex?" Lauren asked, taking a bite of her sandwich.

Tara laughed. "I don't know, but it's what this lesbian is doing because her *lover,* keeps making her come over and over."

Lauren laughed. "I can't help it! I love your body and the way it loves me."

"Oh baby, I'm not complaining!" They both laughed.

"Are you sure sandwiches are okay?" Lauren asked.

"Yes, you know I love sandwiches," Tara said, taking a bite. "Do you think Emily would give me a cooking lesson?"

"Yes, she'd love to cook in that kitchen."

"Would you text her for me and see when she's coming in again?"

"I will."

"Thanks." Tara grinned, leaning over and kissing Lauren.

"I think I'm done," Lauren said in a sexy voice. "How about you?"

Before Tara could answer Lauren's phone rang. Her face lit up. "Here's your chance to ask Emily yourself. That's her ringtone," she said, reaching for her phone on the bedside table.

"Does it feel funny sitting here naked in bed, talking to your daughter?" Tara teased.

"No," Lauren scoffed. "She's not FaceTiming us." She grinned, connecting the call. "Hi honey, you're on speaker."

Tara couldn't help laughing at Lauren.

"Hi Mom, who's with you?"

"I'm at Tara's. Her furniture came today and we just finished setting up the bedroom. You should see it!" she said, grinning at Tara.

"Maybe I can soon," Emily said.

"What do you mean?" asked Lauren.

"I'm coming in to see my momma. I've missed you."

"I've missed you too. Are you coming in this weekend?"

"Mom, you know the weekends are the busy times at the restaurant. I thought I'd come in and spend Wednesday night."

"That'd be great. Tara has something to ask you," Lauren said, smiling at Tara and nodding encouragement.

"Hi Emily. Am I finally going to get to meet you?"

"I hope so. I'd love to see your new home," said Emily.

"I have this awesome kitchen and I'd love for you to give me a cooking lesson and help me set it up. I don't have anything here so I'm starting from scratch. I used to love to cook, but haven't in a long time," explained Tara.

"I'd love to. Let's do it Wednesday. Maybe we can cook dinner or at least I can get an idea of what you have," said Emily excitedly.

"I don't want to intrude on your time with your mom," said Tara.

"She'll be with you, won't she?"

Tara and Lauren looked at each other.

"I will. I can't wait for you two to meet," said Lauren as Tara's eyes widened.

"Me too. I need to meet this woman that my mom talks about all the time," Emily said playfully.

"I talk about her all the time too. I can't wait for you to see how she helped me decorate this place," Tara said.

"Sounds good. I'll see you Wednesday. Can't wait to meet you, Tara."

"Same for me," Tara answered.

"Love you, Mom."

"Love you too, honey." Lauren ended the call and smiled at Tara

"You talk about me all the time to your kids?" asked Tara.

"I'm in love with you and I'm not going to hide it. Besides, we're together a lot and you make me happy so yes, I'm going to talk about you," said Lauren. "She's going to know the minute she sees us together anyway."

"What? Why?"

"The way we look at each other. It's obvious and I don't want to hide it. I'm proud to be with you," Lauren said, getting up and clearing the food from the bed. "I can't wait for you and Emily to meet."

"I'm suddenly very nervous," said Tara.

"Why? There's no reason to be nervous," Lauren said, taking Tara's plate and putting it on the table.

"Yes, there is. I want your kids to like me because I'm going to be in their lives and I'm madly in love with their mother."

Lauren tilted her head. "Madly in love, huh. Well, let me show you just how much I love you back." Lauren crawled back on the bed and pushed Tara down on the pillows.

"Are we ever going to make this bed?" Tara giggled.

"We have pillows now. One thing at a time," said Lauren, leaning down and kissing her with no doubts what was happening next.

Tara chuckled. "God, I love you."

"I know," Lauren said, kissing her again.

13

Tara was pretty sure most people didn't know the side of Lauren that she got to see. She was flirty, sexy, and demanding in the most pleasurable way. This had been undoubtedly the best week of her life. She had moved her things over from the cabin at Lovers Landing and Lauren had stayed over every night since the bed was delivered. She hoped that this was the beginning of their life together. There were times that she was still careful not to overwhelm Lauren because this was all new, but honestly everything felt so right; *they* felt right.

Most evenings they took the boat out for what they liked to call a sunset cruise. In the mornings they drank coffee and had breakfast on the patio if Lauren didn't have to go in to work early. When she did, Tara made sure she had coffee and something to eat before she left. There were a couple of days that she was able to come by for lunch when she was showing property in the area. Lauren liked to tease Tara about becoming so domesticated and taking care of her like a wife from the 60's. They laughed about it, but honestly Tara loved doing things for Lauren. They especially loved this past weekend lazing in bed with their beautiful view of the lake and nowhere to go or anyone to see.

Tara's days were filled with outfitting the house. She'd never done it herself before and found out there were so many things she needed, from simple things like cleaning products and essentials to dishes and glasses that she and Lauren ordered together. More and more it felt like *their* home to Tara and that's how she wanted to keep it.

On many of her trips into town she ended up at the hardware store and made sure to run into Lauren's ex brother-in-law, Matt. She knew that money talked in some circles and wanted him to know that she was willing to support his store even though Walmart was just down the road. Tara was happy and wanted everyone else to be too.

She had just unloaded the car from her most recent trip to town when Lauren came through the door from the garage. Tara smiled, knowing Lauren had parked her car inside next to Tara's just like she lived here.

"There's my love," Lauren said, wrapping her arms around Tara and kissing her.

"Mmm, hello to you."

"What's all this?" Lauren asked, helping unload the bags. "You bought dishes?"

"I didn't want to eat on paper plates when Emily is here tomorrow. I don't care how fancy they are, they're still paper. So, I bought some everyday dishes we can use until our good ones get here. It's a shame IKEA is so far away," Tara said, stacking the plates in the dishwasher.

"Do you like IKEA?" asked Lauren.

"I do. I love to look at everything and can't help but buy something," said Tara.

"We'll have to go one day. It would be an adventure with you."

"Why do you say it like that? Because I have money?"

"Not at all, baby. There's absolutely nothing wrong with having money. You worked hard for it and should enjoy it. I think it would be fun to go through there together and see what you like. I bet I could guess," said Lauren playfully.

"Let's do it. I bet I can choose the things you like," replied Tara.

Lauren stopped putting the groceries away and eyed Tara. "I bet you can. You notice everything."

Tara smiled. "Of course I notice the things you like. I love you." She closed the dishwasher door and turned it on. "How about a beer or a glass of wine?" Tara asked.

"Let's do beer at our spot on the patio. I'll run upstairs and change," Lauren said, walking toward the stairs.

"Do you need any help?" Tara asked seductively.

"Why do you think I want to go to our spot?" Lauren winked and ran upstairs.

Tara laughed and got their beers and went out to the patio.

"I got a text from Emily. She gave me a list of things to pick up for tomorrow night," Lauren said, coming out to their secluded little corner wearing a T-shirt dress.

Tara handed her a beer. "I can pick up whatever you need."

"I'm only working in the morning, so I can do it. She's meeting me here tomorrow afternoon if that's all right," said Lauren, raising her eyebrows.

"I was going to suggest that," Tara said, taking a drink of her beer and gazing at Lauren.

Lauren waited with a smirk on her face.

"What is that look for? I haven't even said anything."

"Go ahead. What was your suggestion?"

Tara exhaled. "What would you say about you and

Emily staying here tomorrow night? I mean, she's helping me out and we'll be having dinner and drinking and…"

Lauren held her hand up, stopping Tara's rambling. "I think that's a great idea." Then she leaned over and took Tara's hand. "I don't want to be away from you either."

Tara visibly relaxed and sighed. "You read me like a book."

"It's not that. Emily is going to know all about us and she may as well see how happy we are. I wouldn't be happy at my place and you here."

"You can still have your time with her. I can disappear tomorrow afternoon or after dinner, whatever you need."

"What I need is for you to relax. We'll have the afternoon so you can get to know one another."

"This is really important to me, Lauren."

"I know it is and I appreciate that." She got up and stood in front of Tara, put her hands on her shoulders and then sat down in her lap. "Now what was it you were saying about helping me undress?"

Tara grinned and captured Lauren's lips in a heated kiss. She ran her hand down Lauren's side and then her outer thigh. She teased her hand under Lauren's dress and up the front of her leg just like the first time they'd had a picnic out here. When her fingers felt Lauren's curly coarse hairs she pulled her lips away.

She grinned at Lauren. "You aren't wearing anything under this dress are you?"

"I think you just found that out. Now what are you going to do about it?" she said with a wicked smile.

There was no denying that Tara had been with many women, but not one came close to stealing her breath and jump-starting her heart the way Lauren did. With just a look or a word she set Tara's body on fire and her soul singing.

Her love was hot, fierce, and all encompassing and Tara was ready to be consumed. She'd never wanted to please a woman the way she did Lauren. It was erotic, passionate, and endless.

Tara smiled back and gave her love what she wanted.

* * *

The next day Lauren walked in and set the bags she was carrying on the kitchen island. She looked out over the living area and didn't see Tara or hear her anywhere.

"Hey babe, I'm home," she yelled.

"Hi gorgeous," Tara said, walking in from the hallway.

"What are you doing in there?" Lauren asked as she began putting food in the refrigerator.

"I was making sure everything was perfect in the guest rooms and bathrooms," Tara said, unpacking the other bag.

Lauren stopped and looked at Tara and her heart began to thump in her chest. "Don't you look nice. Do you have any idea what you do to me when you're wearing those shorts?"

Tara grinned. "I think you may have told me that before, but please go ahead." She finished putting the things away in the pantry and turned around to find Lauren staring at her.

"I'm imagining those long perfect legs wrapped around me in the most sensual way," Lauren said, looking Tara up and down, her voice husky. "And then my hands are caressing your ankles and slowly gliding up over your knees and along your inner thighs…"

"Stop!" Tara said weakly. "Or I'm going to carry you upstairs right this minute and I don't think we have time for that before Emily gets here."

Lauren shook her head, stopping the fantasy. "It's your fault for wearing those shorts."

"I wanted to look nice for you and Emily," said Tara, smiling shyly.

"I swear, people wouldn't believe the Tara I know. Come sit with me a minute before Emily gets here," Lauren said, taking Tara's hand and leading them to the couch.

"You will behave, won't you?" Tara asked before sitting next to Lauren.

"I will, but it's hard." She patted the cushion next to her. Tara sat down and put her arm around Lauren and let out a pleasant sigh.

Lauren turned to her. "Thank you for making today special for me and Emily."

"Let's wait and see if you feel the same way at the end of the day. Emily may not like me, Lauren," Tara said.

"Of course she'll like you. You are enchanting and people love you; you're a fucking movie star!"

Tara chuckled, then said earnestly, "I'm a real person and some people don't like me. It happens."

"You're *my* person and I know you and I know my daughter and she's going to love you. You'll see." Lauren touched Tara's cheek tenderly. "I love you," Lauren said softly, closing her eyes and bringing their lips together in a delicate kiss. Her chest swelled with love and she started to deepen the kiss when her phone beeped on the island.

She pulled back and her eyes widened. "That's probably Emily."

Tara took a deep breath and let it out slowly. "I can't wait to meet her."

Lauren kissed her again quickly and hopped up to get her phone. "She's here," she said, reading the text and walking toward the front door.

Tara got up and waited at the corner of the island, taking one last look around the great room.

"Come on," Lauren said at the front door.

Tara walked over just as she opened the front door. A car was pulling into the driveway and Lauren waved and walked onto the front porch. A woman with dark hair in a stylish messy bun got out of the car. As she got closer it was clear how much she looked like Lauren except for the hair color. Tara looked on as they hugged.

"Hi Mom," Emily said, squeezing Lauren with a big smile on her face.

"You found us," Lauren said, hugging her tightly. With her arm around Emily she turned to look at Tara. She was smiling at them with the happiest look on her face. Lauren felt a catch in her chest as the love hit her. She'd have to share this with Tara later.

"Em, I'd like for you to meet Tara Holloway. She is absolutely the best friend I've ever had," Lauren gushed. She didn't know where that came from, but it was all true.

Tara's eyes widened and she chuckled. "Hi Emily," she said, tilting her head. "It is so nice to finally meet you. I don't know why it's taken so long."

"I'm so happy to meet you, Tara. Has my mom been hiding you away?" Emily teased.

"Oh my God, you are Lauren's daughter." Tara laughed. "No, she hasn't been hiding me. I guess we've never been here at the same time. I'm so glad we are now."

"I am too," said Emily.

"Please come in," Tara said graciously.

"I hope you'll give me a minute to fangirl. I'm a huge fan of your movies," said Emily, walking side by side with her mom.

"Thank you. That's always nice to hear."

They walked into the house and Tara gave Lauren a wink. "This house is beautiful and I'm not bragging. I say that because your mom helped decorate it. Well, help isn't the right word. *She* made it beautiful."

"That's not entirely true. We did it together," corrected Lauren.

Tara looked at Emily and held her hand to her mouth as if sharing a secret and said in a stage whisper, "Not really. Your mom is amazing."

Emily laughed. "I know she is."

"Come look at this kitchen, Emily. You're going to love it," Lauren said.

"Oh wow, you weren't kidding, Mom. This is awesome!"

"Now you see why I need help. This is so much better than I deserve," said Tara.

"Well, we'll fix you up so you feel at home and are cooking fancy dishes for my momma in no time," said Emily, looking at the stovetop and oven.

"For me?" said Lauren.

Emily leaned up against the cabinet, crossed her arms over her chest and looked across the island where Tara and Lauren were standing side by side. "Is there something you'd like to tell me?"

"This kid of mine is such a smart ass," Lauren said, chuckling.

"I learned from the best," Emily said with a smirk.

"Tara and I have been friends for a long time now and she has decided to move here," Lauren began.

"Imagine that," murmured Emily.

Tara chuckled and then looked Emily in the eye. "I'm in love with your mom and she loves me. We're doing this life together and it's amazing. We hope you're okay with that," she said matter-of-factly. She let out a breath and then looked at Lauren. "Oh shit. Sorry, that just came out," she said tentatively.

Lauren laughed. "I think that covers it."

Emily laughed. "You don't have to be a genius to figure it out. Let's see, Tara is all you talk about and has been for years. When she asked you to start looking for property you'd have thought it was Christmas. And when she bought this place it sounded like you were moving in too. Oh and then there's the fact that Tara's gay." Emily shrugged and held up her hands.

Tara and Lauren looked at one another.

"Oh and one more thing. I don't know if I've ever seen you this happy, Mom. So yeah, I'm more than okay with it."

Lauren let out a huge breath and smiled. She put her arm through Tara's and pulled her close. "Do I really talk about Tara all the time?" she asked Emily.

Emily grinned. "All the time."

"Well, I can't help it! Look at her!" Lauren said, grabbing Tara's face in her hands and kissing her quickly.

Emily laughed again and teased, "Do I get to call you Mom, too? Just wait until I tell everyone Tara Holloway is my bonus mom."

"Oh I like you, Emily Nichols. I think we're going to get along just fine," said Tara.

"Now that we have that out of the way, show me the rest of this awesome house," said Emily.

14

As they walked downstairs from the loft Lauren said, "Was there anything else you wanted to do while you were here?"

"You mean besides spending time with my mom and meeting her girlfriend?"

"Is that why you came to see me?" asked Lauren.

"No. I came to see you because I missed you," said Emily, putting her arm around her mother. "I would like to say hi to Krista and Julia if they're around."

"I don't think they had a group come in this week," said Tara.

"I'll text them," Emily said, taking her phone out of her back pocket.

"Wait until you see this patio," Lauren said, leading them to the back door.

Emily's phone pinged and she read the text with a smile. "Julia said to meet them in the bar."

"Perfect," said Lauren.

"Do you want to take the boat?" asked Tara.

"That would be fun," said Emily. Then she looked

around and took in her surroundings. "Oh my God, this is beautiful. It's your own little oasis."

"I know, isn't it?"

"I especially like this little area over here," Emily said, walking to their private little nook.

"It's one of my favorites," Lauren said, squeezing Tara's hand.

Emily chuckled. "I bet it is."

Tara could feel her cheeks start to redden and began to walk toward the dock, hoping no one noticed.

"You must love my mom a lot," Emily said, stopping Tara in her tracks.

She turned around and eyed the younger woman. "More than anything."

"I can tell because I'm sure you don't embarrass easily."

"I'm not embarrassed, it's more like I'm remembering," said Tara, raising an eyebrow and looking at Lauren.

"You're not going to embarrass me," said Lauren plainly.

"Oh I know, nothing seems to embarrass you!" exclaimed Tara.

Emily smiled at their banter. "You'd better stop before you embarrass me."

"That's exactly why I walked away," explained Tara. "Come on. I'll show you the dock. Then we can head over to Lovers Landing. All of a sudden I could use a drink."

Lauren threw her head back and laughed.

"She loves to embarrass me and then on top of that she laughs," Tara said to Emily as they walked down the stairs together.

"Better you than me," said Emily, knocking her shoulder into Tara's.

"I guess so." Tara chuckled. When Lauren didn't follow

she turned around and saw her watching them. "What are you doing?"

"Just looking," Lauren said with love in her voice.

Tara winked at her and followed Emily onto the dock.

"Wow, this is great. You've got a diving board and everything. Are you going to get a jet ski for that spot?" she asked, indicating the vacant slip in the dock.

"I don't know. I'm still a new boat owner," replied Tara.

"You know what you're doing in the boat. You've got a good teacher," said Lauren.

"I can't imagine who your teacher could be," Emily said sarcastically.

Tara laughed, getting into the boat and starting the engine just like Lauren had taught her. Lauren untied the front of the boat while Emily got in. Then she untied the back and took Tara's hand as she stepped in next.

"Let's go, Captain," Lauren said, saluting Tara.

"Oh we all know who the real captain is," Tara said, backing the boat out of the stall.

They took off and Lauren sat in the back of the boat pointing and talking to Emily. Tara couldn't help smiling. She liked Emily and was relieved that she wasn't bothered by their relationship. *One kid down, one to go,* she thought. This was new for Tara. She never really cared if anyone approved of her relationships or dating choices, but with Lauren it was different. She thought her kids might be surprised that Lauren was in a new relationship to begin with, much less with a woman. Deep down Tara wanted Justin and Emily to like her. She didn't want to be their mother by any means, but she did hope they could be friendly.

Tara had gotten close to Julia's daughters Courtney and Becca over the years and thought of them as family. And in the short time she'd known Melanie's daughters, Stephanie and Jennifer, they had gotten along well too. It felt like this was one giant family and Tara and Lauren were part of it. She wanted Justin and Emily to feel that way too. But more than anything she wanted them to like her and approve of her and Lauren's love.

Lovers Landing came into view and she slowed down as they entered the cove. She felt Lauren's hand on her shoulder and then she smoothed her hair down from the wind. Those tiny gestures of love always melted Tara's heart.

She steered them into a vacant slip at the dock and Lauren stepped out to tie the front of the boat. Tara turned to offer Emily her hand as she stepped onto the dock. Lauren did the same for Tara, but held her hand as they walked up to the restaurant and bar.

Julia was behind the bar when they walked in. "Hey!" she yelled. "Who's up for a little day drinking!" She came out from behind the bar and hugged Emily.

"Did I hear something about day drinking?" Krista said, walking in and taking her turn to hug Emily.

"How is our favorite chef?" asked Julia.

"When are you coming to work for us?" added Krista.

Emily threw her head back and laughed. Tara noticed that Lauren did the same thing when she was excited.

"You have a chef," countered Emily. "A very good chef."

"Ah, but she's not you," said Julia.

"What are you doing here in the middle of the week?" asked Krista.

"You know weekends are the busiest times at the restaurant. But I had to come check on my momma. You'll never guess what she's been up to and neither one of you let me know," Emily said, acting miffed.

"Please share," Julia said with a twinkle in her eye. "Tell us, what has your momma been up to."

"She's gone and fallen in love with a movie star!" Emily teased with her best Texas accent.

Lauren looked at Tara and rolled her eyes. Tara thought this was the cutest act she'd seen in ages.

"I heard the movie star was madly in love with her and there for her every whim," Krista said, playing along with a gossipy prattle to her voice.

This made Tara laugh because it was true. "If I could bring some truth to your rumors," Tara said, "just the other day Lauren commented that I dote on her like a housewife from the 60's."

Julia and Krista put their hands to their chests and gasped dramatically.

"I'm here to tell you," Tara paused for a moment. "It's true!" she said with a wide grin. "*The* Tara Holloway is now a lake dwelling lesbian housewife."

"Oh you are not," Lauren said, slapping her on the arm as everyone laughed. "But you do take very good care of me," she said, kissing Tara on the cheek.

Julia went back behind the bar and said, "What's everyone drinking?"

They each got a drink and sat down at a big table.

"Were you surprised about your mom?" asked Julia, now serious.

"Not really. She only talks about Tara all the time. It wasn't too hard to figure out when she told me how she was helping decorate her place. I thought it was time to come home, meet Tara and ascertain her intentions with my mother," she said, narrowing her eyes.

"All kidding aside," said Krista. "These two," she said looking at Tara and Lauren, "are the happiest I've ever seen either of them. And I've known them both a long time. As the person that gave them grief nearly every time Tara came to visit, I can tell you, Emily, that this isn't a fling or a midlife crisis for either of them. This has been such a joy to watch two of my favorite people become best friends, fall in love, and begin a happy life together."

Tara nodded at Krista and then leaned into Lauren as she put her head on her shoulder.

"We used to tease Krista that Lauren had a crush on her because she was always asking questions about being with a woman," said Julia. "Little did we know, those questions were not about Krista; they were because she was falling for Tara. I'm still laughing about that. You got us good, Lauren."

"I wasn't trying to," said Lauren.

"I kept telling them you didn't have a crush on me," said Krista.

"I know we've been laughing and playing, but Emily, do you have a problem with our relationship?" asked Tara.

Emily smiled at Tara and her mom with affection. "I don't. Just please, keep that smile on her face. I like this new mom."

"New mom?" said Lauren.

"Yes. You've always been confident in your job, but Mom, I've noticed in our phone conversations and today how fearless you are now. You say what you want and laugh and I can tell how much you love Tara. I know you want to hold her hand right now. Please don't stop because I'm here."

"I don't know about that, Emily," said Julia. "They can't keep their hands off one another."

"Hmm, that's kind of like you and Heidi when she's here, isn't it Julia?" said Lauren accusingly. "Or you and Melanie, Krista," she added.

Krista grinned. "It's true. You've got the passion we

talked about when you sold me this place. Do you remember that conversation?"

"Of course I do. I'm not talking bad about your daddy, Emily. But I knew something was missing," said Lauren.

"We both didn't have it then, but look at us now," said Krista proudly.

"Speaking of Melanie, I need to meet her. I've heard so much about her and this great love story of yours," said Emily.

"If you'd stay longer than one night then maybe you'd get the chance," said Krista.

"Emily is helping Tara in her fancy kitchen tonight. Do you have fish in the freezer?" asked Lauren.

"I'm sure we do," said Julia.

Lauren looked at Tara and Emily. "If it's okay with y'all how about we let them come too?"

"It's fine with me," said Tara. "If it's okay with my instructor."

Emily chuckled. "I don't mind at all. It's your house," she said, looking at her mom and Tara.

Tara liked the way Emily said that. *It is our house,* she thought, and she'd keep working on Lauren to see it that way too.

"I haven't even told you about the movie premiere yet," said Lauren.

"I want to hear about that too!" said Julia.

"Okay then. You go get your wives and come over at 6:00. We'll have a little impromptu housewarming," said Lauren, squeezing Tara's hand.

"Come get what you need from the kitchen." Krista got up with Emily following her.

"And we'll bring the wine," said Julia.

Lauren leaned in close to Tara and said excitedly, "It's our first party, baby."

Tara couldn't keep the grin off her face. This day was turning out better than she'd dreamed. She brought her lips to Lauren's and kissed her softly.

15

Emily and Tara were working away in the kitchen. Lauren was staying out of their way, but watched them from her seat on the other side of the island. Tara listened and took notes as Emily suggested what pots, pans, and utensils she should get for the kitchen. When they began to prepare the meal Tara was a good student.

Lauren couldn't help the pride that swelled in her chest watching two people that she loved so much working together and having a good time. Tara would look over and wink occasionally and Emily would flash her a smile.

"Are you having fun?" Emily asked, looking at her mom.

"I'm having a great time watching the two of you," Lauren said, shrugging.

"I hope you're paying attention because I'm sure I'll forget some of this," Tara said, desperation in her voice.

"No you won't. You know what you're doing, Tara. It may have been a while since you cooked, but you've got skills."

"Shh, don't say that. Lauren will expect me to cook every night," Tara said in a loud whisper.

"I certainly will," Lauren said, laughing.

"What I love about this," Emily explained as she and Tara mixed spices, "is that this is a way to cook fish or chicken and make it look fancy, but it's really easy to do."

"I love learning these little secrets," Tara said.

They heard voices coming from outside and Lauren got up and looked out the back windows. Krista, Melanie, Julia, and Heidi were walking up the steps from the dock.

"They came over by boat," Lauren said, walking to the back door. "Come in, friends."

Their guests came inside and Lauren showed them the house while Tara and Emily put dinner in the oven. When they came down from upstairs they gathered in the kitchen for drinks.

"This place is amazing, Tara. Welcome to the lake," said Julia.

"Thanks Julia. I'm loving it here even more than I thought," Tara said, smiling at Lauren.

"What can I help you do?" said Melanie.

"First, I'd like you to meet my daughter. This is Emily," Lauren said.

"I'm so happy to meet you. Krista and Julia have told me what a great chef you are. And I have so much respect and admiration for your mom," said Melanie.

"It's nice to meet you. I know my mom is wonderful, but you admire her?" said Emily.

"Yes I do. No one could tame Tara Holloway, until she met your mom."

Tara rolled her eyes as Lauren grinned at her.

"I think it's a match made in heaven. It might have taken y'all a bit to find one another, but it's certainly been a joy to watch your love bloom. And I'm so glad Tara has moved to the lake," said Heidi.

"Thanks Heidi, I appreciate that," said Tara. She put her arm around Lauren. "It feels like home."

"Let's drink to that," said Julia, holding up her glass.

They all clinked their glasses and drank.

* * *

"Okay Melanie, you can help me set the table. We've ordered dishes and glasses, but they haven't arrived yet," said Lauren. "It's a good thing Tara happened to pick these up yesterday or we'd be eating on paper."

They all pitched in to help set the table and get the rest of the meal ready while the fish and vegetables baked.

"Why don't we go outside and enjoy the evening while everything cooks?" Tara suggested.

They all wandered out to the patio and caught up on one another's lives as well as Emily's. A bit later Tara walked inside to check on the food and Krista followed her in.

"I couldn't help but notice Lauren using the word 'we' when talking about the house," said Krista.

Tara raised her eyebrows. "I know. I hope it stays that way." She looked in the windows of both ovens, checking the fish and vegetables.

"Isn't she living here?" asked Krista.

"She has stayed here with me every night since the furniture got here. Every day she brings something else over, whether it's clothes or whatnot. I'm scared to say anything because I don't want to break the spell."

"You haven't asked her to move in?"

Tara shook her head. "Not in so many words. I tell you, Kris, Lauren and I have been friends from the start. I wanted her that first night, but I pushed those feelings aside. From there we grew this rock solid friendship that became so important to me. Even when I wasn't here, we texted or talked on the phone often. She was who I shared my days with even though we weren't in the same town. And then when I asked her to look for a place for me here I hoped that there was more between us..." She paused to take a breath and then looked Krista in the eye. "I'm telling you, I can't imagine my life without her. Even before this," she said, holding her arms wide at the expanse of the room. "She was a vital part of my life and now–" Tara tried to swallow the lump that had formed in her throat.

"I know, I get it," said Krista.

"It's like living a fucking dream!" Tara exclaimed. "I've heard people say that and here I am in the middle of it. It's unbelievable, Krista. What is it about this lake? Is it fucking magical or what?"

Krista chuckled. "I know! It's magical for Melanie and me and in a way for Julia and Heidi, too."

"What's magical?" asked Lauren, walking in and putting her arm around Tara.

"You are," said Tara, leaning down to kiss her. "Excuse us, Krista, I need just a moment." She pulled Lauren into the dining room.

Krista laughed as she walked back outside. "Take your time, love birds."

Lauren wrapped her arms around Tara's neck and pulled her down for a deep, soulful kiss. Tara's arms tightened around her hips as they let their tongues dance in harmony.

They pulled apart each breathing heavily and Tara said, "I'm so glad you came inside. I needed your kiss."

"Why do you think I came in?" Lauren asked, kissing her again just as passionately.

The timer went off on the oven and they reluctantly pulled apart. "I love you," whispered Tara.

Lauren smiled. "I'll go get the others."

Emily came in and helped Tara prepare the buffet. They had everyone fill their plates from the serving dishes on the island and then they ate together as a family in the dining room. When they finished each person took their plate to the sink and Tara herded them all into the living room. Clean up could wait for later.

"This has been such a joy," she said, looking around the room at all her friends. "I've had dinner parties before, but this spontaneous get-together has surpassed all of those."

"Darling," Krista said in her best drawn-out Hollywood accent. "It's the people, don't you know."

Tara laughed. "You couldn't be more right!"

"Mom, I thought you were going to show us your dress for the movie premiere," said Emily.

"Tell us about the movie," Heidi said.

"I have a supporting role, but it was a good part. I wanted to do something special for Lauren and I thought getting all glammed up for a movie premiere would be fun. At least I hope it is."

"Are you kidding! You're going to love it, Lauren," said Krista. "You're going to love Serena, too." She was the designer that also happened to be Krista's assistant's girlfriend.

"I already do!" said Lauren. "She's treating me like I'm a Hollywood star." She took her phone out and began to pull up the dress pictures.

"I've heard there is buzz around your performance," said Melanie.

"That's just studio tactics to get critics to talk about the movie," explained Tara.

"Maybe," said Krista. "But I talked to Libby the other day and she had very complimentary things to say about your performance."

"When did she see it?" asked Tara.

"She and Allison went to an early showing at the director's house," Krista said. "Libby doesn't hand out compliments. You know you were good."

Tara shook her head. "You know how it goes. In the moment you think it's good work, but you're never sure until you see it in the movie."

"I know, but I also know you. Let me remind you that you won the fucking academy award for Best Supporting Actress last year," Krista said, her voice rising with each word.

"That's right!" Lauren said, clapping. "That's the woman I love!"

"We love her too," Julia said, whooping as the others clapped.

Tara laughed and gave them a slight bow. "Thank you."

"Here it is!" Lauren said, showing the picture of the dress to the others.

"Oh Mom, that's gorgeous. Imagine if Tara does get nominated. Then you'll get to go to awards shows and parties," Emily said excitedly.

"Slow down, honey. I've got to get through this premiere and party first," said Lauren.

"Oh Lauren, those Hollywood people are going to eat you up," said Krista. "You'd better have a tight hold on her, Tara. They'll steal her away."

"Oh stop," Lauren said, her cheeks beginning to turn red.

"She's right," said Julia. "I remember going to the Ten

Queens movie premiere and after party. They are going to love your accent. You'd better hold tight to Tara's hand."

"I remember holding Julia's hand and before I knew it she was halfway across the room looking back at me for help. Thank goodness Krista grabbed her," added Heidi.

"Are you serious?" asked Emily.

"Partly," said Tara. "People will fall in love with your mom instantly and they'll want to talk to her and introduce her to other people and then–"

"And then I'll tell them who I'm there with and who I'm going home with," said Lauren, full of sass.

Tara grinned. "Yeah you will."

"Here y'all, look at Tara's dress," Lauren said, showing them her phone again.

"Hollywood won't know what hit them," said Krista, winking at Tara.

The rest of the evening they talked about Hollywood and movies, Ten Queens projects and Emily entertained them with stories from the restaurant. After everyone left and Tara, Lauren, and Emily had cleaned the kitchen, they sat down on the couch.

"Thank you so much for showing me all of that, Emily," said Tara. "I really appreciate it."

"I loved doing it. I want to come back and cook in that kitchen when you get everything done."

"Consider this an open invitation," said Tara.

Emily smiled and nodded, then she turned to her mom. "Mom, I'm guessing you haven't told Justin or Dad about your relationship with Tara."

"I haven't, but I will," said Lauren. "Why?"

"I'm not sure how Justin will react. He claims to always be so busy with work. I'm not sure how you'll get him to stop so you can tell him. I do know he was a big fan of yours because he had a poster on his wall in his room." she said, looking directly at Tara. "I'm sure he was devastated when you came out," she added.

Tara wrinkled her brow. "That's good to know, I guess."

"It'll be fine. What will he care anyway? Like you said, he's always so busy with work. I wonder if we ever cross his mind. You know, I'm going to have to do something about that one of these days," Lauren said. "Don't you be like that, Em. There's more to life than work."

"I know, Mom," she said, giving her hand a squeeze.

"I am going upstairs so you two can have some mother-daughter time," Tara said. She got up and kissed Lauren on the cheek.

Emily got up and gave her a hug. "I'm glad you love my mom. You make her very happy, but now I'm going to find out the real story," she said, winking at her mom.

Tara looked down at Lauren, her eyes wide.

Lauren chuckled, grabbed her face and kissed her on the lips. "Don't worry, honey. I won't tell her the good parts."

Emily laughed as Tara's cheeks reddened.

"Why do I feel like this is just the beginning of my tormented life with you two," Tara said dramatically as she walked to the stairs with the sweet sound of Lauren and Emily's laughter in her ears.

16

Lauren walked into the bedroom and found Tara sitting on the loveseat by the window.

"I thought you'd be in bed," she said, sitting down next to her and putting her hand on her knee.

"Did you know that bed feels very empty without you in it?" Tara said, smiling. "How was your talk with Emily?"

Lauren smiled. "She really likes you. Imagine that."

Tara exhaled. "I'm glad. I like her too. I bet you looked just like her at that age, but with this beautiful blonde hair." Tara smoothed her hand over Lauren's hair and then rested her arm around her shoulders. "You know," Tara began tentatively.

"Yes," Lauren said as she watched Tara carefully.

"I hope it's that easy with Justin."

"You never know with him," said Lauren.

"Justin and Emily are important to me. I want you to know that. It's not just you and me. We're a family, Lauren, including them. I know *we* may be a surprise to them, but I'm not just their mom's girlfriend."

"You want a family?" said Lauren softly.

"You are my family. We have shared our day-to-day lives with one another for several years now and took our time expressing our feelings for one another because of what? Fear? Or maybe patience?"

"What are you trying to say, babe?" Lauren asked, meeting Tara's eyes.

Tara sighed. "Do you remember how you looked at me the first time we met? When we danced together? Because with your eyes you said there's more to me than what you're seeing, give me time."

Lauren smiled. "I do remember it and I also said with that look, I want you to know me and I want to know the Tara you don't let other people see."

Tara smiled. "Sometimes I think the words need to be said. This part may be new for us, but loving you and wanting a life with you isn't. I've wanted that for a long time, but didn't exactly know how to tell you. I asked you to find me a place here because I want to be with you every day. You found this place for *us* and I bought this place for *us*. I've asked you to help with all the decisions because this is *our* home. You bring a few more of your things here each day, so why haven't you moved in? Do I need to say it? Please move into our home with me, Lauren," Tara said earnestly.

"Oh honey," Lauren exhaled. "In case you haven't noticed we've never stayed at my condo."

"I have noticed."

"I don't have any personal things unpacked at my place and I've been there six months. I knew why you asked me to find you a place here, but I guess I've made it into a game. Most of the clothes in the closet are mine and you've given me space in here. I bring a few more things each day, but neither of us ever really said it out loud."

"Well, I'm saying it. This is our home, Lauren. Can we

please move your things in? You don't have to sell your place until the market's right. I am a business woman and understand that, but can we please make it look like our home?"

"Let me ask you this. Do you miss California? Do you miss the people, your house, the life there?"

"No!" Tara exclaimed. "This is my home now, with you. When we go out for the premiere I want you to look around my house and see if there are things we need to move here. Obviously, my clothes and there are personal things I want to move, but there may be some things you like. Let me say this, no one has ever lived with me in that house. I don't want your jealous streak to kick in once we get there."

Lauren laughed. "I'm not the only one with a jealous streak! But I do appreciate you sharing that."

"Okay then, can we move your stuff?"

"Yes." Lauren grinned and kissed her. "Can we do it after we get back from California? It's kind of fun bringing something new every day."

Tara chuckled and shook her head.

Lauren leaned in and kissed her softly. "Was there anything else you needed to say?" she asked, her lips a breath away from Tara's. "Because I'd like to do this," she said, deepening the kiss and putting her arms around Tara.

"Your daughter is downstairs," Tara whispered when they pulled away to breathe.

"Then I guess you're going to have to be quiet," Lauren said confidently as she began to take her clothes off. She dropped her shirt, shorts, bra and undies one by one on the couch while Tara looked on.

"Come on darling, lose those PJ's and let me fill you with my love," Lauren said, crawling on the bed.

Tara slowly raised the tank top over her head and then

stepped out of her shorts. Lauren's sexy smile drew her forward like a moth to a flame. Lauren was the light her soul had longed for.

* * *

"Do you still feel like you're living a dream?" asked Lauren. "It feels like I've worked late every day since Emily was here two weeks ago." She walked up behind Tara and pulled her close then rested her head against her back.

Tara chuckled as she finished arranging the platter of cheese, crackers, olives, and other bite-sized treats. "You have worked late every night this week," she said, wiping her hands and turning in her arms. "And I've missed you," she added, kissing her softly.

"Mmm," Lauren moaned against her lips. "Can we skip dinner? I'd rather do this." She kissed her back eagerly.

"I'm sure you skipped lunch." Tara pulled away reluctantly. "You have to eat something."

Lauren raised her eyebrows.

"Don't even!" Tara said, laughing. She turned around and grabbed the platter. "Let's eat out here."

They went out to the patio and Lauren set their beers down. She immediately started munching on the snacks before Tara even sat down.

"I knew you'd be hungry." She chuckled.

"You take such good care of me," she said between bites. "Mmm, this is good."

"Thank you." Tara smiled.

"This should be the last late day and I finally heard from Justin. He's going to have lunch with me tomorrow while I'm in Dallas."

"Oh good." Tara studied her love. "Are you nervous to tell him about us?"

"Not at all. If he won't come home then I have to go to him. I want to tell him before we go to California."

"Have you thought about what you'll do if he doesn't approve?" she asked cautiously.

"I really don't think he'll care because it doesn't affect his life directly."

"I don't know about that. He may be busy, but it won't always be that way. I want him and Emily to visit or us to go see them. Don't you?"

Lauren wiped her mouth and smiled. "I do want them here, but I also know they have their own lives and I don't get to see them as often."

Tara sighed. "I don't want to be a problem for you and your kids."

"You won't be," said Lauren firmly.

Tara gazed at her as she continued to nosh. "Honestly, I want to get to know them. They are part of you and I can imagine how amazing they are."

Lauren chuckled. "They are pretty good people even if they are mine." She looked at Tara intently.

"What's that look?"

"It surprises me a little that you're so resolute on this. You want a family."

"I do. I've been alone for a long time, but that doesn't mean I didn't want a family. It's kind of like a dream you didn't think would ever come true and here I am living in the middle of it."

"Oh Tara, my love," Lauren said softly.

"You know what else is a dream that's going to come true?" Tara said.

"What?" Lauren grinned.

"I have wanted to take you shopping on Rodeo Drive since the day I met you."

"What? Really?" Lauren exclaimed.

"Yes! I want to make you feel like a queen! I want us to go in all the shops and if you see a dress or a pair of shoes, or a purse, whatever it is, I want to buy it for you! I want to buy it all for you! I want to lavish you with all the things you dream about, but won't do for yourself," Tara said, getting more excited as she spoke.

"Baby." Lauren smiled from ear to ear. "You don't have to buy me things to feel special."

"I know that! What good is having all this money if I can't spend it on you. Do you have any idea what you do for me? This home you've made with me and I'm not talking about the house. I'm talking about the love and comfort I feel when I walk inside our home. I feel your love. That is priceless, honey. You are the only person that has ever given me that. So if I want to spend money on you and buy you a dress. Please let me!"

Lauren threw her head back and laughed. "Well, when you put it that way. Of course you can. What if I see something that I think you should have?"

"Then we'll buy that too!" She grinned.

Lauren beamed at Tara. "This is going to be so much fun!"

"We leave in two days. You'd better get to packing."

"Not tonight. This night is for you and me. I want to gaze out at the lake from the sanctuary of our bed. I've missed our time simply holding one another and ending the day together."

Tara got up and began clearing the table. "How about a bath first?"

Lauren visibly exhaled. "I'm so gonna love you when we get upstairs."

Tara chuckled as they walked inside and put everything in the sink. "This can wait," she said, putting her arm around Lauren and leading them upstairs.

* * *

Lauren walked into the lobby of Justin's office building and found him waiting by the reception area.

"Mom," he said, hugging her. "I hope you don't mind eating in the company restaurant. I'm sorry I couldn't get away, but they have pretty good food."

"I didn't come for the food. I want to spend a little time with my son. Before long you'll be coming home to go hunting with your dad or meeting him at Cowboy games. You won't have time for me," she said, smiling at him and linking her arm through his. He had the most beautiful blond curly hair and soft brown eyes. His smile not only lit up the room, but her heart also.

"Come on," he said, leading her to the buffet. They both filled their plates and found a quiet table away from the main part of the large area.

"You look different, Mom," Justin said, taking a bite.

"I do?"

"Yeah, you look, I don't know, happy," he said.

"Well, that's because I am. That's one reason I wanted you to come home, but since you're so busy." She took a sip of her drink. "Anyway, I'm leaving tomorrow for California."

"California? How cool! Are you going with Tara? Emily told me that she's redone the Hogans' place at the lake."

"Yes, she has a movie premiere and asked me to go with her," said Lauren tentatively.

"That will be so much fun. I've got to come meet her, Mom. Emily said she's just as nice as can be."

"She is and she really wants to meet you too." Maybe this would be easier than she thought. Perhaps Emily told Justin just how wonderful Tara is.

"Have you talked to Dad lately?" Justin asked nervously, changing the subject.

"No, why?"

"I think he's seeing someone, Mom."

Lauren relaxed. "He doesn't have to tell me if he's dating someone, Justin. It's okay. I want him to be happy."

"Well, I thought maybe it would make you jealous and you'd..."

"Stop." Lauren held up her hand. "I want your dad to be happy, but it's not going to be with me."

Justin's shoulders slumped a little, but before he could say anything a man approached their table.

"Justin," he said with a friendly smile. "This can't be your mother."

"Hi Chris." Justin stood up. "This is my mom, Lauren Nichols," he said. "Mom, this is my boss, Chris Dalton."

"Mr. Dalton, so nice to meet you," Lauren said, holding out her hand.

"Could I join you?" he asked.

"Of course," Lauren said graciously.

Justin quickly pulled out a chair and made room at the table.

"Your son is quite talented, but I'm sure you know that," Chris said, taking a seat.

Lauren smiled. "I do, but it's nice when other people notice, too."

"He's made an impact in our commercial real estate department and I have a feeling he gets his skills from you."

"I don't know about that, but he may have learned a few things from me," Lauren said.

"You are a realtor in an area that my wife is interested in purchasing a vacation home," Chris said.

"Oh, I'm sure you're talking about the lake. A lot of my business comes from there. Have Justin give you my contact information and I'd be happy to help her find the perfect home," said Lauren kindly.

"I'll do that. I appreciate it." Chris continued to tell her what an asset Justin was to the company and it filled Lauren with pride.

She was happy to tell him about the property around the lake and the best places to buy. Justin's face told Lauren he was thrilled to see his boss and mother get along so well.

Before long she noticed Justin look at his watch and she hadn't had a chance to explain further about her trip with Tara and their relationship.

"Mom, I wish I could stay longer, but I need to get back to my office," he said.

"Of course," Lauren said.

"I didn't mean to take up your entire lunch, but I enjoyed meeting you," Chris said, standing up. "I'll see you upstairs, Justin."

"Mom, I'm sorry we didn't get to visit more, but I can't tell you how much that means that Chris had lunch with us. He never does that with any of my coworkers," Justin said, obviously excited. "Imagine if you could find them the perfect house like you did for Tara."

"I'm glad. I enjoyed talking to him, but Justin, you have to promise me to come home when I get back from California," she said firmly.

"Okay Mom," Justin said. "I promise. I hope you have a good time."

He gave her a big hug and walked with her back to the reception area. "I love you, Mom," he said and then hurried to the elevator. He waved to her as the door closed and he was gone.

17

"You've had that scowl on your face off and on since you got home from Dallas yesterday," commented Tara while she held Lauren's hand in the back of the car. She kissed the back of her hand. "What do I have to do so you will relax and have a good time?"

Lauren turned toward Tara from where she was gazing out the window. "I'm sorry, babe. I just wish I could've told Justin why this trip was special to me."

"And why is that?"

"Because I'm with you. I want him to know that we're more than friends. I want him to know we're in love."

"He promised to come to the lake as soon as we get back."

"I know, but we'll see if he shows up."

"Look honey, you went to him. It's not your fault his boss showed up at lunch. I know you want him to hear it from you and he will when you get back."

Lauren smiled. "You're right. I'm not going to give it another thought." She scooted closer to Tara. "My darling has planned an extravagant adventure to make me feel like the most loved woman on the planet." She kissed Tara's cheek and whispered in her ear, "What she doesn't realize is that being with her makes me feel that way every day."

Tara gazed into her eyes. She kissed her softly just as the driver turned onto her street.

"We're here, Ms. Holloway," he said, pulling into her driveway.

"Thanks, Gerald," Tara said, grinning at Lauren. "Welcome."

Gerald opened the door for Lauren as Tara got out on the other side.

Lauren gasped as she took in the front of Tara's sleek modern house. "This is amazing!"

Gerald was busy unloading their things from the trunk while Tara waited for Lauren in front of the car. She held out her hand and Lauren took it.

"It's quite different from our home at the lake," Tara said.

"I'll say. This is so modern and I love it!"

Tara chuckled as she walked them through the gate and to the front door. She held the door open for Lauren and for Gerald.

"Gerald, you can leave those there," she said, handing him several bills.

"I'm your driver for the premiere. Let me know your schedule and I'll take care of the rest," he said, bowing his head slightly.

"Oh good! I hoped you were available. Thank you. I'll text you tomorrow," she said, walking him to the gate. She went back in the house and found Lauren roaming around the living room and opening the sliding doors to the outdoor living area.

Tara smiled as she watched her take in the expansive

backyard, pool, and view of the canyon. "This is a little different from the lake, isn't it?"

"Oh Tara!" Lauren exclaimed. "It's beautiful."

"It is," Tara agreed. "You know, I always wanted a house like this when I came to California. The modern architecture screams old Hollywood to me and I loved it."

"Loved?"

"Yes, loved. I mean, I still love this house, but I feel as if a chapter is closing in my life and I'm moving on to the next."

"Hmm, does it have to close?"

Tara took Lauren's hands in hers. "I want to live full time at our lake home. The only acting I want to do now is for the production company I have with Krista, Julia and the others."

"You mean Ten Queens."

"Yes. I've told my agent not to look for roles for me. Unless something is out-of-this-world amazing, I'm considering myself semi-retired. Can you handle that?" she asked, smiling down at Lauren.

"All I want is for you to be happy," Lauren said.

"The happiest I have ever been in my life is the past few weeks with you in Texas. Good God, I can't believe I'm living in Texas!"

Lauren laughed. "It's not all bad. And leave it to the Hollywood lesbians to make their own little paradise on a lake that I just happen to live near."

Tara tilted her head. "I hope you realize how much I love you to move to a state that isn't the most gay friendly, but also, I don't care where I live as long as it's with you."

"I hope you feel that way ten years down the road. Hell, I hope you feel that way a year from now."

"I'll always feel this way about you," Tara said, leaning in and kissing her.

"Mmm, I love you, too Tara," Lauren said.

"Let me show you the rest of the house." She grabbed her hand and tugged her inside.

After the tour, they ended up on the couch in the living room drinking sparkling water.

"Are you tired?" Tara asked. "We can stay in tonight if you want."

"I'm not tired. Did you have something planned for us?"

"I want to take you to Malibu to this little place on the beach that has the freshest seafood you've ever tasted. The sunset is beautiful and I know the perfect spot."

"That sounds heavenly," said Lauren. "We do love a good sunset, don't we?" She leaned into Tara's shoulder.

Tara put her arm around her and they settled comfortably into one another. "We fit perfectly," she murmured, her head resting on the back of the couch.

"We do," Lauren said softly, soaking in this quiet moment of togetherness.

"I've waited my whole life to feel like this and I did with you the very first time we danced and every time thereafter."

"The first time we danced?"

"Yes. You put your arms around my neck and smiled. It felt like taking a deep breath and exhaling. It felt like being exactly where you were supposed to be. It felt like we were the only ones in the room and the only ones that mattered," she said dreamily. "It wasn't sexual, it wasn't friendship, it was simply belonging. It took me a while to figure it all out because I'd never had that feeling before. All I knew was that I wanted it again because it was so complete and I felt content. And whenever we danced or touched I felt it."

"That's beautiful," Lauren whispered.

"Don't get me wrong, my heart also thumped in my chest because I wanted you so badly, but something told me it would happen when it was supposed to. So I enjoyed every touch, every dance, every look, and now I have your heart and you have mine."

Lauren sat up, meeting Tara's eyes. "You do have my heart and you just described what I wanted to tell you, but didn't have the words."

Tara smiled. "Our hearts have been talking to one another for a long time. I'm glad they let the rest of us in on it because you know what I love?"

"I sure do. You love kissing me as much as I love kissing you. I'll never get enough," Lauren said, gently touching her lips to Tara's.

The kiss was warm and soft and Tara deepened it just as the doorbell rang.

Lauren pulled back in surprise. "Are you expecting anyone?"

Tara grinned. "Yes. There's no food in the house. It should be a grocery delivery," she said, getting up and answering the door.

"You think of everything," Lauren said, chuckling.

"I try," Tara said with a wink.

They unloaded the bags in the kitchen and Tara suggested they change clothes. She planned to drive them to Malibu in her convertible and wanted Lauren to have the beach experience in the open air.

"Take your pick," she said to Lauren from inside her closet. "You'll need a hat or a scarf on the drive. You could go with the old Hollywood look and choose a scarf and big sunglasses or any of these hats and caps."

"You have quite a collection," Lauren said as she tried several on.

"I spend a lot of time by the pool and they seem to multiply. Who knows where they all came from."

"Oh, I see. All these women come to swim," Lauren said, wiggling her eyebrows. "And leave things behind."

Tara chuckled. "It's not like that."

"It's okay, sweetheart. I'm teasing. We both have a past and I know who you're sleeping with tonight," Lauren said sassily.

She yelped when Tara grabbed her from behind and spun her around. "I'm spending all my nights with you," she said, kissing her on the neck and playfully swatting her ass.

* * *

They chose their hats and a few minutes later Tara navigated them through the city streets and back roads until Lauren could smell the ocean. Then the water and beach appeared on her left, sparkling with a welcome just for them.

Lauren reached over and grabbed Tara's hand. She closed her eyes and felt the wind, smelled the sea, and captured this moment in her memory forever. When she opened her eyes she saw Tara smiling at her and Lauren knew this had to be a piece of heaven.

Tara parked the car and they walked up to an open air deck hand in hand.

"I can't believe it!" a man exclaimed, smiling broadly as he approached them. "Ms. Holloway, you have come back!"

"Hi Angelo," Tara said, returning his smile.

"The rumors are untrue. You haven't left us."

"What have the rumors said, Angelo?" Tara asked, whispering loudly as if waiting to hear a secret.

"That you have moved away," he said, looking over at Lauren and giving her a friendly smile. "And fallen in love. I think they are not rumors, eh?"

Tara put her arm around Lauren. "Angelo, please meet Lauren Nichols. She has stolen my heart," Tara said dramatically.

Angelo took Lauren's hand in both of his and said kindly, "Welcome. Ms. Holloway is one of my favorite people." He continued to hold Lauren's hand and looked into her eyes as if appraising her soul. "I can see you will take good care of her heart."

Lauren squeezed his hand. "She *is* my favorite person and I promise her heart is safe and loved."

Angelo closed his eyes and released a big breath. "Come, let me feed you the most delicious treats I have caught just for you. I knew this was a special night."

They followed Angelo to a table and a waiter hurried to bring them drinks. He pulled out each of their chairs and said to Tara, "I'm so happy you are here."

"I wanted to show Lauren my absolute favorite place," she said.

"We are honored." He bowed his head slightly. "Prepare to eat!" he said loudly and disappeared into the kitchen.

"Wow," Lauren said. "I love Angelo!"

"I know! Wait until you taste his food."

Lauren looked at her surroundings. The waves crashing on the beach, Tara holding her hand under the table, and the laid-back atmosphere made this feel like a dream. "Are you sure you want to move to Texas? Maybe we should move here."

Tara chuckled. "I'm sure. This is fun for a while, but I love the quiet of the lake."

"You once said that it was always noisy around you. What did you mean?" asked Lauren.

Tara smiled. "The quiet used to scare me. It gave me too much time to think. And by that I mean look at my life.

Believe it or not I didn't always love being single, but I didn't quite know how to share and be vulnerable with a partner either. That is, until I met you. I've never been afraid to tell you things because I knew you wouldn't judge me. I could be just Tara with you."

"Just Tara is who I love. Don't get me wrong," said Lauren, "I love all of you and I understand you have to be different people at times. I know it's hard for you to open up and I'm so glad you trust me. I want to know all of you, darling. I do."

Tara smiled. "That's what I mean. I'm safe with you. And because of that I love the quiet of the lake now."

"You are always safe with me," Lauren said, squeezing her hand.

Angelo sent out plate after plate of the freshest seafood. They shared fish, oysters, crab and shrimp cooked several ways. All of this was accompanied by homemade bread, steamed vegetables, fresh fruit, and Angelo's bubbly personality.

"He makes dinner an event," Lauren said, sipping her wine.

A photographer stopped at the table. "Excuse me, Ms. Holloway, would you mind if I take your photo?"

Tara looked at Lauren and raised her brows. "What do you think?"

Lauren shrugged.

"Sure, just a moment," Tara said, sliding closer to Lauren and putting her arm around her.

Lauren leaned in and they both smiled genuinely at the photographer. He looked at Tara expectantly.

"This beautiful woman is Lauren Nichols," Tara said affectionately.

"Thank you," he said and walked away.

"He's been taking pictures of us all evening so I thought he may as well get a good one," Tara said.

"Will he sell them?" Lauren asked. "I don't know how this works."

"Oh yeah. Angelo wouldn't let him hang around here if he wasn't a decent human being, so I don't mind. I'm not big news though, babe. He might get something for them only since the premiere is coming up."

"Yes you are big news," Lauren said.

"Let's go walk the beach. I have another place I want to show you. We'll come back and say goodbye to Angelo."

They walked along the beach hand in hand, blending in with a few other like-minded people.

"If we walked around our lake like this we'd be turning heads and it wouldn't be because you're a movie star," said Lauren.

"Someday people will see that we're just like any other couple enjoying a romantic stroll. Until then, I don't mind getting looks because it's worth it to hold your hand."

Lauren stopped them and faced Tara. "You are incredible and I love you more every day."

Tara smiled at her. "You are everything to me." She kissed her softly and led her over to a bench that was in front of a beach house.

"I don't remember you mentioning a beach house," Lauren said, sitting next to Tara.

"This is a friend's place where I'm always welcome. You know Allison and Libby from Ten Queens?"

"Of course. I've known them as long as I've known you," Lauren said.

"This is their beach house and available to me whenever I want."

"It's in the perfect place. Look at that sun! How beautiful!"

They snuggled into one another as the breeze coming off the water began to cool. The sun gave an outstanding performance as it fell into the ocean.

"What a wonderful day." Lauren sighed.

"It ain't over yet, baby," Tara said, pulling her closer.

They walked back to Angelo's and said their goodbyes. He hugged Lauren as if he'd known her for years. Darkness fell on the way back to Tara's and Lauren had another surprise when she walked out the sliding doors and took in the twinkling lights as far as she could see.

"What a view," she said, sitting next to Tara.

"It's a great selling point for the house," Tara said.

"Are you selling it right away?"

"I don't know. We could come here for adventures. Justin and Emily might like to come for vacations."

"You'd keep this house so my kids could vacation here?"

"Why not?"

"That's very generous."

"They're family."

"I don't want to think about family or houses right now," Lauren said, getting up. She reached out her hand to Tara. "I'm in Hollywood with a gorgeous movie star."

Tara smiled and led them to the bedroom.

18

Tara closed the trunk and smiled at Lauren. "Next stop, Gucci."

Lauren linked her arm in Tara's and they walked down the sidewalk. "This has been so much fun. I'm not sure what else I could possibly shop for. We've bought dresses and shoes and lingerie." She said the last word with a sexy low voice.

"I can't wait to see you in it either," Tara answered in her own sexy voice. "We've got Justin and Emily something. You found gifts for Krista, Melanie, Julia, and Heidi, but I think I know what *you* need."

Lauren chuckled. "You usually do, but what else?"

"I'll show you," Tara said, opening the door to the store.

They browsed the store and ended up at the handbags.

"Look at this," Tara said, holding up a small tote. "You could use this for work. Your laptop would fit perfectly along with everything else."

Lauren's eyes lit up. "That is beautiful, but I have a tote."

Tara dropped her head and stared at Lauren. "Not like this."

"What color?" Lauren pondered aloud.

"I know what color suits you," said Tara. "I also know which I would choose."

"Oh, you think you know me? Which one?"

"Red, of course. It's a power color. You wouldn't choose it for yourself, but you'd let me choose it for you, wouldn't you, babe?"

"You do know me. I'd love the red, but probably wouldn't choose it."

"Good then, it's a gift." Tara winked. "Was there anything else that caught your eye? Because we're going to the roof for a late lunch and a cocktail."

"They have a rooftop restaurant?"

"They do and we have reservations. Have I told you how much fun this is for me?"

"I can see it in your face, honey. You are glowing!"

"That's because I love you. I always glow now."

"And you're not at all smitten. We'll see when the honeymoon is over, as they say," Lauren teased.

"I don't see it changing," Tara said, shaking her head. "Ever!"

A salesperson walked up. "May I wrap that up for you?"

"Yes," Lauren said. "But I want this small crossbody bag for you, sweetheart. I know you don't really like big purses."

"That's true, but what color? Let's see how well you know me."

Lauren walked over to the smaller bags and looked at the colors. "We'll take this one," she said, choosing a navy blue one. "It'll go perfect with your eyes. How did I do?"

"That's the one I would've chosen." Tara grinned.

Lauren handed the bag to the salesperson and they followed her to the back.

"Shall I put this on your account, Ms. Holloway? I can bring them up to the roof when I have them packaged."

"Thanks, that would be nice," Tara said.

She led them to the elevator and on the roof they were taken to a table near the edge with an expansive view of the city.

"Wow! I keep saying wow and incredible over and over," Lauren said, smiling at Tara.

"I still think it's incredible and I've lived here thirty years," said Tara.

"I can't believe it!" someone said behind them.

Lauren turned around to see Renee Oliver walk up. She was an actress and founding member of Ten Queens, the production company that met at Lovers Landing.

She hugged them both. "I thought you might be in town for the premiere. I'm hearing good things about the movie."

"Thanks," said Tara politely.

Renee looked from Lauren to Tara and back. "Have you two finally taken the leap?" she said, grinning. "Please tell me you have."

Lauren smiled broadly at Tara. "What do you mean?"

"You know exactly what I mean," she said, giggling. "We've been watching you two for three years and wondering when Tara would find the courage. Megan's going to love this." She turned around and waved at her partner, Megan Easterling, the director in the Ten Queens company.

"What's this!" Megan said, joining them. She hugged them both and stood next to Renee.

"They're finally together," Renee said, slipping her arm around Megan.

"I don't think either one of us confirmed that," said Tara, not able to hide her grin.

"Yeah you did. It's written all over your faces," said Megan. "Is this new?"

Tara narrowed her eyes at Lauren. "Yes and no. I asked Lauren to find us a place near Lovers Landing."

"You did! You're moving to the lake?" said Renee.

"I am. Our home isn't far from Krista and Melanie. You'll see at the next meeting." Tara smiled brightly.

"I'm so happy for you both," said Megan. "It was obvious you two had a connection."

"I have never been happier," Lauren said, looking lovingly at Tara.

"Are you going to the premiere?" asked Megan.

"Yes! I feel like a queen. I've got a designer dress and they're doing our hair and makeup," said Lauren excitedly.

"Good for you! It's a wonderful experience and I can see how delighted you are to do it," said Renee, looking at Tara.

"I don't think I've ever looked forward to a premiere like this. And it's because Lauren's going with me," said Tara.

"You're giving me goosebumps!" said Renee. "Love is the best!"

"Getting glammed up with your girl is the best," Megan added. "Just not too often."

They all laughed. Renee and Megan hugged them again and said their goodbyes. The sales person brought their packages up and they ordered.

"That was fun. I never expected to see anyone I knew here." Lauren's phone rang and when she looked at the screen she saw it was a video call from Krista. "It's Krista," she said to Tara as she connected the call.

"Hey you!" Lauren said as she moved closer so Tara could see too.

"Hi! How's the celebrity life?" Krista asked. "You made Page Six!"

"Seriously?" Tara chuckled. Lauren looked at her, confused. "Page Six is the gossip rag in Hollywood," Tara explained.

"What!" Lauren said, surprised.

"Yes, it said 'Tara Holloway was captivated by a beautiful, mysterious blonde last evening in Malibu. Perhaps this is why we haven't seen her out on the town. Could it be love?' And then it had a beautiful picture of the two of you. I sent you a link," Krista said.

"Where are you?" Melanie said, squeezing in next to Krista. "You look like you're in the sky."

"Are you at Gucci?" asked Krista.

"Yes," answered Tara. "We've been shopping all day."

"You should've come with us," Lauren said.

"I can see that," said Melanie. "You look so happy."

"I see a trip to Hollywood in our future," said Krista.

"You were invited," said Tara.

"I know. It's been so long since I've been out there. I forgot how much fun it is," said Melanie.

"Where are you going tomorrow?" asked Krista.

"In the morning we're going to the studio, but we'll be with Pressley and Serena all afternoon up until the premiere," said Tara.

"I can't wait to see y'all," Melanie squealed.

"I'm looking forward to seeing behind the scenes," said Lauren.

"That will be interesting. It's not as glamorous as everyone makes it seem. You'll see," said Krista.

"And then Pressley and Serena are coming to Tara's with their hair and make-up people," said Lauren.

"That will be fun. We may have to video chat y'all," said Krista.

"I'll make sure and have someone text you the red carpet pics," said Tara.

"Thanks. I'll check the internet the next day. Something tells me you'll be on it with that mysterious blonde," said Krista, giggling.

"There is absolutely nothing mysterious about me!" exclaimed Lauren.

"Sure there is! Tara hasn't looked at anyone the way she looks at you. Everyone wants to know your secret," Krista said dramatically.

Lauren laughed. "What's my secret, babe?" she asked Tara, wiggling her eyebrows.

"She gives me joy," Tara said.

"Aww." Lauren kissed her on the lips.

"Dang! Paparazzi would love to have had that photo op," teased Krista.

"Y'all have fun. We miss you," said Melanie.

"Bye," Lauren said, waving at them.

"Bye," Krista and Tara said at the same time, laughing.

The call ended and Lauren pulled up the link that Krista sent to them of the photo from last night. When the picture appeared Lauren gasped. "Look at us," she said breathlessly. "We're beautiful."

Tara leaned in and kissed her cheek. "You are."

"No, Tara, look at us. Look at the love in our eyes. It's beautiful," Lauren said, tearing her eyes away and looking at Tara. "I love you so much," she whispered.

The corners of Tara's mouth slowly turned up. "I love you, Lauren, and when you look at me like that, I feel like the most adored person in the world."

Lauren leaned in and kissed her softly. She pulled away and looked around. "Sorry, I was overcome and had to kiss you."

"Don't ever be sorry for kissing me or looking at me like that."

Their server appeared with their food and Lauren moved her chair back and smiled shyly at Tara.

"Thank you," Tara said to the waiter without taking her eyes from Lauren. When he stepped away she said to Lauren, "Like I said, you fill me with joy."

19

If Lauren had thought she was living a dream before it felt even more so when Tara showed her around the studio the next morning. She got to meet Tara's agent as well as one of her favorite producers.

"Are you sure your agent wasn't upset that you're not actively seeking roles any longer?" asked Lauren as they walked out of the business offices and onto the lot that contained the buildings where TV shows and movies were being filmed.

"Trust me. She'll be fine. I'm not her only client and she lives in a bigger house and a more exclusive neighborhood than I do," Tara said, chuckling.

Lauren squeezed Tara's hand. "I never knew how much I loved holding hands until you grabbed mine," she said, looking over at Tara. "It makes my heart beat fast."

"It makes my heart happy," she said and then she laughed. "I can imagine how we look. Two old women holding hands like teenagers."

"Who are you calling old?" Lauren teased.

"Compared to most of the actors we're about to see,

babe. We're old," Tara said. "But I don't care. I've got a lot of living to do with you."

"Holding hands the whole time," Lauren stated.

They were about to walk into where they were shooting one of Lauren's favorite shows when someone called to them.

"Tara? Lauren?"

They turned and saw Anna Cain, one of the producers that was also in Ten Queens. "I can't believe it. Oh, you're here for the premiere, aren't you," she said, walking up and hugging them both.

"Yes, I was showing Lauren around the studio before we get all dressed up for tonight," said Tara.

"I'm meeting Shelley inside. She'll be so surprised to see you both." She looked down at their clasped hands and raised her eyebrows. Shelley Haskell was her partner and also a producer with Ten Queens.

"I see you're no longer just dancing together," Anna commented.

Lauren grinned at Tara. "Oh we're still dancing, but we have a home near Lovers Landing. You're all invited over at the next Ten Queens meeting. We're having a housewarming while you're all there."

"That's wonderful! So you're full time in Texas?" she asked Tara.

"I am. The only roles I might be interested in would be ours," Tara said.

"I'll keep that in mind. Congrats to you both. Let's go find Shelley, she'll be so happy for you," Anna said, opening the door and letting them walk in first.

They walked into a large area and could see and hear activity deeper into the building.

"Oh my God! I thought I was seeing things," Shelley

Haskell said, walking up and hugging Lauren and Tara. "What are you doing here?"

"They're here for Tara's premiere," said Anna.

"Oh that's right. It's so good to see you both."

"It's good to see you. I'm so surprised to see people I know. We ran into Megan and Renee yesterday," Lauren said, smiling brightly.

"They have their own place near Krista's," Anna said excitedly.

Shelley's face lit up. "I'm so happy for you. When do we get to see your house?"

"We're having everyone over at the next meeting," said Tara.

Shelley looked at both of them and tilted her head. "Some people look like they belong together. That's how you two look. I see a very long happy life ahead for you."

"She knows these things," said Anna, shaking her head and holding up her hands. "She hasn't been wrong yet."

"That's saying a lot when you're talking about Hollywood people," scoffed Tara. She put her arm around Lauren's waist and pulled her close. "But I couldn't agree more. Isn't it awesome when you find your person?" she said, smiling affectionately at Lauren.

"It is," Anna agreed, slipping her arm around Shelley's waist. "No one would believe you just said that." She chuckled.

They all laughed and then went to watch the filming.

After stopping to pick up Chinese food from Tara's favorite restaurant they had a quick lunch before Pressley and Serena got to the house.

"I can't believe I got to not only see a few scenes filmed, but also meet the stars of one of my favorite shows. You did that, didn't you?" she said, smiling at Tara.

Tara simply shrugged and finished loading the dishwasher.

Lauren walked over and put her arms around Tara's shoulders. "Thank you. That was a really nice thing to do."

"I wish I could make you understand how happy it makes me to make you happy," Tara said. "Does that make sense?"

"Yes it does. I love you, Tara," she said, kissing her slow and long.

"Mmm, that was nice," Tara murmured. Then she brought their lips together again. When they pulled apart she said, "We didn't open our fortune cookies." She found them in the bag and handed one to Lauren. They both opened them at the same time.

"Well?" Tara said. "You go first."

Lauren read it and a smile grew on her face. "'You will know when you see it. It will know you when it sees you.'"

Tara raised her eyebrows in question.

"It's true, don't you think? We knew."

Tara nodded. She looked down at her fortune and laughed. "'The love of your life is right in front of your eyes.' Damn, these are spot on today!"

"I'm the love of your life?"

Tara looked at her tenderly. "You are. Deep down I knew I'd find you someday. I believed in my heart that we'd find one another."

Lauren gently cupped Tara's face and kissed her lovingly. The doorbell rang and they pulled apart smiling.

"Here we go," said Tara.

She opened the door and found Pressley and Serena with their arms full and smiles on their faces. "Come in," she said, ushering them inside.

Lauren waited in the living room. They set the garment bags down and walked toward her.

"You must be Lauren," Pressley said, giving her a quick hug. "Krista always has such nice things to say about you. This is your designer and my girlfriend Serena," she said. Pressley was Krista's long time assistant and when Krista decided to take a lesser role with Ten Queens, the company started using Pressley to manage any day to day dealings.

"I feel like I know you; we've texted so many times," Serena said, smiling brightly.

"I know, me too." Lauren returned her smile.

"The makeup team will be here soon, but I wanted to try your dresses on and make sure they were perfect," said Serena. "I expect them to be, but you never know."

"Let's go to the master bedroom. It should be big enough for all of us," Tara said.

"It's been too long," Pressley said, putting her arm around Tara. "I'm going to have to come see that lake. There's obviously something magical about it. Krista's staying and now you're moving there."

"I like the lake and all, but honestly it's Lauren. She's the magic for me," said Tara. "I know, I know. You can't believe I'm talking this way. You'd never expect words like this from Tara Holloway." She laughed.

"I believe it. You were patiently waiting. I could tell when I did see you," said Pressley.

"Really?" said Lauren.

"Yes. She never went out with other women after that first visit to Krista's hideaway and when I saw you there was a calmness around you," said Pressley smiling at Tara.

Tara smiled. "I'm not as calm tonight because I want Lauren to have the time of her life."

"We'll do our part," said Serena, unzipping one of the

garment bags. "For you, Ms. Nichols." Serena handed her the dress.

"It's beautiful," said Lauren breathlessly.

"Come on," Serena said, walking towards the massive closet. "I'll help."

Lauren slipped out of her pants and shirt and stepped into the dress. Serena zipped her up and she started to turn towards the mirror, but Serena stopped her.

"Wait," she said. "Slip these on." She handed Lauren a pair of high heeled designer shoes.

Lauren sat down on the stool Serena brought over. She stepped into the shoes and stood up. This time Serena let her turn around and look in the mirror.

Lauren was speechless. She couldn't believe how beautiful she looked. The woman standing in front of her was poised, polished, and happy. That's what she saw in her eyes. Happiness.

"Just wait until your hair and makeup are done. You are stunning, Lauren. Thank you for letting me dress you."

"You're thanking me! I should be thanking you!" exclaimed Lauren.

"How's it going in there?" Tara asked from the bedroom.

"Stay there," said Serena quickly, walking to the doorway. "You can see her after we get everything done."

Serena unzipped her dress and helped her out of it. She walked out of the closet and unzipped the other garment bag. "Okay Tara, it's your turn," she said, walking back into the closet.

Tara kissed Lauren on the lips as she walked by.

Pressley chuckled. "I can't wait to see you both see one another. Does that even make sense?" she chuckled.

"Yes it does. I can't wait either!" said Lauren.

The doorbell rang and Pressley said, "That's our makeup

team." She and Lauren went to let them in and the glamorous transformation began.

They set up the hair and makeup squad in the master bathroom. Tara and Lauren sat side by side as they were fussed over. Serena and Pressley sat on the counter opposite them and watched, their feet dangling and swinging. Tara made sure everyone had a glass of wine, making it more like a party.

"How are Krista and Melanie? Are they as immersed in wedded bliss as they sound?" asked Pressley.

"They really are," said Lauren. "I've known Krista for a long time and I've never seen her this happy."

"I'm so glad. Krista wanted a life with Melanie, but couldn't make it happen. Thank goodness Melanie did," said Pressley. "Don't you have kids, Lauren?"

"I do. A son and a daughter."

"How have they handled your and Tara's relationship, if you don't mind me asking?" said Serena.

"It's funny. In the three years Tara and I have..." she paused. "We've created this love, haven't we?" she said, looking at Tara in the mirror.

Tara smiled. "Create is a good word."

"In those years my kids were never at the lake the same time Tara was. My daughter, Emily, met her last month and of course loved her. I mean," she said, grinning at Tara, "who could resist her?"

"Evidently you could because you did for a long time," Tara joked.

"We were worth the wait," countered Lauren.

"So worth it," agreed Tara.

"My son doesn't know yet. I tried to get him to come to the lake, but he works all the time. I went to Dallas to tell him over lunch, but we were interrupted by his boss. He promised me he would come home when we get back. I did get to tell him I was coming to the premiere with Tara."

"Do you think he'll be upset?" asked Pressley.

"I really don't know. I don't think so, but..." said Lauren.

"You know, he may feel protective of you, honey," said Tara.

"Protective? What do you mean?"

"I grew up in a small town, just like Justin. I don't have any brothers or sisters, but I have cousins. There were times when they thought they needed to step in to protect their female cousin. There was one particular time when I showed them I could take care of myself and then they eased up."

"Ooowww, tell us the story," said Pressley.

"We were at a party when I was in high school. Yes, we were underage drinking. Like I said, it was a small town. There was a guy, who was also my friend, that got drunk that night and was hanging on me. I kept telling him to stop. I knew he was drunk because any other time he was always respectful. My cousins heard me tell him to stop several times. I saw two of them get up and walk toward us and I knew they were going to beat the shit out of him. I held my hand out to stop them and told them I could handle it. I then turned to the guy and told him quietly what I was going to do to his most prized parts if he put his arm around me again. That sobered him up enough that he stopped, apologized and then went outside."

Everyone laughed.

Tara continued. "You haven't lived with Marcus in several years, but you've only been divorced for a few months. I'm sure he feels like he has to be the big brother to Emily as well as be your protector. It's the same reason your brother-in-law was such an ass at the restaurant. Family is sacred."

"I never thought of it that way," Lauren mumbled.

"That's why they're so important to me. They're my family—at least I hope they will be," Tara said, staring at Lauren in the mirror.

Lauren put her hand on her chest and looked at Tara tenderly. "We'll make them understand that."

Tara nodded and then got a look from her makeup person imploring her to be still. "Sorry," she murmured.

When their hair and makeup were done they got up and Tara said, "I'll meet you in the living room." She winked and then went to get dressed.

"She's going to love this," Pressley said, walking out of the bathroom.

"This is the fun part," Serena said, following Lauren into the huge closet.

Tara got dressed and then went into the kitchen. She got the bottle of wine and topped off her glass and brought it into the living room. She almost dropped her glass when Lauren walked into the room.

Lauren gave her a slow sultry smile and said, "I think you like it." She posed for a moment and then turned around so Tara could see the entire effect. The dress was cut deep in the back and clung to her curves. The front wasn't as deep, but showed off Lauren's cleavage. She had never felt so beautiful and could see the love, want, and passion in Tara's eyes. *I don't think I'll be wearing this dress for long when we get back here.*

"You look stunning," Tara said, finally able to speak.

That's when Lauren saw that Tara wasn't wearing the dress she'd originally decided on. She was wearing a suit with feminine curves. The deep maroon color was so striking with her dark hair and her eye makeup was dark and smoky. The jacket plunged down and hugged her cleavage. Lauren didn't think she'd be able to keep her hands off this exquisite woman.

"My darling," she said softly. "You are absolutely dazzling." Lauren slowly walked towards her. "I can't stop from kissing you, so prepare to reapply your lipstick." She gently touched her lips to Tara's and moaned. "Oh baby, as much as I want to go to this..." she whispered.

"Later, honey. It'll be worth the wait," Tara said softly, kissing her.

They pulled apart and Lauren let out a big breath.

"I think our work here is done," Serena said, grinning.

"Thank you so much for everything," Lauren gushed.

"You are more than welcome. We'll come back tomorrow to get all the stories."

"Have a wonderful night," said Pressley.

The doorbell rang and as Pressley, Serena and the makeup team left, Gerald was waiting to take them to the premiere.

20

They pulled up in a line of cars and limos as they dropped off their passengers on the red carpet. When it was their turn Tara smiled at Lauren and grabbed her hand. "Smile for the camera."

Lauren stepped out of the car and as her eyes met Tara's she gave her the most dazzling smile. Her heart fluttered. Not out of nervousness, but from love. She was the proud woman on this beloved actress's arm. This wasn't her world, but Tara welcomed her into it and made her feel comfortable at her side.

They walked inside the theater and were ushered over to the area for photographs. There were photographers lined up and speaking to the celebrities in front of their lenses. Lauren felt her heart start to pound, but Tara squeezed her hand and gave her a smile that made all the jitters calm.

Tara stepped in front of the photographers and never let go of her hand. She said to them, "This is Lauren Nichols. Make sure you get it right." She grinned at the crowd of photographers. She winked at Lauren and then a man said, "This way, Tara. Look here!"

She put her arm around Lauren and nodded toward the left side of the group.

"This way, Lauren!" a woman shouted.

They both smiled and then turned to face the other side and then it was over.

"That wasn't too bad, was it?" asked Tara as they walked over to the bar to get a drink before the movie began.

"It was at first, but then you smiled at me and everything was just right."

"Hi ladies," Libby Scott said, walking up with a huge smile on her face. "I hoped I'd see you here."

"Hey Libby," Lauren said.

"Hi Lib, how nice of you to come see the movie," said Tara with just a hint of sarcasm.

Libby chuckled. "I'm working. One of the executive producers owns a script that would be perfect for Ten Queens."

"I see. Is that how you saw the movie early? Krista mentioned you'd seen it," said Tara.

"I didn't see the whole thing, but what I did see of you was very good, Tara. Just wait, Lauren. She's going to dazzle you on the big screen. But I hear you are dazzling one another at the lake," she said playfully.

"You could say that," replied Lauren, slipping her arm through Tara's.

"Good for you both. Everyone knew that you'd both figure it out eventually. You can't dance with someone like you two did and not feel it," said Libby. "Allison is here too. We'll catch up with you at the party."

"Oh good. I'd love to see her," said Lauren. Allison and Libby were the other two members that made up Ten Queens.

"By the way, you both look gorgeous. You're not

supposed to steal the spotlight, but I don't think you can help it tonight," she said, chuckling as she walked away.

Tara leaned into Lauren and whispered a kiss over her lips. "Don't worry, I won't mess up your makeup," she said with a wink.

"You can mess up my makeup anytime," Lauren said, quirking one eyebrow.

Tara chuckled and led them inside the theater to their seats. She stopped and introduced Lauren to several people along the way and she spoke with a couple of producers she'd met that morning, impressed they remembered who she was.

They took their seats and it wasn't long until the movie started. Lauren had seen all of Tara's movies and of course she loved them. But it was completely different watching her on the big screen while sitting next to her. At times Tara held her hand or looked over at her and smiled. Lauren glanced over and realized that Tara was nervous. Even after all these movies and performances she could see it affected her.

Lauren squeezed her hand and got Tara's attention. She gave her the most adoring look and mouthed "I love you." That seemed to help her relax. Lauren made a note to apologize for not talking to her about this on the way to the premiere. Now she knew and would make sure Tara was aware that her biggest fan was holding her tight.

Tara had a supporting role, but when she was on screen she commanded the scene. Her talent was obvious and Lauren couldn't help but be proud and at the same time she couldn't wait until they got home to show Tara just what she thought of her performance.

An hour and fifty five minutes later the movie ended and the audience applauded. Lauren leaned in and said,

"You were amazing. I know you don't believe me, but Tara, I've seen all your movies and this was one of your best."

"Thank you, babe. I do believe you and I appreciate it. I'm so glad you were here to see it with me," she said, kissing her on the lips.

"Is it hard for you to watch yourself?" Lauren asked as they let the crowd thin some before leaving the theater. The venue for the party was next door so they planned to walk.

"It is. Even after all these years, you never know what you're going to see. You hope you gave a good performance and it may feel good at the time, but when you see it on the big screen like this, it can be intimidating. Plus, the director is in charge and you hope you've portrayed what their vision is even if you may not agree," she said, raising one eyebrow and grinning.

Lauren's heart swelled with love. "You are amazing, Tara Holloway. I'm so glad you're mine."

Tara's face lit up. "Where did that come from?"

"I'm so proud of you and incredibly happy to be here with you. I'm happy to be with you all the time. You should know that," said Lauren.

Tara tilted her head. "I do, but thanks for saying that. I'm so glad you're here with me, too. Let's go to the party."

"Don't forget to hold my hand. Remember what Krista told me?" teased Lauren.

"Oh I haven't forgotten. Everyone will know you're with me," she said a bit possessively.

They left the theater and made the short walk next door. The huge room had bars in every corner and in the middle. There were people lined up at each one, ready to party. There were several buffet tables set up and the guests mingled, ate, and drank.

Tara and Lauren weaved through the crowd, stopping to

talk to people Tara knew. She introduced Lauren proudly and made sure to include her in the conversations. True to her word Tara held her hand or rested it on her back most of the evening.

"I finally found you," someone said, pulling Lauren away from Tara. Alarmed, she turned around and then realized it was Allison.

"Hi Allison," Lauren said, hugging her.

Tara had an irritated look on her face, but then smiled at Allison. "Hey Ali."

"Oh, don't look at me like that! I'm not stealing your girl away." Allison laughed.

"You certainly aren't," Tara said, her eyes boring through Allison.

Lauren looked at each of them and laughed. "What is wrong with you two?"

"Nothing, babe. Allison likes to fuck with me," said Tara, putting her hand on Lauren's waist.

"I'm sorry, Tara. I was just playing. It's obvious Lauren only has eyes for you. It wouldn't matter how charming I am," Allison said seriously. "Besides, Libby would spank me good when we got home if I upset you."

"Oh, so that's what you're trying to do," said Tara.

Again, Lauren looked at them both and decided she would have to ask Tara about that later. Surely she heard wrong.

"Hey y'all," Libby said, walking up and using her best Texas drawl.

"You're getting good at that accent," remarked Lauren.

"You're the one that would know." Libby grinned. She looked at each of them with a puzzled look on her face. "Did I miss something?" Then she noticed the demure look on her wife's face and said, "What have you done, Allison?"

Lauren put her arm through Tara's and giggled.

"Nothing darling," said Allison. "I was having a little fun with Tara, but she didn't want to play."

"Yeah, I'm sure that was it," Libby said. She looked at Lauren. "What did you think? Your girl was fantastic, wasn't she?"

"Yes she was! I loved it," Lauren said excitedly, pulling on Tara's arm.

"You were great, Tara," said Allison. "The best part in my opinion. I just don't know how well it will do."

"Yeah, I know." Tara exhaled. "We'll see. Audiences will surprise you."

"So true," said Libby. "Have you danced yet? There's a great band playing out back."

"We haven't made it that far yet," said Tara. She looked at Lauren and raised her eyebrows. "We haven't danced in ages."

"Does last week in the living room not count?"

"Oh yeah, of course it counts," said Tara.

Allison shook her head. "I'm not surprised with you two; dancing is definitely your thing."

"Then let's go," said Tara.

"Follow me, we'll join you." Libby grabbed Allison's hand and parted the crowd.

Several people waved as they passed by and some tried to stop them, but Tara held her hand firmly. They stepped through a door and then they were on a patio where the band was playing. Tara stopped and pulled Lauren into her arms and grinned. They began to move to the music and the world fell away.

Lauren was mesmerized by Tara's blue eyes and the twinkle that she'd noticed several times that night. "You're having a good time, aren't you?" Lauren said, her arms resting around Tara's neck.

"I am. Are you?"

"Yes, this has been wonderful. You are very good at introducing me and making me feel included."

"You should be. Have these conversations bored you?"

"Not at all. I was surprised some of the producers you introduced me to this morning actually remembered who I was."

"Most of them are good guys. There are some that are very full of themselves though," said Tara.

"I noticed that after the movie." Lauren chuckled. "But I did enjoy the financial conversation with your producer friend and the studio head. It's amazing to hear the figures they throw around. I mean, in my business we don't move near those amounts of money so it's kind of fascinating to think about it."

Tara's eyes widened. "Does finance get my lover all hot and bothered? Do I need to quote movie profits and losses in the bedroom?"

Lauren threw her head back and laughed. "Do you really think we need any help in the bedroom? I get plenty hot and bothered looking at my movie star lover as it is!" She reached up and kissed Tara just under her ear lobe, that sensitive little spot that she knew made her weak.

"Mmm, you keep that up and we're out of here. Or I may have to pull you into one of these vacant rooms," Tara murmured.

Lauren smiled and relished how responsive Tara was to her touch. If that didn't make her hot, what would, she thought.

The song ended and they stood smiling at one another.

Tara was about to say something when a man gently placed his hand on her shoulder.

"I don't mean to interrupt, but I was about to sneak out and wanted to speak to you for just a moment."

"Hi Robert," said Tara. "Let me introduce you to Lauren Nichols," she said, her arm around her waist.

"It is so nice to meet you," Robert Kinney said, offering his hand to Lauren.

"Robert is the head of the studio, Lauren," explained Tara. "He is the one that finds the best movies and then figures out how to fund them."

"I don't actually do all that, but I oversee it." He corrected Tara with a smile.

"Lauren is a business woman and understands the struggles to find financing when you want something," said Tara.

"Oh?" Robert asked.

"I'm in real estate in Texas. It seems we're always looking for ways to help people purchase the home of their dreams," said Lauren.

Robert nodded. "You do get it then." His eyes narrowed and he said, "Are you the reason the studio is losing Tara? I've heard you were moving to Texas and going exclusively with Ten Queens."

Lauren looked at Tara and raised her eyebrows. Tara grinned. "Lauren would be why I'm moving to Texas. It's time to slow down and she is where I want to be. As far as exclusively for Ten Queens, I want to do more movies with queer representation and good scripts. I've told you that."

"You have and I understand that. Let me say I thought the performance everyone witnessed by you tonight is award worthy and we'll be nominating you. I'm not sure how this movie will be received, but your performance was superb. I guess I couldn't ask for you to leave us in a better way." He chuckled.

"Thanks Robert, I appreciate it. My contract isn't out yet, but I certainly loved working with you and this studio."

Robert nodded. "I'll see you again soon." He turned to Lauren and said, "It was very nice to meet you. I wish you both all the happiness." He bowed his head and then disappeared into the crowd.

"What a nice guy," remarked Lauren.

"He really is. You don't see studio heads like him anymore," said Tara. "Was there anyone else you wanted to meet?"

"Hmm," Lauren said, her eyes sparkling. "Is my date ready to go?"

Tara leaned in close. "You've driven me crazy all night in that dress and all I can do is imagine taking it off of you."

"Then you haven't been paying attention because I know I've undressed you with my eyes at least three times tonight," Lauren said with a sultry smile.

"Let's go home," Tara said, grabbing her hand and leading them through the crowd. She turned to look at Lauren and they both laughed.

21

When they got back to Tara's they thanked Gerald for walking them to the door. Once inside Lauren pushed Tara up against the door and kissed her hard.

Tara was glad Lauren was against her because that kiss made her weak in the knees. It wouldn't take much for her to slide down that door and onto the floor. They pulled apart, both breathing hard.

"Sorry, I've been wanting to do that since I first saw you in that suit," Lauren said, still pushed against her.

"Don't ever apologize for kissing me like that," Tara said breathlessly. She took Lauren's hand. "Come on."

They both giggled as Tara led them outside. She grabbed her phone and pulled up a playlist. "I want to dance with you in the moonlight," she said, grabbing Lauren and holding her tight.

"I'd dance with you anytime and any place," Lauren said, putting her head on Tara's shoulder. "I love you so much."

"Mmm, I love you," Tara replied. She had never felt this

loved, this cared for, this desired, this much desire for someone *ever*. Lauren made her feel beautiful, respected, and adored. As a movie star she felt love and appreciation from fans all the time. And she had felt love from partners and women she dated, but she had never felt like this ever.

"You asked me several times if I was having fun tonight, but did you?" Lauren inquired as she rubbed her hands up and down Tara's back.

"I did have fun."

Lauren leaned back so she could look into Tara's eyes. "You know, I think the most fun for me was noticing how many men and women watched us with smiles on their faces. Some of them were rather salacious looks, but it made me feel pretty damn special when I caught someone's eye gazing at us like that and I could say 'she's mine' with just a look."

Tara chuckled. "You seem to think they were looking at me, but I assure you those hungry looks were for you as well."

"What did you like best?"

"The best part for me is now and a little later," Tara whispered in her ear. "But what I enjoyed was being on your arm as you engaged with the studio heads on finance and then just as easily chatted with my costars, the writers, the staff, producers, everyone!"

Lauren chuckled. "I guess I have the gift of gab."

"No, I think you are kind. You treat everyone like they matter and that puts people at ease."

"You know, we may live in different circles, but you do the same thing. You treat the people you meet at the lake just like you would me or Krista or Julia."

"That's not exactly true," Tara said, nibbling her ear.

"You know what I mean," Lauren said with a throaty laugh.

Tara looked into her eyes and was suddenly overcome with emotion. Tears stung the back of her own eyes when she thought about how truly happy Lauren made her. *This is how it's supposed to be; this is the gift of true love.*

"Baby, are you all right? What's wrong?" Lauren said, concern in her voice and her eyes.

"I'm not sure I ever understood what forever really means. You have this idea that it means until you die and is some obscure word tossed around when you're in love. But I understand it now. I belong to you. We belong together and that is a feeling that I haven't experienced. I believe we're together from here on out; to the end of time. That's what you have put in my heart. Do you know what that means to someone like me? To someone that has never truly wholly belonged? My heart isn't searching any longer for the one it loves. It's found you and now," she said, taking a breath, "now I get to live in all this happiness we created...forever." Tears spilled from her eyes.

"Oh Tara, my sweet darling, this is the love they write poems about, make movies about, and you're exactly right. We get to live it." Lauren crushed her lips to Tara's and kissed her with abandon.

Tara didn't think she'd ever tasted anything so sweet and hot all at once. She let Lauren make love to her mouth with her tongue and lips and thought her heart just might explode in her chest.

"You are everything I ever dreamed of and I knew you had to be out there somewhere just for me, Tara Holloway. Do you hear me? You are just for me," Lauren said, claiming her lips once again.

Desire along with love raced through Tara's body. She

wanted to feel Lauren's skin on hers, she wanted Lauren to mark her as her own.

It was as if Lauren heard Tara's thoughts because she pushed her away, grabbed her hand and hurried them to the bedroom.

* * *

Lauren was breathing like she'd run a marathon by the time they walked through the bedroom door. She wanted Tara desperately, but turned and put her hands on her chest, stopping them both. "Let's slow down," she said, staring intensely into Tara's eyes. "We have forever, right."

"That's right," whispered Tara.

Lauren looked Tara up and down. She ran her hands up and over Tara's shoulders and down her arms. She unfastened the one button holding her suit coat together and gently eased it from her shoulders. "I've wanted to take this off you all night." The dark maroon lace bra that greeted Lauren made her heart speed up again.

"There was a time when I could go braless underneath an outfit like this, but no more," said Tara.

Lauren looked into her eyes and said hoarsely, "You are the most beautiful woman I've ever seen. Can't you see that in my eyes?"

"I do. You make me feel like the most beautiful woman in the world," exclaimed Tara.

"Because you are," Lauren said, taking Tara's lips with her own. She held Tara's face between her hands and then ran them down her back. She unclasped Tara's bra and slid the straps down her arms. She cupped Tara's breasts and exhaled. "So beautiful," she said softly. She ran her thumbs over Tara's nipples and watched them harden, begging her to take them in her mouth.

She leaned down and sucked one into her mouth and moaned. Tara held on to Lauren's shoulders.

"I'm yours," she mumbled.

Lauren smiled as she made her way over to Tara's other breast and sucked it in with softness and then gave her a firm nibble.

"Damn," exclaimed Tara.

Lauren knew Tara was extremely aroused when she swore and this made her smile.

Tara grabbed her shoulders and began to turn her around. Lauren understood and raised up her hair so Tara could unzip her dress. She took her arms out and started to let it fall to the floor but thought better since it was a designer piece made just for her.

Tara held the dress while she stepped out of it and laid it carefully across a chair. When she turned back around Lauren stood in front of her in matching dark blue undies and bra, still in high heels.

"Breathe, baby," Lauren said playfully as she watched Tara's mouth open slightly.

"Do you have any idea what you're doing to me?" Tara said, her eyes widening.

"Yes, we're grabbing forever and making it ours," Lauren said, kicking her shoes off. Then she grabbed the front of Tara's pants and unbuttoned them.

She stepped out of them and laid them with Lauren's dress. She turned around and Lauren unclasped her own bra and let her breasts free.

"Good God, Lauren. *You* are beautiful!" Tara said, closing the distance between them.

Lauren stopped her with a look and said, "Together."

They both slowly lowered their lace undies and stood naked in front of the other. Lauren reached out her hand and offered it to Tara. Together they climbed onto the bed and lay down on the nest of pillows facing each other.

"You keep saying that you're mine," said Lauren softly. "I belong to you, Tara. Not in a possessive way, but in an absolute, unconditional, everlasting way."

Tara ran the back of her fingers down Lauren's cheek and rested them over her breast. Lauren could feel herself shudder at the gentleness of her touch. Her skin was flushed and hot wherever Tara touched.

She edged closer to Tara so she could run her hand down Tara's side and rested it on her hip. Her eyes met Tara's dark, deep blue ones and she inhaled. She took in the sexual energy between them, but also the love. There was so much love.

Tara trailed her hand down and across Lauren's stomach until her fingers became entangled in Lauren's short curly hairs. Lauren gasped and raised her leg. She looked into Tara's eyes and her hand moved across Tara's body the same way, but she didn't stop. Her fingers slid into Tara's wetness and they both moaned.

Tara closed her eyes momentarily engulfed in all the sensations Lauren swirled through her body. Then she opened them and her fingers found the wetness she craved.

Again, Lauren moved closer and this time she pushed a finger inside Tara and thought they'd both come that instant, but she held out. "You feel so good," Lauren moaned as she pushed deeper.

But then Tara slid her finger inside Lauren and she groaned louder. "Oh my God, that's even better." Lauren didn't know which she loved more at this moment, being inside Tara or Tara being inside her. All she knew was it had to be the best feeling in the world and she never wanted it to end.

Their eyes met and as if their bodies were leading them next came their lips. This kiss was soft and tender and wet. Their tongues and fingers danced together like the perfect partners they were. They found a rhythm among the moans and aroma of love.

"I'm close baby, but I want us to do this together," Lauren said greedily.

Tara took her other hand and held Lauren's hand firmly inside her. "Right there," she whispered.

They were staring into one another's eyes when they glazed over and the orgasms hit them. Neither said a word as it shot through their bodies and then spread over their entire beings. They held one another like this for several moments, simply staring and letting their hearts marry, imprinting this moment in their memories forever.

22

The next morning they were sitting on the patio leisurely having breakfast when Tara came back out after refilling their coffee mugs. She set Lauren's in front of her and started to walk off when Lauren grabbed her wrist.

She pulled her down for a kiss and then said, "Last night was incredible."

Tara smiled and retook her seat. "Best night I've had in..." She looked up and then around, pretending to think. She grinned at Lauren and completed her statement with wide eyes. "Ever!"

Lauren laughed. "These nights with you keep getting better. Growing old with you is going to be the best."

Tara laughed with her. "Hey, I had an idea and wanted to run it by you."

"Let me have it," said Lauren.

"I would like to take both of my cars to Texas. And instead of somehow shipping them with the furniture I thought we could get Justin and Emily to fly out here with us and we could drive them back together."

Lauren's brow furrowed. "Like a family road trip?"

"Exactly. We could take turns riding with each other and I could get to know them better," said Tara.

"Babe! That's a fucking awesome idea!" exclaimed Lauren.

"Oops, you've been around me too long. Your language!" Tara said, aghast, grabbing her chest.

"Seriously, what a good idea."

"Do you think you could talk Justin into taking off a few days?"

"This not only sounds like fun, but something he'd like, so yeah, I think I could. He won't come home to see me, but I think he'd do this."

Tara sat back and beamed. "Good! I want to go through the house today and mark the things we want to move to Texas. You'll help me, right?"

"Of course. As you keep telling me, it's my house too."

"It's not just a house. It's our home," stressed Tara. "I've always had houses before, but the lake house with us in it, that feels like home."

"It is our home," Lauren said, correcting her earlier statement.

Tara was smiling at her when her phone rang. She picked it up and scooted over toward Lauren. "It's Krista."

She connected the call and Krista and Melanie's faces appeared on the screen. "Hey y'all," Tara said.

Krista started laughing, "Listen to you with your Texas drawl. How does it feel to be the talk of the town?" teased Krista.

"What do you mean?" asked Lauren, looking at Tara curiously.

"There are so many pictures of the premiere on various sites and you two are in lots of them," she explained.

"Really? I hadn't checked yet," Tara said, handing the phone to Lauren and picking up her iPad. "I did send you the photos from the shoot on the way into the theater."

"We got those," said Melanie. "You two were stunning! I loved the suit, Tara. Did you change your mind about the dress?"

"Yes, that suit called to me." She chuckled. "And I thought it looked perfect with Lauren's dress."

"It did," said Krista. "Lauren, you looked incredible. How many times did they try to steal you away from Tara?"

Lauren giggled. "None! But Krista, I caught several people staring at us when we danced and it was kind of fun to stare right back at them."

Krista and Melanie laughed. "Oh, I love it. I knew you'd enchant Hollywood just as you do Tara."

"I don't know about that," said Lauren timidly.

"I do. You should have seen her, Krissy. She was fucking talking finance with Robert and Harry and they were listening! And then my two co-stars cornered her and wouldn't let her go when Allison and Libby walked up."

"Oh my God, I would have loved to have seen that! Allison Jennings doesn't wait on anyone." Krista laughed.

"You should have seen Tara in the movie!" said Lauren excitedly. "All the party stuff was fun, but y'all, Tara was amazing. Prepare to fall in love when you see it!"

Tara looked at Lauren and smiled shyly.

"I already love her," said Krista playfully.

"Me too," said Melanie. This made Tara look at the screen in surprise. "You know I do. You love me too," teased Melanie.

Tara laughed.

"That makes me want to see the movie now for sure," said Krista.

"You mean you weren't going to see it?" asked Lauren, bewildered.

"Yes she was. She likes to tease Tara. You know how they are," said Melanie.

Lauren breathed a sigh of relief. "Oh good, I didn't want us to have a problem, Krista," she said sternly.

"Wow, what happened to the sweet woman that had a crush on me?" said Krista, grinning.

"I didn't have a crush on you! Julia and Heidi thought I did." Lauren chuckled.

They all laughed and then Lauren's phone pinged with a text message. She ignored it and continued her conversation with their friends.

"What are you doing today?" asked Melanie.

"We're deciding what to move to Texas and I'm hoping I can get my movie star girlfriend to take me back out to Malibu for seafood," said Lauren.

"Surely you're bringing the beach painting in the bedroom with you," said Krista.

Lauren looked over at Tara and said, "Why would Krista know about the painting in your bedroom?"

A slow smile played on Tara's face. "I know you're not jealous and you're fucking with me. Tell her Krista."

"That painting has been in all her bedrooms in all her houses since I've known her. It's the first big purchase she made after her first big movie role," explained Krista.

Lauren grinned and wrinkled her nose. "I had you going there for a second." She laughed.

"Oh no you didn't," said Tara, tickling Lauren's side. Her phone pinged again three times in succession.

"Someone is looking for you," commented Melanie.

Lauren reached for her phone and Krista asked Tara, "When are you coming back?"

"Tomorrow," answered Tara. She looked over at Lauren and could see a worried look on her face. "Is everything all right, babe?"

Lauren shook her head while she replied to the text. "Evidently Justin saw some of those pictures and is losing his mind." When she finished the message she looked up at Tara with worry in her eyes. "He's very upset."

Tara nodded. "We'll figure it out," she said calmly.

"Hey," said Krista. "I'm sure he's just surprised."

"That's why I wanted to tell him before we came out here," Lauren said, tears of frustration pooling in her eyes.

"It'll be okay, Lauren. I'm sure he'll come home now and you can have the conversation you wanted in the first place," said Melanie.

"He plans to be there waiting for me when we get back," said Lauren.

"Oh," murmured Tara.

"I think we should let y'all go. Listen, Lauren, we're here for you. We'll do whatever you need. I'm happy to talk to him if you want. Julia would too."

"Thanks Krista," Lauren said, sighing.

"We'll see y'all when we get back," said Tara.

"Bye," Krista and Melanie said in unison.

Tara put the phone down and pulled Lauren into her arms. "It'll be all right."

Lauren let Tara hold her for a few moments and then sat back.

"What did he say?" Tara asked gently.

"He said someone in his office showed him pictures from the premiere. He wants to know what's going on. He said it looked like we were a couple and it made him sick. I wanted to call him, but he said he couldn't talk to me right now. He said he'd be waiting at my house when we get back tomorrow," said Lauren, crestfallen.

Tara took Lauren's hand and tried to meet her eyes. Before she could say anything Lauren said softly, "We make him sick." With a frown on her face she added, "How are we going to fix that?"

Tara took a deep breath. "He's shocked. And on top of that he was at work. Emotions are flying through him right now. Probably some he doesn't understand." She paused and said, "Lauren, look at me." When her eyes finally rose to Tara's she continued. "Everything will be all right, I promise,"

"How can you promise me that?" she said with tears in her eyes. "How can we be happy when my son thinks we're horrible? And how can I be happy without you, Tara? And how do I break your heart? We just found one another," she cried.

"Slow down, baby. Slow down," Tara said soothingly, grabbing Lauren's hands. "That's not going to happen. What we created is strong and it's built on love. Justin doesn't know that. When he sees the love, when he feels the love we have, he'll understand. It won't always be happiness. We will be challenged. That's when we have to trust one another and trust our love. I trust you Lauren with all that I am and I trust this love we've created," Tara said, nodding.

Lauren stared at Tara and began to nod too. "Trust our love," she murmured.

"That's right. Trust our love."

"I'm scared, Tara. I do trust you and I trust our love, but my kids have never doubted me as their mother and that's how Justin's text sounded."

"It was a text. You don't know that. He was shocked,

honey. It makes you say unkind, confused things. Trust our love."

Lauren nodded again and then tried to smile. "And things were going so well."

Tara smiled at her. "They still are. This is just a little bump in the road." Tara's eyes widened. "That's it!"

Lauren looked at her. "What's it?"

"The road trip. That's how we're going to show him," stated Tara.

"He won't go on this road trip with us," said Lauren sarcastically.

"Then you have to convince him."

Lauren stared at Tara and let the idea bounce around in her head. Tara was right. If he was stuck in a car with them he'd have no choice but to listen and see how happy they were. They weren't horrible; they were happy. "Convince him to come with us," she said, nodding at Tara. "Emily could help with that," she added, thinking out loud.

"Now you're talking," said Tara, encouraging her.

Lauren gazed at Tara and a smile creeped onto her face. If anyone could make this all right it would be Tara, but Lauren had to get him to agree. She had until tomorrow evening to figure out how.

23

As they got closer to the lake, Tara felt more and more nervous. She kept her eyes on the road, but wasn't really focused on driving.

"I know we talked about this, but you do understand why I should talk to him alone first, right?" Lauren asked as she pulled Tara's hand into hers and held it in her lap.

"Of course I do. Honestly, I'm not sure I'd want to be there for this first conversation," replied Tara.

Lauren chuckled. "Hey now, you're the one that keeps talking about having a family."

Tara glanced over at her and smiled. "I know and I do. I'll just unpack for us both and wait nervously on the patio drinking beer." She scoffed. "Wouldn't that be great, to meet Justin for the first time while I'm slobbering drunk."

This time Lauren laughed. "You're very charming when you're drunk."

"I thought I was charming all the time," said Tara, turning into their driveway.

Lauren chuckled. "Oh God, how much I love you," she

said, squeezing Tara's hand. "Justin is going to have to understand."

"He will," Tara said softly.

Lauren eyed her love. "I think you're more nervous about this than I am."

Tara parked the car in their garage. "I am. I don't want to lose you, baby. I just found you. But I'm not going to come between you and your son," said Tara emotionally.

"You won't. As a very smart, extremely beautiful woman told me, everything is going to be all right. And that means you and me will always be an us, including these kids of mine that I have no doubt you will make yours, too."

Tara stared at Lauren for several moments and sighed. The corners of her mouth started to turn up and she said, "Smart and extremely beautiful, huh?"

"That's right. She's my hot, hot girlfriend and there ain't no way I'm going to let anyone else get their hands on her," she said sassily.

Tara rolled her eyes and got out of the car. "Lauren Nichols, only you could make me smile when we are in the most serious situation of our relationship!"

They met at the back of the car to get their bags from the trunk. When they walked into the house Lauren dropped her bag by the couch. "I know it's serious, honey, but I trust in our love. I'm also not naive to the fact that there will be people that don't understand it, but my son is not one of them. He needs to be educated, that's all."

"I know who's going to educate him," Tara said under her breath. She grabbed Lauren's bag and walked towards the stairs.

"Where are you going?" asked Lauren.

"I'm taking your bag upstairs like the loving partner I

am. I thought you might want to change before you go to your house and talk with Justin."

"You are a loving partner," Lauren said quietly as she followed her up the stairs.

While Lauren changed into more comfortable shorts and a top, Tara unpacked their clothes. She began to sort them into piles for laundry when Lauren walked up behind her and rested her head on her back.

"For some reason I can't imagine you unpacking and sorting your own laundry and here you are doing that for me," she said, hugging her from behind.

Tara turned in her arms and smiled. "If you haven't figured it out yet, I would do anything for you including your laundry."

"I know that," Lauren whispered. She buried her head on Tara's shoulder and they held one another for several moments.

"Are you ready to leave?" Tara asked, pulling back.

"Yes, I'd better get going." She sighed.

They walked downstairs hand in hand and Tara walked out to the garage with her. A noise caught their attention and then they saw a car pull into the driveway. Krista and Melanie got out and waved.

"Did you just get in?" asked Krista, stopping at the back of the car.

"Yep," said Tara. "Lauren was just leaving."

"We wondered if you wouldn't mind drinking a beer with us," Melanie said to Tara.

Tara smiled, knowing her friends had come over to wait with her. Last night they had called Krista and Melanie and filled them in on what happened with Justin and their plan to hopefully calm his objections.

"I'm sure there is beer in the refrigerator. Let's go out to the porch," said Tara.

"We'll meet you there," Krista said with a wink to Lauren. She and Melanie walked into the house leaving Lauren and Tara alone.

Lauren gently laid her hands on Tara's cheeks and leaned in for a kiss. "I'll call you later. I may end up staying there tonight if he doesn't come around," she said delicately.

Tara's eyes widened and she took a deep breath. "I hope that doesn't happen."

"Me neither, but if I have to I will, for us." She held Tara's face firmly and looked into her eyes. "I'm not going to leave you. Justin will come around."

Tara nodded. She wasn't sure, but she thought Lauren was saying this as much to herself as to Tara.

Their lips met in a sweet soft kiss and before it could become more Lauren pulled away.

"I love you, Tara Holloway. I wish I had the words to tell you how much," Lauren said, a little breathless.

"I love you, too," Tara said softly as tears stung her eyes. She gave Lauren a slow sweet smile and took a deep breath. "Go on, so you can hurry back to me."

Lauren smiled back at her, got in the car, and Tara watched her drive away.

"Please listen to your momma, Justin," she said softly, swallowing the lump in her throat. "Please give us a chance. Please give *me* a chance." She inhaled deeply, let it out, and walked into the house.

She grabbed a beer and went out to the porch to join Krista and Melanie.

"How was your flight?" asked Krista.

Tara looked at her like she was crazy. "Really? Small talk?" She sat down, put her face in her hands and let the tears fall. There was no way she could hold it in one more second.

"Oh honey," Krista said, getting up and kneeling in front of her. Melanie got up and stood behind Tara, rubbing her back.

After several moments Tara dropped her hands and sat back. Hot tears stained her cheeks and she tried to smile. "Thanks for being here. I'm scared to death I'm going to lose her or come between her and Justin. Why does this have to happen to us? Why can't people understand that two women can love each other just like a man and a woman, just like two men? Why does it have to be so fucking hard?"

"Hey, hey, hey," said Krista firmly. "You are not going to lose Lauren. I know Justin. He can be a little fucker, but he's a smart kid and was always kind. When he gets to know you it's going to be awesome, but sickening for us because you'll have someone to be an ass with. Because we all know you can be an ass!"

"Hold up," said Melanie, stepping around in front of Tara. "You haven't been an ass like you usually are since the day Lauren kissed you. It's like something changed. Oh wait, I know what happened." She grinned. "All this time you were searching for your heart. You found her so you're not this asshole anymore. You're happy, almost sweet Tara now, so there's no room for anything else."

"Hmm, I think you're onto something, babe," Krista said with a twinkle in her eye.

"Aren't you two hilarious," deadpanned Tara.

"I love you and Lauren together. Your happiness has changed you both. I have been around Justin and he's not homophobic," said Krista. "I think you were right when you said he was shocked and that can make you say hurtful things."

"All I want is a chance. I want him to see how happy his mom is now. I wonder if he realizes how important that is in life. Lauren and I know because we're older and we've lived in the unhappiness. He's young and I hope we can make him understand that."

"He adores his mother," said Krista. "He may hunt and love the Dallas Cowboys just like his daddy, but he's a momma's boy."

"What if he asks her to leave me? I don't want her to have to choose," Tara said, tears brimming in her eyes once again.

"He won't. Lauren will talk him into this road trip idea of yours and that's when you'll get your chance," said Krista.

"I've only met him once, Tara, but he seemed like a good guy. Of course he is because Lauren raised him," Melanie said, holding up her hands. "You're looking at this the wrong way. Put your positive panties on and stop with all this negative bullshit!"

Tara's eyebrows shot up her forehead. She looked at Krista. "Positive panties?"

"The first time I've heard that, but I like it. Put on your positive panties. Come on, Tara, you are the most charming, charismatic person I know. Justin will fall in love with you just like everyone else."

"Your wife is sitting right here, Krista," said Tara, embarrassed by the compliments.

"She's right! You are the most charming and charismatic person we know," agreed Melanie. "This is the biggest role of your life!"

"That's just it; it's not a role. I can't study for this one. I don't know the first thing about being a mom," said Tara dejectedly,

"That's not true. Ask my girls or Julia's girls and they'll

tell you you're better than a mom. A kid needs someone they can trust and talk to. Just imagine doing that for Justin and Emily. You have so much life to share with them," stressed Melanie.

Tara considered everything her friends had said and nodded. "All I can do is be myself." She took a drink from her beer.

"Now you're getting it." Krista nodded.

"Thanks y'all," Tara drawled in her new Texas accent.

24

Lauren's heart began to beat quicker and she had a sick feeling in her stomach as she pulled into her driveway and saw Justin's pickup. She still couldn't believe he had texted those hurtful things to her. Did he really think of her that way? She hoped Tara was right and in his surprise he had fired off those texts. She took a deep breath and got out of the car.

She walked into her living room and Justin jumped up from the sofa where he'd been watching TV. He turned it off and said quietly, "Hi Mom."

Lauren looked at him sternly, measuring him with her gaze. "Justin," she stated. He looked away from her and sat in the corner of the couch. She sat down in the other corner and tried to calm her racing heart.

"You need to know that I asked you repeatedly to come home so I could tell you about Tara," she began. She noticed he flinched at the mention of her name. "When you wouldn't I came to you. But I couldn't very well tell you when your boss joined us and you were so pleased with how engaging I was and how much he seemed to like me. I wasn't disgusting then, was I?"

Justin looked down at his hands. "I'm sorry I said that Mom. It's just that Eric came into my office and shoved his laptop in my face. He kept saying, 'Look that's your Mom isn't it'. I couldn't believe it. One of the captions said something like 'Has this beautiful blond tamed Tara Holloway.'"

"Gee, Justin, did it bother you that they called me a beautiful blond?"

"No, but you're my mom! Do you know what a player Tara Holloway is? It was one thing that y'all had become friends, Mom, but she's just out for–" Justin didn't finish his sentence.

"That's funny, Justin. Isn't Eric the friend that goes out every weekend and comes in on Monday and tells you about the women he's been with? Isn't he your friend and you have even gone out with him a few times?"

When Justin didn't say anything Lauren continued. "You know, Tara defended you when I read your texts yesterday morning. She said that you were shocked and when that happens people say things they don't mean."

Justin looked up at her with surprise on his face. "She did?"

"Yeah, she did. Let me tell you something, Justin, you can't believe everything you read in those gossip rags, but I thought you knew that. Tara is not a player."

"Wait, Mom, I didn't mean those things I texted to you and I'm really sorry," he said, his voice full of remorse.

Lauren inhaled and released a breath. "The best thing I have ever done in my life and will always be the best thing is being your and Emily's mom, Justin. That is the absolute best. But you and Emily are older now and don't need your parents as much. I think you have grown into good people.

For many years your dad and I focused on you and Em because we wanted to give you the best life."

"You did!" he exclaimed.

"But now that you are discovering the world on your own, your dad and I realized we had neglected ourselves and our relationship. I will always love your daddy and we will always be friends, but that's all there was." She paused as Justin hung on to her every word. "Justin, I needed more in my life than a friend and you kids."

"You told us that."

"Three years ago I met Tara at Krista's."

Justin interrupted her then. "You changed, Mom, when Krista came back to town and brought all those lesbians with her," he whined.

"Do you hear yourself? I thought you liked Krista."

He sighed. "I do like Krista."

"All those lesbians? Really?"

He sighed again. "I didn't mean it that way. This is so confusing."

"I'm trying to explain it to you, son."

He nodded and Lauren picked up her story. "When I met Tara, I knew exactly who she was and knew her reputation. But something connected between us that very first night. She saw something in me that told her I was worth waiting on because she knew I was trying to figure things out with my marriage." Lauren took a breath. "And I saw something in her that told me she wasn't what all those magazines said. From that night on, Justin," she emphasized his name to be sure he listened, "she didn't go out with another woman."

He looked at her, seeming not to believe her.

"That's right, no one. We became friends. By that I mean we called each other, we texted, and we spent time together when she came to Krista's. I needed a friend like her that didn't know your dad because all my other friends did. Some of them thought I was crazy to leave him. They didn't believe that there could still be passion at our age."

Justin looked down at his hands.

"I'm not trying to embarrass you, but come on. You know what I mean."

"You are still my mom and I never expected to talk about this with you," he said, his eyes wide.

Lauren chuckled. "I know. Tara listened to me when I told her what I was seeking. She didn't know Marcus, so I didn't have to worry about her opinion of him. As we got to know one another better she confided in me that she believed her person was still out there, too. Yes, she had dated a lot of women, but just because their pictures appeared in magazines and on the internet didn't mean she slept with them."

Justin looked at her again with surprise.

"That's what I was trying to tell you. She's not really the player the magazines made her out to be. And even if she was, it doesn't matter now. Because as we got to know one another better and became closer we realized we were looking for the same thing and found it in one another."

She paused again to make sure he was still listening. "I'm not naive, son. Tara lived in Hollywood and is a movie star. Why would she want to be with a real estate broker in Texas? And I'm not about to move out there, away from you and Emily and the business I've built."

"She'd be lucky to have a woman like you!" he exclaimed.

Lauren quirked an eyebrow and looked at him. "You didn't think so yesterday. Anyway, when she asked me to find her a place here I knew she loved me and was doing all she could to be with me."

"But why her, Mom? Why a woman? Are you in love with her?"

"It's her, Justin, and she happens to be a woman. I didn't set out to find a woman or a man. I wanted to find where I belong. I don't know how else to explain it. Yes, I'm in love with her and feel like she is the person I was meant to be with in this life."

"This is so much, Mom." Justin sighed.

"I know it is, but I need something from you," she said.

He looked up at her with his brow furrowed. "What do you need from me?"

"I need a promise."

"A promise? Okay, what am I promising?"

"Nope, I want your promise first. Maybe then I can forget those horrible things you said to me. Because Justin, the first thing I wanted to do when I walked in this house was slap you across the face for being so disrespectful. I wasn't planning on telling your father," she said firmly.

"Okay, I promise," he said hurriedly. "You know I didn't mean those things!"

"I do, but they still hurt."

"Oh Mom, I'm so sorry. What is it you need me to do?"

"Tara is moving here. Next week a moving company is loading up and shipping her furniture. She has two cars in California that she doesn't want to send with them. So you and Emily are going to fly to California with Tara and me and drive her cars back."

"What!"

"You are going to go back to work and take care of whatever you need to and tell your boss you need next week off."

He looked at her wide eyed. "And Justin, I will not hesitate to call him."

"We're driving two cars back here. I'm not riding with her," he grumbled.

Lauren chuckled to herself. "You don't have to."

Justin looked at his watch. "When are we leaving?"

"Day after tomorrow."

Justin stared at her and she could see the wheels turning in his head. "Then I'm going back tonight, so I'll have all day tomorrow to get things organized."

"Are you sure you're able to drive back? You're not distracted?"

"No, Mom, I'll be fine."

"Then you think about why it took something like this to get you to come home to see me. I'm sure if your dad called you to meet him at next Sunday's Cowboys game you'd be there."

Justin looked down at his hands and mumbled, "Yes ma'am."

"One other thing, Justin. Did you see how happy I was in those pictures? Shouldn't that matter?"

He looked up and nodded. "Yeah, Mom, your happiness does matter."

Lauren nodded and got up and held out her arms.

He rose and walked into them. She held him tight for several moments before whispering softly, "Give us a chance."

He pulled away, looked her in the eye and nodded. "I'll text you when I get home tonight."

She smiled. "Thank you."

He started towards the door and she said, "Hey Justin." She waited for him to turn around. "I love you."

He gave her a small smile. "I love you too, Mom."

She waited for him to leave and then sat back down on the couch. That went better than she'd thought it would. She had no doubt that Justin would eventually come to love Tara. The love she had for both of them, as well as Emily, was immeasurable and there was no way she was giving up any of them. She turned off the lights, got in the car, and drove to what she now considered home.

When she came into the house she could see Tara on the back porch with Krista and Melanie. She poured herself a glass of wine and walked out the back door.

Tara jumped up and looked at her expectantly.

Lauren walked over to her, looked into her eyes, leaned up and kissed her. She pulled away and couldn't stop the smile forming on her face. "We got our chance," she said.

"Yes!" Tara exclaimed, hugging her tightly.

Lauren held out her glass, trying not to spill it, and laughter filled the air.

"He's going with us?" asked Tara, her eyes bright.

"Yep. He went back tonight to get things ready at work." Lauren sat down in the empty chair next to Tara's.

"That's all y'all need, a chance," said Melanie.

"He'll try to be stoic, but he won't be able to resist Tara for long," said Krista. "And when he sees how happy you are there's no way he'll remain upset. Besides, Emily will be with you too. She already loves Tara."

Tara exhaled. "You keep saying he can't resist me and I'm charming, but I don't exactly know how I do that. I'm just me."

"That's all you need to be, baby."

"Yeah, if you try to be someone you're not, that will be disastrous," said Krista.

Tara smiled and nodded. "Road trip! This is going to be epic."

They all laughed and it wasn't long until Krista and Melanie left.

"I'm ready to go up," Tara said. "How about you?"

Lauren joined her at the bottom of the stairs after locking the back door. She put her arms around Tara's neck and said, "I was hoping you could help me relieve some of this stress I endured today."

Tara grinned and looked into her eyes. "I don't think the stress will be gone until after this road trip."

Lauren's face turned serious. "He apologized for the hurtful texts and he listened to what I told him about the friendship we built and the love that came from it." She took Tara's face into her hands. "I will not lose either one of you. It's going to be okay. Now, take me to bed and make me yours." With that she kissed Tara passionately and pulled them up the stairs.

25

"Thanks for driving us to the airport," said Tara as she got out of the car.

"We're glad to do it because it's an opportunity to do a little shopping," said Krista as she opened the trunk. "Plus, we'll get to see Justin and Emily."

"What she really means is she wants to see if you all get on the plane in one piece," Melanie said playfully.

Lauren laughed. "You never know."

"I think it's a nice touch, you chartering a private plane, Tara," said Krista.

"I hoped maybe we could all talk and have a good time. You can't do that on a commercial flight even in first class," said Tara. "Besides, my darling and her kids should be treated special." She put her arm around Lauren.

"Aww, thanks, love," Lauren said, kissing her on the cheek.

"We're about to see how special they feel because here they come," said Krista.

Justin and Emily got out of their shared ride.

"Did you know they were coming together?" asked Tara.

"Nope. Emily probably met Justin at his apartment to make sure he'd come," said Lauren. She waited while Justin and Emily walked towards them.

Emily smiled at her mom and hugged her. "Hey Mom." She turned to Tara and said, "Thanks for the trip to California."

Tara grinned at her. "Thanks for helping me."

"Hey Mom," Justin said quietly, giving her a hug.

Tara saw him close his eyes as he hugged her and it made her heart lurch. She swallowed down the emotion that suddenly caused a lump in her throat.

"Justin, I'd like you to meet Tara Holloway," said Lauren, turning to her with a smile that said everything will be okay.

Tara saw him swallow and meet her eyes. "It's nice to meet you," he stated.

"Hi Justin, it's nice to meet you. Thanks for going on this trip with us."

He nodded and then turned to Krista. "Hi Krista, how are you?"

Krista smiled at him and chuckled. She leaned in and said, "I'm probably better than you right now."

He released a nervous chuckle.

"You remember my wife, Melanie?" said Krista.

"I do. How are you liking lake life?" he asked.

"I love it, but I'm sure it's because of the people." She grinned at Krista. "Your mom has helped me feel right at home."

Justin smiled. "Yeah, she's good at that. I'm not sure you'll meet a kinder person."

Lauren stood straighter. "Why thank you, Justin."

"It's true, but he should be kissing up," Emily said, loud enough for the others to hear.

"Everything is ready, Ms. Holloway," the pilot said, walking up.

"Thank you." She turned to the others and raised her eyebrows. "Thanks again for the ride. We'll see you in a few days," she said to Krista and Melanie.

"Come here, you," Krista said, giving her a hug.

Melanie took a turn and whispered in Tara's ear, "You've got this. Enjoy."

Tara smiled at her then grabbed her and Lauren's bags while the others said their goodbyes.

"Here babe, I can get that," said Lauren.

Tara thought she saw Justin wince at the term of endearment toward her.

Once they were all settled on the plane the pilot taxied to the runway and took off. It wasn't long until they were able to unbuckle and relax in the comfortable seats.

"Does anyone want something to drink?" asked Tara.

"Are you trying to impress us with the private plane and the drinks?" asked Justin.

"Well, hell yeah, wouldn't you?" said Tara.

Justin flinched at Tara's honesty and almost smiled.

"What do you have in there?" asked Lauren. "How about a mimosa?"

Tara looked in the refrigerator and found a bottle of premixed orange juice with champagne. "You've got it. Anyone else?"

"I'll take one," said Emily.

"Justin, there's beer and other hard seltzers in here or soft drinks and sparkling water," said Tara.

When Tara brought Lauren and Emily their drinks, Justin got himself a beer. Tara grabbed a sparkling water and sat back down next to Lauren.

"You know, Justin, you shouldn't be so quick to judge

Tara for her money. Wait until you see the lake house," said Emily.

"I wasn't judging her for her money," said Justin.

"There's nothing wrong with spending the money you make. I saw how hard Tara had to work for it. Making movies is a lot harder than I ever imagined," said Lauren.

"What's so hard?" asked Emily. "I mean, I always hear about long hours and getting up early to be at the studio."

"There's that," said Tara. "Really, the hard part is making people believe you're someone else on camera. You have a camera, a sound person, the director, hair, makeup and wardrobe people standing less than six feet away and you're supposed to convince the audience you're in an intense conversation with your co-star while you're spying on a criminal. Or let's say you're sitting on a sofa having an intimate moment with a love interest, and there's ten people hovering around you. It's amazing how they can make a scene look like it does with that many people around."

"How do we know you're not being someone else right now?" asked Justin.

"Justin," Lauren said.

"No, that's a good question. Honestly Justin, being happy isn't an act. Your mom makes me smile all the time." Tara smiled at Lauren. "She makes me feel happy inside. Have you ever felt that?" she asked. "I haven't very often. Don't get me wrong, I haven't had a bad life, but being with your mom makes me understand a lot of the cliches you hear about love. Like, 'you complete me,'" she said dramatically, looking at Lauren. "For me, it's a feeling inside that is calm and at the same time excited for what comes next. It may be a look, a smile, a trip." She widened her eyes at Justin and Emily. "Or a song, a boat ride; it could be anything, but it's looking forward and you know someone is going to be with you. Someone that makes you breathe, makes your heart beat, makes you live." She looked at Lauren with love in her eyes.

She shook her head and looked at Justin and Emily. "I'm sorry." She could feel her cheeks redden. "That just came out. But that is who I am."

"You don't have to be sorry," said Emily. "Now I know how much Mom means to you."

"Then maybe now you can see why I like doing special things for her and the both of you. I'm not necessarily trying to impress you; I'm loving you," said Tara.

Justin and Emily didn't say anything but both smiled and nodded.

"I need to see you back here," Lauren said to Tara, getting up and going to the back of the plane.

Tara looked at Justin and Emily like a child about to be scolded. They both shrugged and grinned at her.

Lauren pulled Tara behind the wall that divided the main cabin from the restroom and bar area and kissed her lovingly. When they pulled apart Tara was dizzy with love.

"All those things you said," Lauren whispered, "that's how I feel. I can't wait for what's next. And even if it's nothing then as long as I'm with you I'm happy."

"I didn't mean to say that to them, though," said Tara apologetically.

"I think they loved it. They now know how much you love their momma and respect her."

"I do," whispered Tara earnestly.

"Do you think I could get a refill?" Emily called from her seat.

Tara laughed and winked at Lauren. "Coming right up."

They settled back into their seats and Justin said, "Mom told me the other night that you can't believe everything in those magazines. What do you do when they print lies about you?"

Tara exhaled. "I guess it depends on what they're saying and how bad it is."

"I was trying to tell him you are not the player that they tried to make you out to be," Lauren said, putting her hand on Tara's arm.

"Here's what I know about being a player," said Tara.

Emily interrupted and said, "Listen up, Justin."

"Ha ha, very funny," said Justin.

"If you have lots of money, a pretty face, and are successful, the women will come to you. Leaving Krista broke my heart, but I felt like I would die if I stayed in the closet any longer."

When Tara said that, Lauren grabbed her hand and held it. Justin looked at their hands but didn't seem offended by the gesture.

"I went on these lavish vacations with different women because I was so happy to be free. I was free to love and be who I really am. I had enough money that if my career ended because I came out I could start over somewhere and do something else. That's how my reputation started."

Lauren squeezed her hand, giving her strength.

"I didn't like the perception that I was a player because of how I feel about sex, trust and intimacy. And the truth is, your mom saw all that in me the first time she looked into my eyes. Right?" said Tara, looking over at Lauren.

"I saw a woman who was looking for the same thing I was. I just didn't know how we were going to get there. But yes, I knew you weren't the player everyone tried to make you out to be. Especially after we danced the first time."

"You danced?" said Emily.

"Yes—Justin, don't cringe, but I was at Krista's enjoying

karaoke with all those lesbians and they were dancing," said Lauren playfully.

"Mom," said Justin, shaking his head.

"We sang and danced with one another," said Lauren.

"You mean with the other Hollywood people?" said Emily, a bit star-struck.

"Yes, but," Lauren looked at Tara, "after I danced with Tara the first time I didn't dance with anyone else and haven't since."

"Really?" said Tara.

"Yep. I guess my heart knew something the rest of me didn't yet, but I didn't want to dance with anyone else."

"That's so romantic," said Emily.

"We are annoyingly sappy and you don't want to hear about that," said Tara. "Justin, I didn't know how to drive a boat when I bought the lake house, but your mom has taught me. Do you know anything about jet skis?"

"A little. A friend of mine has one. Are you thinking about getting one?"

"I always wanted a motorcycle or scooter when I was young, but never got one. Jet skis seem like motorcycles on the water," she commented.

Justin began to tell them his knowledge of jet skis and the conversation turned to other topics as they soared toward California.

Tara knew she'd like him and he seemed to be relaxing somewhat around her, but he would still ask a pointed question here and there. At least she felt like there was hope they'd be a family.

26

When they got to Tara's house she gave Justin and Emily the tour and then told them to meet her and Lauren by the pool. She went to the kitchen, grabbed a few snacks and went outside. Lauren was waiting for her with a smile.

"What are you smiling about?" she asked, setting the crackers and chips on the table and sitting next to her on the couch.

"Come here," she said, grabbing Tara's face and kissing her soundly.

Tara pulled away and looked at the sliding doors to see if Justin and Emily saw them.

"I need your lips on mine." Lauren grinned. "Stop, honey," she said, turning Tara back towards her. "They're going to see us kiss from time to time. They need to get used to it."

"But it might make them uncomfortable. I don't want to do that," explained Tara.

"Oh babe, it'll be fine. Kiss me and I'll let you go."

Tara looked at the door again and then kissed Lauren as

she asked, but she couldn't pull away. Lauren's soft lips felt so good on hers and she sank into the kiss and let Lauren fill her with love.

"Now that's more like it," Lauren moaned.

"That's what you do to me," Tara said, catching her breath.

"Here they come," whispered Lauren, grinning.

Tara leaned back and shook her head. "You are too much."

Lauren laughed. "I know." She looked at her kids. "Was there anything you wanted to do or see? There's a fancy place we want to take you for dinner. It's on a rooftop and I think you'll love it, Emily."

"Aren't we leaving tomorrow? I thought the whole idea was to drive these cars back," said Justin.

"It is," said Tara. "But that doesn't mean we can't have fun before we hit the road."

Justin looked from Tara to his mom. "This isn't a vacation for me."

"It could be," said Lauren.

"Not really," he replied.

"Fine. We can hit the road tomorrow and we'll stop along the way because I don't know when we'll get to make this drive. I'm looking forward to seeing our country."

"We can at least drive down Sunset Boulevard and see vintage Hollywood on the way to the restaurant," said Tara. "You know, I'm not selling this house. You are both welcome to plan trips out here and use it anytime you want. Before you ask, Justin, no, I'm not trying to buy you or impress you. I'm not retiring just yet and will still come back here from time to time so I'm keeping the house for now."

"This would be a great place to have a girls vacation," said Emily.

"Or a mother daughter trip," said Lauren.

Emily's eyes widened and she smiled. "It would."

Justin didn't say anything.

"Look, having money is nice, but that's not what your mom and I are about," said Tara, wanting to clear the air. "Taking you to fancy restaurants is fun for me. I thought Emily would be interested because I know someday she'll have her own. And Justin, I never had anyone that could do this for me, so being able to do it for you gives me joy. But honestly, for me," she said looking at Lauren and smiling, "there's nothing better than you coming home from work and having a glass of wine or a beer while I make us dinner. I know that sounds boring to you." She looked at Justin and Emily. "Of course we like to watch movies and TV," she added honestly. "But sitting on the couch and holding hands is the best." She grinned at Lauren.

"You cook?" asked Justin.

"She's a good cook," said Emily. "Have you tried those recipes we made together?"

"I did the one with chicken for us not too long ago."

"How was it?" she asked.

Tara looked over at Lauren. "It was delicious," said Lauren. "It might not have been quite as elegant as yours, but it was just as tasty."

"Yeah, I need to work on my presentation," admitted Tara.

"But not with me," said Lauren.

"Why not?" said Emily. "You're special too."

"That's what I told her," said Tara.

"You already make me feel special enough. If you do that at dinner you're going to expect me to do the same when it's my turn to cook," said Lauren.

"No I won't."

"You have planned so many romantic things for us to do I'll never catch up," said Lauren.

"What are you talking about!" exclaimed Tara. "You found the lake house!"

"She's right, Mom. That house is full of romance," said Emily.

"Are we making you uncomfortable, Justin?" asked Tara.

"Not really. I didn't realize how unhappy you were, Mom, but when I stopped and took notice, you've changed. Since the divorce was final you're happy again. At first that bothered me, but I get it now," he said.

"I think you're brave, Mom. You left what you knew, what was comfortable and went after what made you happy. Tara is the lucky one because she has you," said Emily.

Lauren's mouth fell open at both her children's words.

"I am the lucky one. No doubts," agreed Tara, taking Lauren's hand in hers.

"I can't believe this! Who are you people? I swear, Tara, these two *look* like my kids," said Lauren.

Justin and Emily laughed.

"We're finally understanding all those lessons you tried to teach us growing up, Mom," said Emily.

"Yeah, we're thinking of others and not just ourselves. How many times did you have to tell us that?" Justin chuckled.

"A few," said Lauren. "Seriously, it was hard leaving your dad. He is a good man and great father. But I knew there was more for me in this life. I hope you'll understand someday, but for now I ask that you respect me and Tara."

"I do, Mom," said Emily with a smile.

"I'm working on it. It's still new for me," said Justin.

"That's all I can ask," said Lauren. "Enough seriousness.

Let's change and go for that drive. How about it, babe?" She smiled at Tara.

"Let's go," she said, getting up and pulling Lauren up with her.

In the bedroom Lauren put her arms around Tara's shoulders and held her close. "How about that," she said in her ear.

"Those are good people you raised, but they are so lucky that you're their mom," said Tara.

"Right now I'm feeling thankful that we found one another. Do you know how wonderful it feels to wake up every day and know I get to spend it with you? That fills my heart and makes life matter."

"I do know how wonderful it feels," she said, kissing her tenderly.

"Let's spend the rest of the day like a family," said Lauren.

That really made Tara smile and they quickly changed clothes.

Back in the living room Lauren led them to the garage and Justin stopped.

"You've got to be kidding me," he exclaimed as he saw Tara's red convertible.

"Wow," said Emily.

Tara smiled. "Now you see why I want to bring it to Texas. It's a Maserati. I always wanted a fancy red convertible. Do you both know the movie Krista and I made with our friends?"

"Duh, it won the Academy Award," said Emily with awe.

"I got this after that movie," said Tara.

"It's beautiful," said Justin.

"Thanks. I'm sure you'll drive it at some point on this

road trip," she said, opening the driver's side to her four door Audi SUV.

"This is going to be fun," she heard Justin say softly.

Lauren looked over at her and grinned as she got in the passenger seat.

"You know," Tara said, looking at Justin and Emily in the back seat. "We can go to an elegant restaurant anytime. Would you mind if we did something else?"

"Heck yeah. I work at a fancy restaurant. I appreciate you wanted to take me to this one, but it's fine with me. What did you want to do?"

Tara looked at Lauren. "Let's go to the beach. That's what families do."

Lauren's eyes lit up. "Can we see Angelo?" Tara nodded. "Let's do it," said Lauren. She turned to the kids. "Want to go to Malibu?"

Emily nodded excitedly, but Justin said, "I didn't bring a swimsuit."

"No worries, son. Come on," Lauren said, getting out of the car.

They walked back in the house and Lauren said, "Emily, you won't believe the swimsuits that Tara has out in the pool house."

Tara explained, "When you have a pool people leave things like swimsuits, hats, glasses, towels. It's ridiculous." She looked at Justin. "Don't worry, I have guy suits, too." After a few moments she came out of the pool house and handed Justin three different suits. "They have all been laundered. Try them on."

They all went inside to change and when Tara walked into the bedroom she stopped and stared at Lauren. "Are you kidding me?"

"What?" Lauren grinned devilishly, twirling around in the one piece suit showing plenty of cleavage.

"I won't be able to keep my eyes or hands off of you if you wear that!"

Lauren chuckled. "Yes you will."

Tara shook her head and then caught the swimsuit Lauren threw at her. "I want to see you in this," she demanded.

She changed and walked out of the bathroom to Lauren's wide eyes.

"I didn't think your legs could get any longer. You are a beautiful woman, my love," she said, walking over and putting her arms around her. "This is a great idea." She smiled and kissed her.

"I want them to have a good time."

"What about me?" Lauren pouted playfully.

"I'm taking you to your favorite place," said Tara.

Lauren chuckled. "My favorite place is with you."

Tara touched her lips to Lauren's and let the kiss wrap her in love. When they pulled apart she whispered, "I love you."

"And I love you," Lauren said, her forehead pressed to Tara's. "Thank you for treating my kids with such love. They don't realize it yet, but they will."

Tara smiled. "We'd better go before they wonder what happened to us."

They went back out to the garage, but this time they all got in the convertible. Tara took them along the same roads she'd driven days earlier with Lauren. This time she pulled up to Allison's beach house. They would walk to Angelo's seafood restaurant via the beach.

"Before you ask, Justin, no, I don't own this place, but I know where they hide the key," said Tara, getting out of the car. She looked at Justin and Emily. "You've done that before, haven't you? Your friends aren't at their place at the lake, but you know where the key is and they wouldn't mind." She winked.

Justin and Emily looked at one another and grinned.

Lauren studied both of her kids. "Wait? Have you done that." Before they could answer she said, "Stop, I don't want to know."

Justin and Emily laughed and got out of the car before their mother could change her mind.

27

It was a perfect afternoon and evening for the beach. They took turns splashing in the cold water and walking along the shore. Lauren and Tara sat down on the bench where they'd watched the sunset before and held hands.

Their laughter drifted down to the beach and Emily turned around where she was sitting in the sand. She nudged Justin, who was sitting next to her, and they watched them for a few moments.

"Were you surprised when they told you?" asked Justin.

"They didn't really tell me," said Emily, looking at her brother. "I went to the lake to see Mom and she asked me to help Tara set up her kitchen. It was obvious when I first saw them how much they loved one another. The way they looked at each other, they couldn't have hidden it if they wanted."

"It doesn't bother you?"

"Not at all. You know, if I hadn't seen them together it may have been different. But Justin, she practically told us. Whenever I talked to her Tara's name always came up. They were like best friends that didn't live in the same town. Did she not talk about her to you?"

"I kind of remember her talking about her, but honestly I didn't pay attention like I should have," he said.

"If this shows us anything we need to stay in touch with one another and listen. Have you talked to Dad lately?"

"I actually talked to him last night. I asked him if he knew about Mom."

"Did he?"

"He said he'd heard that Tara bought a place and Mom was living there. Then he told me very plainly that he wanted Mom to be happy and it wasn't any of his business who she was seeing."

Emily nodded. "That's what Mom told me about him. You know, we're a family with Dad and we're a family with Mom. We get them both. And now we get Tara, too. If you haven't picked up on it, she really wants us to be a family. I don't think it's just to please Mom either. I think she wants us."

"She doesn't know us," said Justin.

"Sure she does. She's heard Mom talk about us for years now. She's known Krista and Julia for a long time too and they know us. I think that's why this trip is so important to her. She wants to get to know us. And by the way, Mom tried to tell you so you wouldn't be surprised."

"I know. I've been a dick about coming home because I'm working a lot. But I should've known when she kept asking me. I thought she was just lonely because the divorce was final."

"She asked us to come in several times to meet Tara over the years and we didn't. That's on us. I like Tara. As far as I'm concerned she's family now and we're better for it. Look at them," she said, gazing in their direction. "Have you ever seen Mom so happy? She's always touching Tara and you can tell Tara adores her. She was happy with Dad, but not like this. Why would we want to get in the way of that?"

"No argument from me," he said.

Emily jerked her head around and looked at him. "You're okay with Tara?"

"Yeah. How can you not like her? And Mom is crazy about her."

"So she's part of the family?"

"Yes, I just don't want Tara to know yet. This is kind of fun," he admitted with a grin.

"You are evil," Emily said, shoving his shoulder and throwing her head back in laughter.

"What's so funny?" Lauren said, walking up holding Tara's hand.

"We were just talking about how happy you are and that we approve," said Emily.

Lauren eyed them both. "You shouldn't lie to your mother like that," she said, walking toward the water with Tara.

Justin and Emily laughed again.

They played in the water, walked along the beach and enjoyed the afternoon together.

"After the sun sets let's walk to Angelo's," said Lauren. "I'm getting hungry."

"Me too," agreed Justin.

Lauren put her arm around Tara and watched the sun fall into the ocean. Justin and Emily sat on the beach in front of them. The sky was a beautiful deep orange and cast a halo around them. Her heart filled with emotion as she looked upon her family, the people she loved the most all in one place. Tara had brought her kids back to her when they were once too busy to bother. Granted it didn't begin under the happiest of circumstances, but she knew they'd get there.

"Thank you," she whispered into Tara's ear.

She looked at her, confused.

"I'll explain later," she said with a soft smile. "I love you."

Tara smiled and love radiated from her eyes, filling Lauren even more.

"Let's eat," said Emily, hopping up.

Lauren winked and grabbed Tara's hand as she pulled her up. "Follow me," she said, leading them down the beach towards the restaurant. Tara explained to them that Angelo was an old friend. They liked to say that they both started here at the same time. Tara hit it big and Angelo's restaurant got its first big review all in the same week. She came here to celebrate and they had been friends ever since.

Tara led them up onto the outdoor dining deck from the beach. When Angelo spotted them he rushed over.

"I cannot believe it! My eyes deceive me! Tara Holloway is back again this week and with her most beautiful Lauren."

Tara turned to Justin and he held up his hand. "It's okay. I know you didn't plan this."

She eyed him, but before she could say anything Lauren grabbed her arm.

Angelo looked at Emily and Justin. "These must be your beautiful children," he said to Lauren.

She beamed with pride. "They are. This is my daughter Emily and my son Justin."

Angelo shook both of their hands. He showed them to a table in the corner that was out of the view of the patrons inside the restaurant.

Before Tara sat down he said in her ear softly, "What a beautiful family."

She grinned and nodded.

"Please tell me you are hungry? I have the freshest, most beautiful shrimp and oysters to go along with the seafood feast I shall prepare for you."

"We are starving! Bring it on, Angelo," exclaimed Tara.

As the dishes began to arrive they dug in with gusto.

"Oh my God, honey. Taste this," Lauren said to Tara and put the bite in her mouth.

The pleasure was obvious on Tara's face and she moaned in delight. "What is that?"

"It's a scallop, but I don't know how he cooked it," said Lauren.

Angelo brought out another dish of shrimp and Tara asked him. "What is this scallop dish? Is it new?"

"Ah, you like?"

"Very much," said Lauren, taking another bite.

"You know, Angelo, Emily is a chef back in Dallas. She is helping me get my culinary skills back. Could I persuade you to give her this recipe so she can teach it to me?" implored Tara.

Angelo studied Tara and made a show of considering her question and then a smile began to spread over his face. "How about you come back to the kitchen with me and I'll show you."

"I'd love to," Emily said, getting up.

"You have to promise not to take it back to your restaurant in Dallas. When you open your own place then you can use it," he said.

Emily's face lit up. "Yes sir!" she exclaimed.

They shared the scallop dish with Justin and he tasted it. "That's really good, but I'm telling you I think this is the best shrimp I've ever eaten and I've eaten a lot of shrimp!"

Lauren chuckled. "I told Tara when we were here before that you would love that dish."

Justin looked up at her and smiled.

"What's that look?" she asked.

"I don't know. With so much going on when you were here, I'm surprised you were thinking of me." He shrugged.

"I'm your mother. I think of you a lot more than you know."

"Yeah. Em and I were talking. We've both kind of been absent from your life lately. I'm sorry about that."

"Thanks. I know you have your own lives, but every now and then it's nice to hear from you."

"I know."

Angelo came back with Emily and topped off their drinks.

"I've got you, Tara. We'll be making this in no time. Thanks Angelo," Emily said, taking her seat.

"It was my pleasure," he said, nodding slightly. "My friend, there is a photographer roaming the restaurant. Would you like me to steer them away?"

Tara looked at Lauren who turned to her kids. "They love to take Tara's picture and we're news. What do you think?"

"You didn't mind," said Emily.

Lauren smiled. "I want everyone to know that Tara Holloway is now taken," she said possessively.

Tara's cheeks reddened and she looked down, mortified.

"Well you are," said Justin. "It's fine with me if they take your picture."

"Oh no. They'll want the whole group," said Angelo.

Tara shrugged and he walked away.

"Does this happen to you often?" asked Justin.

"Sometimes. It depends on if I have something coming

out. The movie released last week so I'm big news for now," she explained.

A photographer walked up and looked at Tara expectantly. "Is it okay?"

"Sure, but get their names correct," she said.

Before he took a picture he wrote down all their names. He zoomed in on Tara and Lauren and then asked if Emily and Justin could scoot in closer.

Lauren had her arm around Emily and was holding Tara's hand while Justin sat next to Tara. They all smiled and when he was done Lauren whispered in her ear, "Our first family photo."

Tara grinned. "And we were all smiling."

"Progress. One step at a time." She winked.

They finished their meals and said their goodbyes to Angelo. There was just enough light to walk back down the beach to their car.

"What a fun day," said Emily, getting in the back seat.

"It surprisingly was," agreed Justin.

Emily glared at him and shook her head. He gave her a sly smile back.

"Will he send you those pictures?" Emily asked Tara.

"Angelo will have them. He's supposed to text them to me," answered Tara.

"Would you share with me, please?" she said. Looking at her brother she added, "I think we make quite the happy family."

Tara looked into the rearview mirror and could see them smirking at each other. She smiled to herself and glanced at Lauren. She loved this family already.

28

"What smells so good? Is my dear sweet sister cooking breakfast treats?" said Justin, walking into the kitchen.

"No," Emily chuckled, sitting at the island. "But dear sweet Tara is."

Tara smiled and set a plate with a hot fresh omelet down in front of her. She turned to Justin. "Coffee?"

"Yes please," he said, sitting down next to his sister.

Tara poured him a cup and set it down. She slid the sweetener and creamer across the island to him. "You can start on pancakes," she said, handing him a plate. "Would you like an omelet? I have veggies and cheese if that's okay."

"I'd love one, thanks."

"By the way, good morning," said Tara with a smile.

"Good morning." Justin smiled between bites. "These are delicious," he mumbled.

"Thanks," said Tara, turning back to the stove.

"You really can cook," he mumbled.

Lauren walked in and put an arm around each of her kids shoulders and said, "Good morning."

"Morning, Mom," they replied.

Then she walked around the large island and put an arm around Tara's waist and kissed her on the cheek. "Do you need any help?"

"I need your breakfast order, my love," she said softly with a smile.

Emily looked over at Justin and nudged him. As he forked in another bite he looked at her and then at his mom and Tara.

He smiled and rolled his eyes. "I saved you a pancake, Mom," he said, getting her attention.

"Thanks," she said, turning away from Tara. She got a cup of coffee and sat on the other side of Justin.

Tara plated Justin's omelet and handed it to him.

"Thanks," he said, meeting her eyes. She waited for him to take a bite and she was rewarded with a moan of pleasure. "You weren't kidding about cooking, Tara. I would've never thought it."

"There's lots of things you wouldn't expect," said Lauren, smiling at her.

"Eat up everyone. We have a long way to go," said Tara, looking over the island at what she hoped was her family.

"Where to today?" asked Emily.

"We're going to the Grand Canyon," said Tara. "It may be too late to see it today, but we'll be able to drive through tomorrow. Have you ever been?"

"Nope," Emily said. Justin shook his head.

"It will take your breath away," said Tara. She was pleasantly surprised they had never been and would get to experience it with her.

* * *

They finished breakfast and quickly got ready to leave. Tara talked to the moving company that would be there later today.

"Lauren and I will drive the convertible first and you can take the Audi," she said to Emily and Justin.

"Sweet," said Emily, grabbing the keys.

"Oh no, I get to drive first," said Justin, wrestling them away from her.

"You just thought you wanted kids," chuckled Lauren, getting into the passenger side.

Tara laughed. "Follow me."

They pulled out of the driveway and the family road trip began.

"I sure did enjoy last night," said Tara, glancing over at Lauren. "It doesn't matter to you where we are or who is in the house, does it?" Before she could answer Tara added, "I think you like to do that because you know it makes me blush."

Lauren chuckled. "You are adorable with red cheeks, but believe me I like to do that because I love you and it seems I can't get enough of you. Do you have any idea how much joy I get from rocking your world like that?"

"Rocking my world." Tara laughed.

"Seriously babe, it feels so good to make you feel good. Does that even make sense? It's a new feeling for me and I love it. It's quite addictive, I think."

"Would this be the honeymoon phase?"

"I don't know about that," said Lauren. "I hope it doesn't stop."

"You would know. I've never had a honeymoon," said Tara.

Lauren thought about what Tara said for a moment. "Yes, but you've had relationships. I guess the beginning is like a honeymoon. It was different with Marcus. We were both working and came back to our lives and then had kids. With you, I come home from work every day and there you are. I have to say, I love it."

Tara laughed. "This may surprise you, but I love it too. I like being a housewife." She laughed again and looked at Lauren and shrugged.

"Is that what you are? A housewife? You're the sexiest housewife I've ever seen," said Lauren.

"All I know is I think about you all day long and I can't wait for you to come home."

"Maybe you have too much time on your hands," suggested Lauren.

"No I don't. Does it bother you?"

"Not at all. I just don't want you to get bored and–" Lauren didn't finish her thought and looked out the window.

"And what?"

Lauren didn't answer.

Tara took her hand and pulled it into her lap while she kept her other hand on the wheel. "I'm not going anywhere, Lauren. That is, unless you do."

Lauren looked at her and exhaled. "I just worry that you're going to get bored and want to move on."

"I thought we were in this forever. Didn't we talk about that?"

"We did."

"I meant it. Honeymoon or no honeymoon. Living at the lake or wherever. I don't care where we live as long as we're doing it together. Please don't waste another moment worrying if I'll get bored. I won't," she stated firmly.

Lauren squeezed her hand. "Okay." She gazed at Tara

and asked, "If you could go on a honeymoon, where would you want to go?"

"Hmm, that's a good question. Where would you want to go?"

"Oh no, I asked you first," said Lauren. She watched as Tara considered her question and an idea began to form in the back of her mind.

"I think I would want to go to a beach. We both like the water. Or we could go to the mountains if you'd rather." She glanced over at Lauren.

"I'm not sure either. I could see us somewhere romantic that doesn't have a lot to do because I think we'd be more interested in one another than sightseeing," said Lauren.

Tara nodded. "You are absolutely right." She kissed the back of Lauren's hand and looked in the rearview mirror. Justin and Emily weren't far behind them.

"Most people get married before they go on a honeymoon. Have you ever wanted to get married, babe?"

Tara sighed. "I used to think I wanted to be married, but I've never been in a relationship with anyone that I wanted to marry. I liked the idea of marriage, especially when we finally got the opportunity to do so. The older I got, it didn't seem to be as important. I like what Krista and Melanie did. They felt like they married years ago and they are obviously pledged to one another from here on out. And then there's Julia and Heidi. They married as soon as they both were out of college and started a life together. What about you? Do you want to get married again?"

"The right person would have to come along." She waited for Tara to glance her way and winked at her. "I wonder what would happen to Hollywood if Tara Holloway got married. It might never be the same," she teased.

"Ha ha," deadpanned Tara.

"When I decided to leave Marcus I knew our marriage was over and I haven't thought about marrying again. I guess 'I've been there, done that' as they say."

"Does it really matter? We've fallen in love and plan to live our lives together. Now, if I can just convince your kids to come home for Christmas," Tara said, grinning at Lauren.

"I think you've won them over. Justin likes to be a hard ass, but he's softening."

"I hope so because we could really have fun together, don't you think?"

"We already are!" replied Lauren. She settled back and eyed her beautiful lover. Tara may say it doesn't matter and earlier it didn't to Lauren, but now she liked the idea of marrying Tara. Lauren Holloway had a nice ring to it. *Hmm*, she thought.

They stopped to go to the restroom and stretch their legs. Tara suggested they change partners and she got in the Audi with Emily while Lauren drove her and Justin in the convertible.

* * *

"This is the coolest car, Mom," said Justin as they followed behind Tara and Emily.

"It's fun to drive too," replied Lauren.

"Do you think Tara will let me drive it?"

"I'm sure she will. If it were me I'd make you trade me something."

"Like what?" he said.

"Maybe a promise to visit. Look what it took to get you to come home," said Lauren.

"But it got me here," sing-songed Justin.

"And for that I will always be grateful to *Tara*. Without her you'd still be in Dallas working," she sang right back.

"Tara is not at all what I expected," said Justin.

"I tried to tell you. I hope you'll be around more and get to know her better. There is a lot that would surprise you."

"I can see that you're crazy for each other. I don't guess you worry that it will last?"

"Nope. I know it will. Do you really think she'd move to Texas if she wasn't sure?"

"Does that mean you're going to get married?"

"Hmm, I don't know. Would that bother you?"

"Does it really matter if any of this bothers me?" said Justin.

Lauren glanced over at him. "I know you're not homophobic and I know you want me to be happy. Tara is a good person, so what about this could bother you?"

"I guess I'm wondering...if I didn't like it, would you leave her?"

"Are you asking me to choose?" said Lauren with a steely gaze.

"No, that would be dumb. You shouldn't ever have to make a choice like that. You're right, I can see Tara is a good person and for some insane reason she wants us to like her so bad. I mean, what does she care if we like her or not, as long as you do."

"Well, you do happen to be a big part of my life!"

"I know that, but it wouldn't harm your day to day life," he said.

"She wants you to like her because you are important to *her*."

"Because *you* are important to her."

"It may have started that way, but she knows who you are because I talk a lot, if you haven't noticed in the past twenty-eight years, and she thinks you and Emily are pretty incredible people."

"She does?"

"Look, Justin, family is important to Tara and you're it. You might just like it," said Lauren.

"You know, Mom, the divorce was hard on me, too. The family I knew broke apart and that was hard to understand. All these years I was in a stable family and knew what part I was, where I fit. And then it broke apart and everything felt unsettled. If that happened to me I can't imagine how it affected you," he said sincerely.

Lauren sighed. "You know the last thing I wanted to do was hurt you."

"I know, Mom. We've talked about this. I was surprised how much it bothered me though. I'm glad you and Tara found each other. I'm sorry I freaked out the way I did a few days ago. I think we've started a new family with Tara."

Lauren looked over at him as tears stung her eyes. "Tara would be so happy to hear you say that. I know I am."

"Don't cry, Mom. You're driving a very expensive awesome car. Be careful," said Justin.

Lauren chuckled.

"Don't tell Tara, Mom. I'll ride with her tomorrow and tell her myself. Okay?"

"Okay."

"Hey, maybe I'll trade her," he said with a devilish grin.

"Justin," Lauren said warily.

"I'm kidding, Mom!"

They both laughed and Lauren honked the horn with joy.

29

The next morning they planned to meet at the motel restaurant and have breakfast before driving to the Grand Canyon.

Tara opened the sliding glass door to the balcony for a breath of fresh air while Lauren finished getting ready in the bathroom. She was about to step onto the balcony when she heard Justin on his own balcony next door.

"Yep, we're going to the Grand Canyon today," he said.

Tara assumed he was on the phone since she couldn't hear another voice.

"I'm telling you she's not like that," he said rather forcefully.

Tara's eyebrows shot up her forehead. She didn't mean to eavesdrop and started to clear her throat when Justin raised his voice.

"Listen motherfucker, I'm telling you, you've got it all wrong! And if you don't stop saying that shit I'm going to hang up. I'll see you when I get back, Eric."

Tara knew they had to be talking about her and was

surprised at Justin's tone. She was about to close the sliding glass door when Lauren walked into the room.

"Fuck off, man. You can't believe the shit you read. I've gotta go."

Tara could hear him close his own door.

"What was that?" asked Lauren.

"Justin was on the phone with Eric when I opened our door." A smile grew on Tara's face and she said, "He was defending me to Eric." Tears burned the back of her eyes.

"He was? I'm not surprised. He may give you a hard time, but he's not going to let anyone else talk about us."

"You think?"

"I do."

Tara shook her head, still smiling. She held up her hands with her fingers crossed.

Lauren chuckled and grabbed her face and kissed her. "Let's go have breakfast with these kids that are quickly becoming your biggest fans."

"I thought you were my biggest fan," she teased.

"And much more," Lauren said, kissing her again.

* * *

They took the Audi to the Grand Canyon and drove through the park, stopping to get out and walk. Tara and Lauren stood looking out at the expanse with their arms around one another.

"It is truly amazing," said Lauren reverently.

"I know," said Tara, just as quiet.

"This will sound sappy, but as vast as this Grand Canyon is it doesn't compare to the love I have for you, Tara."

"Oh babe," Tara said, turning to Lauren to look into her

eyes. "And the eons it took to carve this natural wonder doesn't compare to how long I'll be loving you."

They stared at each other and then their lips met in a kiss as natural as it was to breathe. It was soft, sweet and full of love. When they eased away, they smiled and once again took in the incredible vista.

On the way back to the motel Emily said, "You're right, Tara. That did take my breath away. Pictures don't come close to showing the beauty, the enormity, and vastness. Thank you so much for bringing us. I'm not sure I would have come here otherwise."

"I'm glad you enjoyed it. Maybe we can come back and do a little hiking. Lately I've been hiking around the lake. Have you hiked there? You probably have all your life," she scoffed.

"Not really," said Emily.

"I have," said Justin. "Where have you gone so far?"

"Krista showed me a place where we rode bikes through the woods and ended up at a beach. It was the coolest thing," she said.

"I know where you're talking about. Have you been to the cliffs where everyone jumps off?" he asked.

"Yes. We go there every time I come to Texas," she replied.

"There are some trails over there too. I'll show you next time I come visit."

"I'd love that. Thanks."

They made it back to the motel and loaded the cars. In the parking lot Justin turned to Tara and Lauren. "Is it the kids' turn to drive the convertible?" he asked with a boyish grin.

"You don't want to do that," Emily said to Tara.

Tara and Justin stared at one another then with a sly

smile she said, "If you have any balls, you'll drive that car as it's intended."

Justin couldn't hold back a grin and before she could change her mind he said, "Emily, get in the car."

They jumped in the car and backed out of the parking place leaving Lauren and Tara standing at the back of the SUV.

Lauren swatted Tara on the arm and said, "Why would you say that to him!"

Tara picked her up and twirled them around hugging her. "He smiled at me!"

Lauren couldn't help but smile at her. "Oh my darling, he can't resist you." She laughed.

They got in the car and went after them.

"I still can't believe you said that."

"Do you really think I bought that car to drive the speed limit on the interstate? Come on, honey."

Lauren laughed.

"Oh, would you text Emily and tell her the driver pays the ticket."

Lauren chuckled. "I think you know what you're doing after all." She texted and quickly got a response from Emily. "I also told her to slow down until we could at least see them. This road is straight and goes on forever."

A few minutes later they caught sight of Tara's red convertible and smiled at one another. The traffic flowed and it didn't seem like any time had passed before they crossed into New Mexico. It was time for a break and they followed Justin down the exit ramp to a convenience store where they could walk around and get gas and snacks.

"How are we switching up this time?" Emily asked when they were refueled and ready to get back on the road. "There's just so much sibling love we have to share."

"I'll ride with Tara," said Justin. "Which car?" he asked, looking at her.

Tara smiled and looked at Lauren. "You choose."

Lauren chuckled. "It's fine. Y'all can take the convertible."

Tara said, "Yes," quietly under her breath. "You can drive," she said to Justin.

He nodded and went around to the driver's side and got in. Emily went to the SUV and hopped into the driver's seat.

"Looks like we're being chauffeured," said Lauren. She walked over to Tara who was about to get in the convertible and whispered, "Don't be scared. You've got this."

Tara chuckled and kissed Lauren on the lips. She winked and got in.

They got back on the interstate and headed east.

"This is such a sweet car," said Justin.

"It is fun to drive. I didn't know you were such a car guy," said Tara.

"Anyone would love this car. It's so much fun; at least it is for me since I drive a pickup."

"Oh wow, this is so low to the ground compared to that," said Tara.

"Yeah it is," he chuckled.

"Do you and Emily see much of each other in Dallas?"

"We text or talk to each other pretty often and sometimes meet up on the weekends when she has time."

"I don't have any siblings and feel like I missed out sometimes."

"That's kind of a bummer."

"I had a bunch of cousins that felt like brothers though."

"You know, Tara, I wanted to tell you," he began and paused. "I'm sorry for the way I reacted when I found out about you and Mom. That's not the person I am. I'm ashamed I texted those things to her and hope she can forgive me."

"She already has," said Tara. "I know it had to be a shock."

"It was, but since she and Dad separated I feel like I need to watch out for her, which is dumb because I'm never home and didn't come to see her when she asked me several times. I'm an asshole and plan to do better."

"You know, Justin, my cousins thought they had to look out for me since I didn't have any brothers so I get that."

"I know Mom can look out for herself and now she has you. I don't think I was jealous of that. I guess I let my dumbass friend, Eric, convince me you were out to hurt her." Before Tara could say anything he continued. "I know that is the farthest thing from the truth."

"It is. The truth is that I can't believe how lucky I am that your mom loves me. It surprises me every day!"

"Really," he chuckled. "You are so different from what I thought."

"I hope that's a good thing."

He laughed. "It's a very good thing. Mom told me that you really want us to be a family. Is that because you didn't have any brothers or sisters?"

"No. I never was in a relationship where I thought about having kids and I didn't really see myself as a mom. My parents are gone, so it's just me, but now I feel differently about it. I mean, having a family and being a part of one is life to me." She paused and turned toward Justin. "I think you've got the best mother in the world, Justin. I certainly don't want to be a bonus mom or whatever they call it now. I really just want to be a friend to you and Emily and want you to know that you have someone else you can come to if you need them, whether it's help or if you want to share something good. I think having people you can count on is important in life."

"Do you have people you can count on since your folks are gone?"

Tara smiled. "I do. Of course I have your mom, but I can count on Krista and those rowdy cousins I spoke about earlier. Julia has been my friend for a long time and now I have Melanie. We've become good friends, too. How about you?"

"I have my parents and Emily and we may fight like brothers and sisters do, but we'd do anything for one another. I'm pretty close with my Uncle Matt, but you know... I'd love to have someone else in my corner," he said, glancing over at her briefly and grinning.

Tara smiled at him. "I've actually met your Uncle Matt."

Justin's eyebrows climbed up his forehead. "How did that go?"

Tara chuckled. "Well at first he was very, shall I say, cautious. But as I started to spend more and more money in his store and donated to several things in the town, he began to come around."

Justin laughed. "Uncle Matt is okay. He was upset about the divorce, too. Not that it's really any of his business. I think he was looking out for his brother. It's that guy code thing. I kind of understand it because I felt that way toward Mom until I realized she was fine."

"Your mom is the smartest, most courageous person I know. Do you realize how good she is at her job?"

"Well, I know she's successful. We're both in real estate, but I'm in commercial which is different."

"Justin, at the premiere she mesmerized two of the studio heads talking about finance. I'm not sure you know how good she is. And then to be so brave and step out of what she knew the way she did. That takes courage."

"I guess I didn't really think about it like that."

"She doesn't settle and neither should you. She might be afraid, but that doesn't stop her from going after what she wants and what she knows is there for her."

"You mean you, right? Y'all were friends, but there must have been some kind of connection for you to move away from LA to a small town in Texas."

"It wasn't a connection. It was Lauren. I love her so much," Tara said, suddenly emotional. "Oh fuck. Sorry Justin. Sometimes it overwhelms me. Wow."

Justin smiled. "It's okay. Maybe someday I'll feel like that about a woman."

"I hope you do. It's awesome, frightening, and the best thing in the world all wrapped into one." She laughed.

He looked over at her and smiled.

"Hey, you have brown eyes. You don't see that very often on someone with blond hair."

"No, I guess you don't," said Justin.

"My mom had the softest brown eyes. They were a lot like yours, light brown. It was like looking into a warm, comforting hug. Unless she was angry." Tara laughed. "They were dark brown then. I always hoped if I ever had a kid that they'd have her eyes."

"That must have been nice when you were having a bad day," said Justin. "Maybe I'll have a kid with light brown eyes like your Mom's."

"Maybe," murmured Tara, looking out the window.

30

They stayed overnight in some little town in New Mexico between Albuquerque and the Texas state line. The next day they got up and spent the day driving until they pulled into the driveway of the lake house.

"I'm so glad to see our beautiful home," said Lauren with weariness in her voice.

"You don't want to drive a few more hours today?" teased Tara.

"No! Let me out of this car!" she said, opening the door when Tara stopped the car.

"Wow," said Justin, getting out of the SUV and looking up at the house. "I've only seen this from the water. I had no idea it was this nice."

"Ha," Tara scoffed. "Only the best for your momma."

"I know that's right," said Justin.

They had settled into an easy banter of teasing since riding together. Their bond strengthened as they acknowledged their love for Lauren over the last couple of days.

"Go on inside, babe. I'll get your bag," Tara said, grabbing their things from the trunk.

"I'll let you. Thank you," she said, opening the front door.

"Come on Justin, I'll show you around," said Emily.

Before they could get inside they heard a car coming up the driveway. Krista and Melanie pulled up and got out carrying something.

"We brought dinner," said Krista, smiling. "I knew you'd be too tired to cook."

"How thoughtful," said Tara. "Lauren is inside. Go ahead."

Melanie followed Justin and Emily inside and Krista waited to walk in with Tara.

"You got here in one piece," she remarked.

"And so did my cars," chuckled Tara.

"I want a ride with the top down," said Krista.

"Absolutely." Tara grinned, shutting the trunk.

"So?"

Tara looked at her friend and visibly exhaled. "I love those kids." She smiled and added, "I think they like me and we're going to be a family."

Krista smiled back at her. "I never doubted you, my friend. They don't realize how lucky they are yet."

"I don't know. I think I'm the lucky one."

Krista put her arm around Tara and they walked inside.

*** * * ***

Everyone pitched in to grab plates, glasses, and utensils. They filled their plates and gathered in the dining room.

"Nothing says welcome home like sharing a meal with friends and family. Thank y'all," Lauren said as she looked around the table. She held Tara's eyes and knew what she was going to do after everyone left and it was just them again.

The next day they were all sitting around the great room after a boat ride. Lauren and Justin had a spirited conversation about real estate while Tara and Emily talked about what recipes they wanted to try next.

Tara was searching for a movie they all wanted to watch when Emily said, "I guess this was our first family vacation."

"Only if it was a success," said Tara, sitting next to Lauren on the couch.

"It was," said Justin, sitting in the chair, smiling at Tara.

"Welcome to the family," said Emily, getting up from the end of the couch and standing in front of Tara with her arms out. Tara got up and Emily hugged her tight.

Justin had his arms open when Emily let her go. That was all Tara could stand. The tears began to fall down her cheeks.

"Oh no," said Justin. "We didn't mean to make you cry."

"You have no idea how happy you've made me," sniffled Tara.

Lauren pulled her down on the couch and held her in her arms.

"I think we're getting the idea," said Justin, chuckling. "You know, it's fucking awesome for us, too." He sat down on the couch next to Tara.

"Whoa, what?" said Lauren.

"We were born into our family and our parents are kind of stuck with us," he said, looking over at Emily. "But this is special, Tara, because you actually *want* us. I have to say that feels really good because you didn't have to do that."

"I agree," said Emily. "We can tell that you really want us to be a family because you love us, not just because you love our mom. It feels nice. We want to be a family with you, too."

Now Lauren had tears in her eyes.

"I knew it," said Tara. "I knew I would have the best fucking family ever! I just knew it!"

Lauren laughed between her tears. "Now that's the Tara Holloway everybody knows!"

They all laughed and hugged.

"If we're having family movie night we need popcorn," Justin said, hopping up and wiping a tear from the corner of his eye.

"I know where it is," said Emily. "We've got it. We'll be right back," she said as Justin followed her over to the kitchen.

"I love you so much," Tara said, holding Lauren close. "And I love your kids."

"I think they just became your kids too." She looked at Tara with such love and kissed her tenderly. When they pulled apart she whispered, "I wonder if they'd miss us if we snuck upstairs."

"Damn kids. When do they go to bed?" teased Tara.

"We heard that." Justin cackled from the kitchen.

Laughter filled the room as love filled their hearts.

* * *

Emily and Justin stayed the rest of the week. They went boat riding every day. Emily and Tara cooked something scrumptious every night. True to his word, Justin took them to the cliffs and around the back side they hiked to the top and enjoyed the beautiful vista.

Emily and Justin visited with their dad and that side of the family, too. One night they all went to Lovers Landing and were treated to karaoke. They heard Tara sing to their mom and watched them fall deeper in love. They danced along with Krista and Melanie and even Julia and Heidi came to visit and party with them.

"What a week," said Tara as she held Lauren close while they danced to a slow song.

"It was one of the best of my life," said Lauren, nuzzling her neck.

"Mine too. This was better than winning the Oscar."

"What?" Lauren pulled back to look into Tara's eyes.

"It's true. Family is better than anything."

"Well, family is good, but I can think of a few things that are even better. When Justin and Emily go home I'll show you what I mean," said Lauren with a sexy smile.

"Mmm, I can't wait," Tara said, kissing Lauren softly.

"After they leave tomorrow, will you go on a boat ride with me?" Lauren clasped her hands behind Tara's neck.

"I'd love to go on a boat ride with you," replied Tara.

The next morning Tara cooked breakfast as had become their routine. She loved the big island where they could sit and talk while she prepared waffles. There was fresh fruit, butter, and syrup to go along with the fresh, fluffy feast.

"Emily is going to want to hire you when she opens her own place, Tara. These are so good," said Justin between bites.

"Thanks J, but I'm not that good." Tara chuckled. "Hey, I appreciate y'all taking my rental car back for me."

"Listen to you," said Emily. "You'll be talking Texan in no time."

"What'd I say?"

Lauren chuckled. "Y'all," she said with an exaggerated drawl.

Tara laughed. "I didn't even realize I said it. Y'all are

rubbing off on me. I'll need a dialect coach for my next role."

"Oh honey, you've got a long way to go to sound Texan," teased Lauren.

Tara shrugged. "Hey, before I forget, we're having a housewarming party next month when all those divas from Hollywood come to Lovers Landing for a meeting. We really want you to come."

"Oh, that sounds like fun," said Emily.

"Courtney and Becca will be here and so will Melanie's girls Stephanie and Jennifer," said Lauren. "It will be wild."

"Count me in," said Justin.

"I'll text you both the date when we know for sure," said Tara.

They finished breakfast and it wasn't too long until they packed up to go back to Dallas. Lauren and Tara walked them to the car.

"Thanks for everything," Justin said, hugging Tara.

"Thanks for helping me get the cars back, but more than anything thanks for giving me a chance."

"You know, you'd have been a good mom, Tara," he said, smiling at her. Then he walked over and hugged his mom. "I love you, Momma. I promise to come back soon."

"I love you too, Justin. Remember what I told you, work isn't everything."

"I'm beginning to understand that," he said.

Emily hugged Tara and then her mom.

"I want to hear about all the new dishes Tara is cooking for you, Mom," she said as she got into the car.

Lauren nodded. "Y'all text me when you get home."

"We will," they answered in unison.

They watched them drive away and Lauren said, "Come

on, babe. I'll help you clean up the kitchen and then we can go for that boat ride."

"Sounds good."

It wasn't long until they were walking down to the dock and Tara said, "Where are you taking me?"

"Mmm, you'll see," said Lauren, getting into the boat and starting the engine.

Tara looked at her curiously and untied the line, gently pushing them away from the dock.

"What a glorious afternoon," said Tara.

"It really is. I love this time of year. It's no longer hot, but it's not too cool," she said as she pushed the throttle down to speed up the boat.

They skimmed along the water and Lauren glanced over at Tara. She had her face turned to the sky with her eyes closed, letting the sun warm her skin. Tara was the most beautiful woman Lauren had ever seen. Sometimes her heart stopped when she looked at her and other times it beat faster than it ever had before. How she loved her.

"I can feel you looking at me," said Tara with her eyes closed.

"You're so beautiful I can't look away."

Tara opened her eyes then and looked over at Lauren. She tilted her head and furrowed her brow.

Lauren reached for the throttle and pulled it back so they glided along the water. She cut the engine. "Does this look familiar?"

Tara sat up and looked around. They were in the middle of the lake. In one direction they could barely make out the cliffs. Behind them they could see the beginning of the cove where their house was nestled. Around the bend, Lovers Landing would come into view. Tara looked back at Lauren and recognition bloomed on her face.

She smiled slowly and leaned over until her lips almost touched Lauren's. "This is where we first kissed." Then she brought their lips together.

"Very good," Lauren said proudly. "You're learning your way around." Lauren looked at her and smiled. "I need to ask you something. Well, I need to tell you a few things first."

"What is it, baby? Is something wrong?" said Tara, concerned.

"Oh no," Lauren said breathlessly. "Everything is so right." She took Tara's hands in hers. "When I first talked to Krista all those years ago," she said, shaking her head, "I asked her if she thought there had to be more out there for us." She chuckled. "And look at us now? She's living her best life with her soulmate and love of her life." She smiled. "I never dreamed that what I was hoping for and looking for could be this wonderful, this life-changing. I didn't know I was capable of loving someone the way I love you," she said, her voice cracking and tears pooling in her eyes.

"Oh babe," Tara said softly.

Lauren put a finger over Tara's lips, quieting her. Then she kneeled in front of her and said, "Tara, you know I love you. I finally found the *more* that I knew in my heart was out there. You were in my heart and I want your last name."

Tara looked at her, seeming confused. "My last name?"

"Yes and the way I can get it is if you'll marry me. Will you?" Lauren asked, her voice hopeful.

"You want to get married?" she asked with tears now pooling in her eyes.

"I do, baby. I want to marry you. I didn't think it mattered, but it does. Will you marry me? I want to call you my wife."

"Yes!" Tara said, reaching for Lauren's face and gently

pulling it to hers. The kiss was soft and wet and so luscious. "Let's do it now. I'll marry you right now."

Lauren chuckled. "Wait. I've got to do this right." She reached in her pocket and pulled out a ring.

"You have a ring?"

"Yes. This was my grandmother's. It's always been important to me, but I've never worn it. And now I know why. It was meant for my wife. It was meant for you," she said, sliding it on Tara's finger.

"Lauren, it's beautiful," said Tara, admiring the ring.

"It fits. Why am I not surprised?" She chuckled. "We were meant for each other, Tara. It just took us a little longer and we had to live a few lives before it was our turn."

"I love you, Lauren. I didn't know love could ever feel this good, but every day you make it better. All I ever need is you." She brought their lips together again and this time Lauren deepened the kiss until they both had to gasp for breath.

"Let's go home," Lauren said.

"I am home," Tara said, kissing her again.

31

The next morning Tara and Lauren pulled into Krista and Melanie's driveway. They got out of the car giggling and walked around to the back door.

"Good morning," Melanie said from where she sat on the back patio. "What a nice surprise." She looked from one to the other and couldn't keep from smiling. "What are you two giggling about?"

"We need a favor," said Tara. "Is Krista around? We need both of you."

"She's right inside; I'll get her." Melanie got up, her brow furrowed, looking at both of them as she opened the door and yelled inside. "Hey babe, Tara and Lauren are here. They need a favor." Melanie turned back to Tara and Lauren. "You two are up to something."

"We are," said Lauren, wide-eyed.

"Would you like a cup of coffee?" Melanie asked as they waited for Krista.

Before they could answer, Krista walked out of the house and said, "Hey y'all. What's up?" She walked over and eyed her friends as they smiled from ear to ear.

Tara and Lauren looked at one another and then said in unison, "We're getting married!"

"Wow!" said Melanie. "Congratulations!"

"Yay!" said Krista, applauding.

"We need your help though," said Tara.

"Sit," said Krista. "Let me get coffee?"

They both nodded and Krista ran inside to get coffee and once they all had a cup they sat around their patio table.

"Okay," said Melanie, grinning. "How can we help?"

"Well," said Lauren. "We've been into town and applied for the license. We have to wait 72 hours before we can get married."

"So we have three days to plan a wedding?" asked Krista, clapping her hands together again.

"Not exactly," said Tara, grinning at Lauren. "We're going to get married at the Grand Canyon."

"Oh wow!" exclaimed Melanie.

"We'd like you to marry us, Krista. And we'd like you to be our witness, Melanie," explained Lauren.

Krista's eyebrows shot up her forehead and Melanie's face lit up with excitement.

"Are you busy Thursday?" asked Tara, chuckling.

Krista and Melanie looked at one another then Krista said, "You're serious."

"Yes we are. We could fly to Flagstaff Thursday and drive into the Canyon Friday morning and do it. We have the place picked out. We were there last week," said Tara matter-of-factly.

"Back it up, kids," said Melanie. "I want to hear this romantic story. What happened on that family vacation?"

Lauren laughed. She took Tara's hand. "Krista, do you remember when you introduced me to Melanie?"

Krista thought about it. "At the party we had when Melanie and the whole family surprised me."

"Yep. We were talking just before Tara got there. Anyway, you asked me why I immediately liked Melanie when I had been cautious with Brooke. I told you it was because of the way you love each other. And then I said it was the way Melanie looks at you with certainty and security."

Krista's face lit up. "And you said 'I hope someone looks at me that way.'"

Lauren nodded, her face glowing. "Tara looks at me that way," she said, gazing into Tara's eyes. "I want to call her my wife. I want her last name."

Melanie's hands were over her mouth, tears in her eyes.

Krista beamed at Lauren and Tara. "I'm so happy for you!" She jumped up and pulled them both into a hug.

"Does that mean you'll do it?" Tara asked.

"Yes!" they exclaimed.

* * *

Friday morning Tara parked their rental car and they all walked out to the same place Tara and Lauren professed their vast and endless love.

The sun was shining, the air was crisp and it was peacefully quiet. What a perfect moment for a wedding, Lauren thought. Her heart was furiously beating from excitement. She was about to become Lauren Holloway, wife of Tara Holloway. For the life of her she couldn't explain why this was so important to her, but it was. Tara was all for it and just as excited.

Lauren had to admit proposing to Tara was one of the most meaningful moments of her life. She had no doubt they would spend forever and beyond together, but marrying Tara felt like destiny. How syrupy did that sound, she thought as a chuckle bubbled from her throat. But she and Tara didn't care. They were on this path together and they were up for each adventure, every detour, or simply staying home. It didn't matter because they'd be together.

"Are we ready?" asked Krista.

Tara smiled at Lauren and raised her eyebrows in question. "I'm so ready," she said.

"Here we go," said Lauren. She took out her phone and video called Justin.

At the same time Tara video called Emily.

"Hey," said Tara. She held the phone so Emily could see them both as Lauren did the same with Justin.

"Where are you?" asked Justin.

"We're at the Grand Canyon," said Tara.

"What? Again?" said Emily.

"Yes," said Lauren. She turned the phone around and said, "Say hi to Krista and Melanie."

Tara did the same thing so Emily could see them.

"After you left Sunday, your mom asked me to marry her," explained Tara. "I said yes!" She grinned.

"Oh my God!" said Justin.

"Anyway, I wanted to do it that day before she changed her mind, but you have to wait three days. So here we are. Krista is going to marry us and Melanie is going to hold the phones so y'all can be here too," said Tara.

"Like she's going to change her mind." Emily laughed.

They handed the phones to Melanie and stood in front of Krista.

"Here we are on this beautiful morning in this amazing wonder of nature to celebrate love in its most natural pure form. Love between two hearts, two souls, and two minds.

Lauren, you asked to go first," said Krista, smiling at her old friend.

Lauren faced Tara and held her hands. The smile on her face brightened the morning even more. "Loving you has opened a part of my heart no one else could. When I see you my heart thumps in my chest, when I hear you my heart sighs with relief, and when I feel you my heart beats with the love you put there. I am forever yours and promise to hold you close for all time."

Krista handed her a ring that was one gold strand and one silver strand braided together, representing their two lives coming together as one. There was one square emerald that sparkled brightly in Tara's ring that reminded her of the love in Lauren's green eyes.

Lauren slid the ring onto Tara's finger. It fit snugly next to her grandmother's simple band she had given Tara when she proposed.

Krista smiled at her dear friend and said, "Tara, it's your turn."

"I always believed there was a special someone just for me. I never gave up as the years continued because I could feel you pulling me towards you. I had this classic movie scene in my head about what it would be like when our eyes met. But when you looked at me it was even better. With your eyes you simply said, I'm the one your heart has been waiting for. You have wrapped me in your love and given me not only a home, but also a family. You are my forever and beyond. I won't let go."

Krista handed Tara a ring that looked just like hers except it had a blue sapphire that shone brightly, just like Tara's eyes did when Lauren looked at her. They'd found the rings at a jeweler's in Dallas three days before. They both felt like it was meant to be when they asked if the gems could be added and the jeweler could not only do it, but also have them ready for the wedding.

Tara slid the ring on Lauren's finger with such joy and love. Her eyes did indeed sparkle just as the sapphire did. Lauren looked up at her with the same brightness and joy in her face.

Krista put her hands over theirs. "You have claimed one another, you have nurtured one another, you have declared your love to your family, friends and to the universe. It is with great joy and honor," she said, smiling into their happy faces, "that I pronounce you married. May the light of your love smooth your path and calm the waters of your life together. You may kiss!" she shouted, a hint of an echo surrounding them all.

Lauren grabbed Tara's face and stopped to look into her beautiful bride's blue eyes momentarily and then she kissed her wife for the first time. When their lips met flashes of her life zoomed through her mind and then she saw hints of a future full of laughter, love, and contentment. She realized that was what Tara made her. She was content.

They pulled apart to the cheers of their kids on the phones joined by Melanie and Krista.

"What now?" asked Justin. "Where are you going on your honeymoon?"

"Yeah," said Emily. "Is that our next family vacation?"

"No!" Lauren and Tara said in unison.

"We don't know yet," said Lauren, blowing them kisses.

"Thanks for letting us be there," said Justin. "Congratulations!"

"Wait until I tell everybody who my stepmother is," laughed Emily.

Tara's eyes got big. "I'm not your stepmother!"

Justin and Emily laughed.

"You shouldn't have let them see your weakness," said Lauren, sighing.

"They're not scaring me off," said Tara, putting her arm around Lauren.

"Call us when you get home," said Justin.

"Bye and congrats," said Emily.

They ended both calls and Melanie handed them their phones.

"May I present Tara and Lauren Holloway," said Krista sweetly.

Lauren beamed. "I'm so happy!"

"We're so happy for you," said Melanie.

"I think we should go to Vegas and have a party," said Krista.

Tara and Lauren looked at each other and grinned.

"There's a helicopter at the entrance of the park, waiting to take us to Vegas," said Tara.

Krista and Melanie looked at one another in surprise.

"We had to thank you for doing all this with us. What better way than a night in Vegas. Shall we?" asked Lauren.

"Let's go!" said Krista. "You are always full of surprises, Tara Holloway!"

They were whisked away and spent the day taking in Las Vegas. They gambled a little, spent the afternoon being pampered at the spa, and then dressed up for an exclusive rooftop dining experience.

"This is where we part company," said Tara. "Y'all are off to a show and we are going to the honeymoon suite."

"I can't thank you both enough for doing all of this with us," said Lauren. "You have made this day even more special."

"You have taken the phrase 'doing it our way' to new levels," said Melanie.

"I guess it isn't that different from a wedding at a venue. Our venue was mobile and you were our wedding party," said Tara. "I wouldn't want it any other way."

"It would have taken us a lot longer to find each other if we hadn't had you, Krista," said Lauren.

"And if you hadn't come back to save my friend, Melanie, who would have calmed me down after my first kiss with Lauren?" said Tara.

"You are both more than welcome. I do have a question though," said Krista.

"What's that?"

"I know Lauren is going back to work when you get home, but what are you going to do, Tara?"

Tara grinned at Lauren and then looked at Krista. "I'm going to be a housewife."

"I wouldn't have believed it if I hadn't heard it with my own ears," said Krista, shaking her head.

"Come on, babe," said Melanie. "These newlyweds have plans."

They all hugged and left the restaurant. Krista and Melanie took the elevator down to the theater and Lauren and Tara took the elevator up to the honeymoon suite on the top floor.

Several hours later Lauren leaned back into Tara's arms as they looked out the floor to ceiling windows at the lights of the Strip. She didn't expect their lovemaking to be different just because they were now married, but it was. Every touch, every kiss felt shared and more intimate. Every sound, every scent spoke to her soul and was seared there for all time.

"What are you thinking, Mrs. Holloway?" asked Tara.

"I never knew changing my name would bring me such joy," said Lauren.

"Maybe it's how you went about changing it," said Tara, nibbling below Lauren's ear.

"Mmm, maybe," moaned Lauren. She turned in Tara's arms and looked into her sparkling blue eyes. "I have never been this happy. There have been happy times in my life, but Tara, you have filled my heart to overflowing."

Tara smiled at her wife. "I didn't realize how important having a family and being a part of one was to me until you put that in my heart. I will never feel like I missed out again. You have given me so much more than you know, baby."

Lauren's heart swelled with love. "I didn't realize until I kissed my wife at the Grand Canyon what I was feeling. The truth is, I'm content, honey. I have never been content in my life. All I need is you. I want to go to sleep in your arms every night and have you wake up in mine every morning."

"That is bliss," said Tara. "And I will be happy to oblige."

"I need one more thing from you," said Lauren, tightening her arms around Tara's neck.

"Name it," Tara said quickly.

"Promise me we will grow old together because I'm going to need many more years with you," said Lauren, her voice dripping with love.

"I promise," said Tara.

Lauren pulled her wife down and kissed her with passion, promise, and love that even the Grand Canyon couldn't hold.

FIVE YEARS LATER

"I think everything is ready," said Tara, coming out of the guest room.

"Honey, you had everything ready two days ago," teased Lauren. "Come sit with me a minute before they get here," she said, patting the couch.

Tara plopped down next to her and exhaled heavily.

Lauren threw her arm around Tara's shoulders and kissed her on the cheek. "Take a breath."

"I just want everything to be perfect for our granddaughter's first visit," said Tara.

"I don't think Ruby is going to remember this trip since she's only a month old," Lauren said, pulling Tara into her side.

"Sure she will. Don't you think she remembers meeting us at the hospital? She'll remember feeling safe at her grandmas' house and want to come back again and again." Tara lowered her head to Lauren's shoulder. "I love you, sweetheart. Thanks for giving me this family," she said quietly.

"I love you, too." Lauren kissed the top of Tara's head. "Justin said he had a surprise for you."

"Who knows with him. Let's see, there's the time he surprised me with those expensive steaks that he thought would be fun for us to grill. Even though he hadn't noticed or listened when we told him on numerous occasions that we were not eating meat."

Lauren chuckled. "He ate steak for days. And then remember when he got us that framed print overlooking the Grand Canyon and he was sure that it was the spot where we got married."

"And when we opened it, it wasn't the Grand Canyon at all. It was Bryce Canyon," said Tara, laughing. "That's our boy."

"I've never seen him take to someone the way he has you," Lauren said, turning to look into Tara's eyes.

"I understand where the term 'bonus' comes from when talking about blended families. Justin and Emily are such a bonus in my life. I couldn't imagine being happier when I knew you loved me and we were spending our lives together. Then here they came, jumping right in the middle of us, with a bit of coaxing when it came to Justin, but nonetheless they seem to like spending time with us," said Tara, her voice thick with emotion and amazement.

"It's because you love them and show them in many ways. I'll never forget that day when Justin said the difference was that you wanted them."

"I did want them and still do. And then Justin married Mandy. She couldn't be a more perfect partner for him," said Tara.

"I know. And now we have sweet little Ruby. I'm telling you, she looks so much like Justin did."

Tara smiled and wrapped her arms around Lauren.

They held each other close for a few moments. "I love our life," murmured Tara.

"I love being Mrs. Lauren Holloway," said Lauren, leaning back and gazing into Tara's eyes. "Did you know I have the hottest wife?"

"Is that so? I didn't know women were hot in their sixties unless it was from a hot flash." Tara giggled.

"You'll be hot to me in our eighties and nineties," stated Lauren. "Remember, you promised me years!"

"I remember, but slow down, we don't have to get there yet. It took us long enough to finally find one another and I don't want to rush one moment with you," said Tara, closing the distance between their lips and softly kissing the woman that could speed up her heart with a look, a touch, or a sound.

Lauren and Tara's phones both pinged on the coffee table.

They ended the kiss, but didn't let go. "They're here." Lauren smiled.

Tara put a hand to her ear, pretending to listen. "I hear Ruby calling for her Gran."

"Are you sure? I think she was saying Mimi," said Lauren. She grabbed her phone and looked at the text message.

Tara got up and they went to the door. When they opened it Justin's pickup pulled into the driveway. He waved and got out, opening the back door. They walked to the truck and before they could say anything Justin held his finger to his lips.

Mandy came around the front of the truck and said, "She's asleep. It's her nap time and she may wake up."

"But it's okay if she doesn't. Is that what you're trying to tell us?" Tara chuckled as she hugged Mandy.

"She's a lot happier after a good nap. That's all I'm saying," said Mandy, hugging Lauren.

"How are *you*?" asked Lauren. "You look great."

"Thanks. I'm not sure I believe you, but I feel like we're getting better at functioning with less sleep."

"Hi son," Lauren said, hugging him as he held the baby in her carrier.

"Hi Mom." He smiled. He reached out an arm for Tara and hugged her next.

"Come on in. Let's see if we can keep our hands off of her while she finishes napping," said Tara quietly.

They all went inside and left the baby in her carrier in the guest room while they gathered in the kitchen.

"We were just talking about the different surprises you've brought us over the years," said Lauren, teasing her son.

He laughed. "I swear they shipped the wrong print. The one I saw was the Grand Canyon."

"We believe you. That's why the correct one is hanging in our bedroom," said Tara.

"I do have a surprise for you and this time it's a good one, but you have to wait because Ruby is in on it," he said.

"When is Emily supposed to be here?" asked Mandy.

"Anytime," said Tara. "She texted a couple of hours ago that she was on her way."

"She's still bringing her friend, right?" asked Mandy.

"Yes, why?" asked Lauren suspiciously.

"No reason," said Mandy nonchalantly.

"Spill it," said Tara. "What do you know?"

"I know that her friend is the assistant to the head chef at a rival restaurant. And I know that Emily really likes her."

"She mentioned meeting someone, but wouldn't elaborate," said Lauren.

"She told me that she wanted us to meet her friend and not make a big deal about it," said Tara.

Justin laughed. "Are you kidding me? Em has a girlfriend. I'm shocked she didn't ask us to be on our best behavior."

"I'm sure she didn't ask because she knew you'd try to embarrass her," said Mandy, staring at Justin.

"I won't do that, although it is tempting," said Justin.

"Not a good idea," warned Tara.

"Oh, so now she's your favorite," Justin said playfully.

Tara dropped her head and looked at him and rolled her eyes.

The door opened and Emily said loudly, "Hello! Anyone home?"

Lauren hurried into the entryway followed closely by Tara. She playfully smacked Justin on the arm as she walked by.

"Hey honey," said Lauren, pulling Emily into a hug.

"Hi Mom," Emily squeezed her mom and smiled at Tara over her shoulder.

Tara hugged Emily when Lauren let her go. "I'm so glad you're here."

"Me too. I have a new recipe for us, but first," Emily said, turning to her friend. She put her arm around her. "Mom, Tara, I'd like you to meet Ava Andress. Ava, these are my moms, Lauren and Tara."

"Welcome to our home," said Lauren graciously.

Tara was savoring how Emily introduced them and caught her eye and smiled. Emily winked at her. Tara turned to Ava and said, "We're so glad you're here."

"Let me just say that I'm a big fan and get that out of the way," admitted Ava.

Tara chuckled. "Thank you. That means a lot."

"She's even better in person," said Lauren, smiling at Tara. "Y'all come in," she added, ushering them into the great room. "Mandy and Justin are in here. Ruby is sleeping."

Emily put her arm through Tara's and whispered, "Thanks. When I told her you were my bonus mom she melted."

"I'm glad I could help." Tara chuckled but secretly she was elated.

While Emily introduced Ava to Justin and Mandy, Lauren said, "We'll check on Ruby and then get everyone drinks."

She and Tara crept into the guest room and watched Ruby sleep.

Tara put her arm around Lauren. "Did you hear how Emily introduced us as her moms?"

"I did and I loved it," said Lauren.

"Isn't it funny how little things like that can mean so much," said Tara softly.

"We're a family," said Lauren, pulling her close. "Come on. We'll be in trouble if we wake this precious baby."

They went back out and made sure everyone had something to drink. The conversation was lively as Emily and Ava talked about their good natured rivalry and how it had quickly turned into more. Justin and Mandy told several comical stories of what new sleep deprived parents do.

Mandy held up the baby monitor and listened. "I think our little jewel is stirring," she said. She smiled at Justin and nodded.

"Do you want to come with me to get her?" he asked Tara.

"Of course." She looked at him with pure joy.

They walked into the room and could hear Ruby's peaceful coos.

"Sit on the bed," said Justin as he unhooked the straps of the infant carrier. He took Ruby in his arms and smiled down at her.

Tara took a framed picture off the bedside table and gazed at it. Justin sat down next to her and she said, "Would you look at this?"

"That was when we went to California to drive your cars back."

"Yep, our first family photo," said Tara, putting the picture back on the table.

"That's when you charmed your way into my heart and I remember a particular conversation we had in the convertible," said Justin.

Tara looked at him with her brow furrowed.

He put Ruby in Tara's arms and said, "This is your surprise. Look at her eyes, Tara." He gave Tara a moment to gaze at his daughter and let recognition sink in. "Her eyes have turned from the blue she was born with to the most beautiful light brown eyes. They're a little like mine. Do they look like your mom's?" He looked at Tara.

"Oh Justin. They do!" she said around the lump in her throat. "You're going to have to give me a second."

Justin put his arm around Tara's shoulders and rubbed her back. "There's no way I have the words to express just how important you are to me and how happy I am that Mom married you. I'm happy for her, but you know I'm a selfish prick and it's all about me."

Tara chuckled as she gently bounced Ruby and stared at her happy little face with those light brown eyes.

"I'm happy she found you because you've made me a better person. You've opened my eyes to things I never thought about and you've been a friend that I didn't know I needed but am so happy I have. You were right when years ago you said I didn't need another mom because I had the best one."

Tara nodded, remembering that conversation.

"Ruby has the best mom now, but she really needs a grandma like you. And through her I hope every time you look into her eyes you'll see the love I have for you. Because Tara, when her eyes changed I almost died. I told Mandy this is the one thing I can give to you that shows how I feel." Tears pooled in his eyes as his voice cracked.

"Oh Justin," Tara said, sniffling. "You are now my favorite. I'm sure Emily is listening. I'm sure everyone is listening," she joked. "The baby monitor is right there."

After just a few moments she heard something in the doorway and looked up to see Lauren with Mandy, Emily, and Ava standing behind her. They all had tears in their eyes.

"You know I was teasing, right?" she said to Emily.

Emily nodded and grinned.

She looked at Justin and said, "Don't ever try to surprise me again. You'll never top this."

Ruby let out a little squeal as if on cue.

Justin laughed. "We'll go get her a bottle and give you and Mom a minute." He got up and walked to the door. "Let's see, we'll be back in ten years or so. Surely she'll be sleeping through the night by then."

They laughed as they left the room. Lauren sat down and put her arm around her. She laid her head on Tara's shoulder and looked at her granddaughter as she smiled up at them.

"When I first laid eyes on you, Tara Holloway, I thought, look at this gorgeous woman. She is so full of herself and yet

I'm drawn to her like a moth to a flame. I watched you and right then I decided I might get burned, but it would be worth it. I admit I wondered what it would be like to be with you way before I should've been having those thoughts," said Lauren, chuckling.

"Oh you did? And?"

"And never in my wildest dreams did I think you would make my life so rich, so full, so complete. I thought it was just you and me, but was I ever wrong."

"Look at us now, baby," said Tara. "We have great kids and they have awesome partners and look at this! They gave us Ruby! Do you have any idea how much fun I'm going to have showing her off to Krista and Julia!"

Lauren laughed and ran her finger along Ruby's cheek. "Like I said earlier, we're a family. Your family." She squeezed Tara's shoulder.

"Our family," Tara said, turning to face Lauren. Then she looked down at Ruby and said, "We're your grandmothers and we kiss a lot because we love each other so much."

Then Tara leaned in and touched her lips to Lauren's like she'd done so many times. This kiss was a promise of years to come filled with laughter, kids, grandkids, friends, happiness and love, so much love.

ABOUT THE AUTHOR

Small town Texas girl that grew up believing she could do anything. Her mother loved to read and romance novels were a favorite that she passed on to her daughter. When she found lesfic novels her world changed. She not only fell in love with the genre, but wanted to write her own stories. You can find her books on Amazon and her website at jameymoodyauthor.com.

As an independent publisher a review is greatly appreciated and I would be grateful if you could take the time to write just a few words.

On the next page is a list of my books with links that will take you to their page.

After that I've included the first chapter of No More Secrets, Book Two in The Lovers Landing Series. It is the never-ending love story of Krista and Melanie.

ALSO BY JAMEY MOODY

Live This Love

The Your Way Series:
Finding Home
Finding Family
Finding Forever

It Takes A Miracle
One Little Yes

The Lovers Landing Series
Where Secrets Are Safe
No More Secrets
And The Truth Is ...

NO MORE SECRETS
CHAPTER 1

"Say something!"

"There's nothing to say."

"You've always got something to say," Julia Lansing said, eyeing her best friend.

"Not this time, Jules," Krista Kyle replied, gazing at her beloved lake. It had been three months since that disastrous walk down the aisle; well, it was more like an almost walk down the aisle.

Before that she was living her best life or at least she thought she was. She was an award winning actress and now producer. The production company, Ten Queens, she founded had produced the biggest blockbuster to date with queer women acting in leading roles with a queer storyline. It was more than a movie about gay people in the gay community. It followed queer people in everyday life; living life. Krista was extremely proud of the company and the quality entertainment they were creating.

She had started the company not long after she and Julia had purchased this old run-down lake resort and turned it into the best kept secret in Hollywood. Lovers

Landing was the secret hideaway Krista and Julia had created for the closeted queers in high profile careers where being out could harm them professionally. Sadly that was the way the world still worked in some circles, but Lovers Landing was a place they could come and be themselves.

They could hold one another's hands without fear it would end up on social media in a matter of minutes. There was a private beach, a restaurant with romantic little nooks for secluded dinners and a bar with nightly karaoke. Each couple had their own cabin that backed up to the water with gorgeous sunrise or sunset views. It was romantic, peaceful, and more importantly secluded. Secrets were safe, people were happy, and love flourished.

It was during their inaugural season that everything almost ended before it began. Krista, Julia and Lovers Landing hosted many happy couples that first summer, but a journalist that made a name by outing lesbian stars heard about the hideaway.

Krista made it her mission to keep this journalist from ruining her and Julia's dreamland for closeted lovers. What she didn't plan on was falling in love with the journalist, but then again does anyone ever plan on falling in love?

Brooke Bell was a talented writer with her own secret when she came to Lovers Landing. Krista was determined to save the resort, but in the process she saved Brooke, too. She helped Brooke see her worth and rewrite her career out of the depths of sensational sleazy journalism into an Academy Award winning screenwriter.

They fell in love fast and hard. It was a whirlwind romance and they worked side by side with their other Lovers Landing friends and made the movie they were all now known for. Three months ago on the night they received their academy awards the group boarded a plane and came to Lovers Landing to celebrate.

Caught up in the success, joy, and love Krista and Brooke thought it would be a great time for a quick wedding. Their friends would already be there and it would be a fun surprise. Now that Krista looked back on it; it was her insane idea to get married. Brooke was just going along like she had for the last three years until she didn't.

Julia reached over and took Krista's hand and squeezed.

"Don't do that Jules, you'll make me cry," Krista said, looking out over the water. "That is if I had any tears left." Krista chuckled sarcastically, "Ironic, isn't it? I once encouraged Brooke to cry and told her that tears were healing. If that wasn't the biggest line of bullshit!" She shook her head, "All I've done is cry and nothing is healed. So my dear friend. I don't have anything to say."

"I have tried to be patient with you, Krissy. You've got to talk about it so you can go on."

"Go on? Where am I going, Jules."

"You haven't been back to LA. You've barely been out of your cabin."

"I've been working. I'm reading scripts for new projects."

"Krista, come on."

Krista sighed. "Look Julia, I've lived it over and over. It was my fault."

"What? Your fault? What do you mean?"

"I knew Brooke lived with considerable guilt over how she treated her first love. I am the dumbass that suggested she contact her. I thought she would see that this woman had a good life and it would ease the guilt."

"You had no way of knowing Brooke was still in love with her," Julia said supportively.

"First love is a mighty strong emotion, isn't it," Krista said, smiling sadly at Julia then looking away.

Julia furrowed her brow, "It is. Are you sure you're talking about Brooke?"

"I am," Krista said, convincingly. "God Jules, we were walking down the deck, hand in hand. Brooke Eden's "Got No Choice" was playing through the sound system. I looked out and could see you and Heidi holding hands smiling at us. And then Brooke stopped," Krista said, remembering.

"We were remembering our own wedding for a split second when we saw Brooke simply quit walking," Julia recalled.

"She stopped and said, 'I can't do this'." Krista shook her head. "That really is all that needs to be said, Julia. Brooke reconnected with her first love and will probably live happily ever after with her. That's it. That's all. I'm not supposed to have a partner. Karma, history or whatever has shown me over and over and this time I get it. I'm listening. I'm done."

"What? No way!"

"Yep, I'm done. I'm fifty-three years old and that's enough. I'm also done talking about this."

Julia started to object but Krista stopped her.

"I mean it, Jules," she said, looking over at her best friend.

Julia looked at her for several moments and then exhaled. "Okay, but you're going to have to help me here this week."

"The latest group just left. We have a week off before the next one gets here and then the next week is our Ten Queens meeting. What do you need help with?"

"I know it's our week off, but I'm doing someone a favor," Julia replied.

"A favor?"

"Yes. A family contacted me and wanted to rent out a couple of the cabins."

Krista chuckled, "You explained to them that this isn't exactly a family resort."

"Of course I did, but they were persuasive. Besides, it doesn't hurt to be nice occasionally."

"You're always nice. What did you do, Jules?" Krista said, narrowing her eyes.

"This family came here years ago, probably when we worked here in high school. They wanted to recreate special memories they had here for their kids. They promised they wouldn't be any trouble. They simply want the cabins and I agreed to let them use the paddle boards."

"What about the restaurant? It will be closed. What about the boats and the bikes?"

"I told them the restaurant would be closed and I gave them access to one boat."

Krista eyed her friend and shook her head. "Why would you do that? Lots of people contact us and don't realize we're not a family resort. You explained it and they still want to come?"

"I told them it was our off week and they were fine with it."

"Of course they're fine with it. They'll have the place to themselves. I'm not sure this is a good idea, Jules."

"It's done. You wouldn't even know they're here, but turns out I need to be gone Tuesday. I'll check them in tomorrow. All I need you to do is take the boat keys to them Tuesday afternoon."

"Why can't you give them the keys tomorrow?"

"Because the marina has both boats in for service. They picked them up today and will bring them back Tuesday."

Krista stared at Julia, not sure she was getting the whole story. "You'll check them in tomorrow and you need me to take them the keys. That's it?"

Julia nodded. "That's it. I don't know why you're making a big deal. It's not like you've done anything around here the last three months anyway."

Krista jerked back as if Julia had hit her.

"I didn't mean that the way it sounded, Krissy. What I mean is that you haven't been to the office

or even the beach in a very long time. You are supposed to be my partner in this place. I've tried to go easy, but I need your help."

"Don't give me that shit. I know Becca has been running this place and doing a fantastic job. She is your daughter and you taught her well. You are not going to make me feel guilty for taking some time to myself."

Julia narrowed her eyes and stared at Krista. "Don't you get it. I miss you! You're my best friend and I barely see you."

Krista softened. "I know, Jules. It's easier to work on these scripts than think about what happened. I couldn't watch all these happy couples holding hands and having fun. It was too much." Krista took Julia's hand and smiled. "I will take care of this family and I will be right beside you when the next group comes in. How's that?"

"You will? They seem really nice."

"I will."

Julia chuckled. "I'd almost like to see their faces when the superstar Krista Kyle brings them their boat keys."

Krista laughed with her. "You haven't called me that since we worked here over thirty years ago."

"I remember those happy times."

"Me too, Jules. Me too."

Krista looked over the water thinking back to when she

was twenty-one years old and working side by side with Julia at this resort. Her biggest care then was when she could steal another kiss from Melanie Zimmer. Those were the days. Simple and sweet. If only she'd known.

No More Secrets:

When Krista Kyle's world is turned upside down, there's only one person that can save her.

First love is a mighty strong emotion. Krista knows this and has been given several chances over the years to have the life she dreamed of, but something always got in the way.

Melanie Zimmer has loved Krista Kyle for over half her life. She now has the courage to do something about it. All she has to do is help Krista find hers and she knows just the place.

Does Lovers Landing still have the magic that brought them together over thirty years ago? Will Krista finally be brave enough to hold on to her true love?

This is the second book in The Lovers Landing Series. Come along on this first love, second chance romance and see if Krista and Melanie can find their courage in one another.

Get No More Secrets

Printed in Great Britain
by Amazon